Thanks t
reading!

J Sugis Lith

QUICK FIX

Other Titles by J. Gregory Smith

Thrillers

A Noble Cause (Thomas & Mercer, Kindle Bestseller U.S., UK and Germany)

The Flamekeepers (Thomas & Mercer)

Darwin's Pause (RedAcre Press)

The Paul Chang Mystery Series

Final Price (Book One, Thomas & Mercer)

Legacy of the Dragon (Book Two, Thomas & Mercer)

Send in the Clowns (Book Three, Thomas & Mercer)

Young Adult

The Crystal Mountain (RedAcre Press)

Short Stories

"Heroic Measures" (Amazon StoryFront)

"Blenders" (*Insidious Assassins*, Smart Rhino Publishing)

"The Pepper Tyrant" (*Uncommon Assassins*, Smart Rhino Publishing)

"Something Borrowed" (*Zippered Flesh: Tales of Body Enhancements Gone Bad*, Smart Rhino Publishing)

"Street Smarts" (*Stories from the Ink Slingers*, A Written Remains Anthology, Gryphonwood Press)

J. GREGORY SMITH

QUICK FIX

RedAcre Press

This is a work of fiction. Names, characters, organizations, places, events, and incidents are either products of the author's imagination or used fictitiously.

Copyright © 2018 J. Gregory Smith

All rights reserved.

This book or any portion thereof may not be reproduced or used in any manner whatsoever without the express written permission of the publisher except for the use of brief quotations in a book review.

Published by RedAcre Press

Cover design by Malcolm McClinton

Printed in the United States of America

First Printing, 2018

ISBN 978-0692147368

For Julie

Chapter 1

Fishtown; Philadelphia, Pennsylvania

I was over at Kelly's Korner playing pool with the guys and trying to pocket the nine-ball -like that would solve anything- when in walked that hipster, douchebag, lawyer, Richard Fenster, in his short-sleeve dress shirt, ear gauges, and a loud red tie.

He stood in the middle of the room, as if the regulars hadn't noticed this beanpole clown already, and called me out.

"Mr. Kyle Logan!" Fenster used what he must have thought of as his courtroom voice.

Kelly's wasn't trendy enough for the likes of Fenster to grace with his presence, but apparently he wanted to make a point. It wasn't enough for him to serve me papers from Beth filing for divorce, he had to do it in front of my friends.

Besides representing my wife, Fenster was also banging her silly. Back when Beth had first dropped that bombshell I'd vowed to take the high road. I'd even asked the guy to call me Kyle, for the sake of civility.

Then this.

I clung to that thought, determined to ride out the humiliation with beer and shots as soon as he left. I walked across the room, but my arms wouldn't reach to accept the envelope he was waving at me. I'd known it was coming. I wasn't going to change anything, but this juvenile dig was too much.

"Send it to my house, *Dick.*" I stood there with the whole place staring at us.

"Name's Richard." He held it out to me and I didn't move. "Suit yourself." He started to walk away and I figured he'd leave them at the little place where I rented a room.

Instead, he turned back and flung the envelope, Frisbee-style. "You're still served!"

It twirled toward my face like it was in slow motion, but I couldn't move a muscle. One pointy corner raked along the side of my nose. Then it dropped at my feet.

My muscles unlocked. I raced toward him, no thought at all of my bad leg, and spun him around. I can remember the smug expression on his face, the little bit of a smile that just touched his stupid beard.

Right before I slugged him in the mouth.

Even before he hit the floor I could see by his eyes that he was out. A zing of pure joy shot through me, better than I'd felt in a long time. The sound of cheers and scattered applause snapped me back to reality. Had I killed him? I've been told I don't know my own strength.

Lucky for me he was just KOed. And when he woke up soon after he was POed.

Fenster was all, "I'm pressing charges!" though he sounded mushy when he spoke. I hadn't broken his jaw, but the loose teeth and split lip would make smirking painful for a while.

The cops and the ambulance arrived at the same time. By then the scar tissue I'd popped felt like fire and my knee was beginning to swell. That was okay. Been there, done that. I could hobble with the best of them, and the pain reminded me that at least my leg was still attached to my body.

QUICK FIX

That night the cops tossed me in the drunk-tank, even though I was sober. The next day I was deemed safe to return to the community, but felony assault charges went onto my booking sheet.

Beth showed up the next day at the row house where I rented a bedroom. She even asked about my leg before screaming at me. Eventually she slowed down enough to hear my side of it. I believed her when she said that while she'd agreed to file, she thought Fenster would use a process server like a normal person. She was tough but never vicious.

Fenster was the icing on the cake anyway. Maybe Beth and I shouldn't have dragged things out the way we did. We'd drifted apart long before I'd gotten hurt in Iraq, and when she suggested we wait to finalize things until I'd recovered, I milked the situation a bit. Fenster didn't seem like the patient type and his repeated insistence for Beth to *move up* may have caused my heels to dig in. Still, to serve me in public like that crossed the line.

It wasn't a good time to tell her that she looked good. Her chestnut hair was cut short in an expensive-looking coif. Her cashmere sweater probably cost as much as the new tires I needed on my truck. It made me think of the way she'd stressed out about the hole in her sweater on our first date in college.

I asked if an apology and paying his medical bills might get Fenster to drop the charges. She didn't laugh, which was considerate, but the unspoken *hell no* came through loud and clear.

* * *

One week later; Kelly's Korner

I signaled Dave, the latest owner of Kelly's, for another round. He'd already poured it and slid the brimming mug toward me. Somehow he didn't spill a drop. "Glad you came back."

"Returning to the scene of the crime," I gave him a smile I didn't feel.

Dave wiped his hands on a stained apron and lowered his voice. "I was talking with some of the guys, the ones that were there that night. They're willing to testify that you were provoked."

Provoked. Maybe I had been, but things are never that simple. Not for me, anyway. The muted chatter and click of balls at the pool table behind me told me the guys were trying to figure out how to approach me. Or avoid me.

"I appreciate that. I'm still trying to decide who to use for my lawyer."

"I know some people."

I waved my hand. "No, I'm good. I have some calls out. Maybe I should stick with the public defender."

Dave made a sour face. "Don't be stupid."

I'd never figured him for a legal expert. "I'll have the financial hardship angle covered. As of this afternoon I'm on unpaid leave until this case is resolved. After that I'll probably be plain old fired."

"Delivergistics said that?"

I could still see the pained look on my boss, Cliff's, face. I think it was the first time in my life when someone said how sorry they were, and I believed them. "Company policy. Doesn't matter who buys my version. I have a felony assault charge. Until it goes away I can't work for them."

"Damn. That sucks."

QUICK FIX

I drained my beer and watched the suds crawl back to the bottom of the mug. "I guess I shouldn't have mentioned that while opening a tab."

Dave shook his head. "Don't worry about it. I wish I'd been here. I'd have tossed that asshole out before he had a chance to take things so far."

Dave left to serve another customer. He'd heard all about what happened. I didn't need to rehash it with him. But he was a good listener. Part of the job.

I don't make a habit of beating up lawyers, or anyone else for that matter, even if they deserve it. Usually. The thing was, while I hated the mess my life had become, I wasn't now, nor would I ever be, sorry for punching that punk's lights out.

I chugged my beer and hoped it'd quiet my thoughts. Not tonight; it just set them loose.

* * *

Dave had brought me enough beer to get me thinking about making the painful hobble to the bathroom, but not enough to stop thinking about Fenster, Beth, and the train wreck our marriage had become.

The knee would heal up, the marriage wouldn't, and both hurt. Life limps on.

Red Connor left the pool table and approached when I slid off the barstool. "How's it going, Kyle?"

He'd been there last week, front row seat.

"Could be better, but I'll live."

"Did Dave talk to you about lining up a good lawyer?" Red walked with me toward the men's room. The

5

big guy worked for the roofer's union. A couple years older than me but still shy of forty, he was a lifer. We met on a project after my old man had pulled strings to get me into the shop.

"Yeah, he did. Thanks, and I just may need to take you up on that." I liked Red, he'd at least pretended to understand when I chose to leave the secure but slow seniority track. At least Pop never lived to see me go.

Red studied my face. "Shame it didn't leave a big cut. You could get pictures. He started it."

"I'm too tough for my own good, I guess." I shook his hand.

* * *

Outside of the bathroom it felt like I'd pissed away my buzz along with the beer. Even so, the knee felt better than I had any right to expect. That, and I was so used to a certain level of pain I hardly noticed it anymore.

Then I spotted another asshole looking for me. He was a shifty, scheming weasel who'd con his own mother. In fact he had. I had no idea what he wanted with me tonight. Ryan "Anything for a Buck" Buckley.

My best friend.

Chapter 2

Kelly's Korner

"Go away for a few days and what happens?" Ryan crossed the room and pointed to a just-opened table.

The guy was a true pain in the ass and got into enough shit to fill a cesspool. The difference was nothing ever touched him, but everything stuck to me.

"Whatcha drinking?" He waved to Dave who began to draw a pitcher.

"Some of your beer, I guess. How was the flight back?" I asked.

Ryan stood just five foot eight on a good day, and looked something like a leprechaun with sunburn. No shit, one time he grew a beard and out of nowhere people left boxes of Lucky Charms at his spot in the mess hall. His haircut was the only military thing about him yet both of us worked for a supply logistics company with a large military contract. Our work had us in and out of hot zones in the Middle East all the time.

"You know, deadheading in a jump seat all the way from the Sandbox."

Odd, Delivergistics sent us commercial unless there was a reason to rush us somewhere. "What was the big hurry?"

"I heard you were in trouble. So I came running." The gleam in his eye told me not to waste time pressing the point.

"You missed the fun." I gave him the short version of what happened. The way he nodded told me he knew more than he let on.

"So Cliff won't budge?" Ryan worked for him as well. "Maybe I could say something."

"Not his call. Company policy and they can't get caught cutting corners. He said contractors are under the microscope right now."

Ryan's eyes were getting that crazy twirl. "But if the charges went away?"

I held up my hand. Ryan thought he could talk his way out of anything. "You don't know this lawyer. I half-think he pulled this crap just to get me to pop him."

"At least you got your money's worth."

"Doubt it. I think he has *Born to Sue* tattooed on his ass."

"Have to ask Beth," Ryan grinned at me.

"You looking to sue me too?" I held up a fist but couldn't help smiling.

Ryan turned serious. He glanced around, but nobody paid any attention to us. "What if I told you there was a way to keep working for Delivergistics and afford a decent place to live to boot?"

"Who do I have to kill?" I joked.

"Nobody's going to get killed." Ryan didn't smile.

My guts iced over. "Your timing stinks. I'm in enough trouble already."

"My timing is perfect. And haven't you ever heard of fighting fire with fire?"

"You asked me to meet you here and so I came. Why?" It came out edgier than intended, but I was getting tired.

"I need your help. And I think you need mine."

I knew I should have stopped him there, but I said, "Go on."

Ryan spoke in his shifty voice that was so low I turned my right ear to him. The left one hadn't worked right since our last adventure in a truck over in Iraq.

"Got an arrangement set up and it's going to come off next week. Things are moving faster than I expected. This is a real window of opportunity thing." That rang false. Ryan only came across as a seat-of-the-pants deal maker, but he always planned things out in detail.

"And you heard about my problem and decided last second to do me a solid?"

Ryan shrugged. "Let's call it win-win. I need a driver for two nights of work, and the guy I was going to use got stopped on a DUI. The son of a bitch had warrants I didn't know about and now he's in lockup."

"I'm lucky to be out myself." Not really. I had a clean record and this was my first offense. "I'm not eager for a trip back so fast."

"That's what makes this so beautiful. Officially, nothing illegal will happen. This is a true victimless crime. Before I go on, in or out, you can't say a word."

"Don't be an asshole."

"Promise."

"Fine, I promise, as long as we're not talking about murder or something."

Ryan gave me that *all's right with the world* Chiclet flasher. "That's my boy, Kyle." He leaned in toward me. "What do you know about Aztec sculpture?"

"Not a damn thing." Where the hell was this going?

"Me either. And lucky for us, neither do the Pennsylvania State cops in charge of seized property."

"So?"

Ryan looked like he was going to burst. "So, a certain drug kingpin got all his property seized and it turns out he was really into ancient art. This guy died in jail and the state is sending all the property to auction."

"How do you know this?"

"A guy on the inside of the property room I work with sometimes tipped me off."

"Whoa. You want to rob a police station? Are you out of your mind?"

"Rob sounds so," he paused, "violent. We're going to move an inconsequential crate from right under their noses. And they're going to pay us to do it."

All I could imagine were cameras and facial recognition leading the cops to my house before I even got home. "I'm not looking to live on the run the rest of my life."

"Don't be so dramatic. You haven't heard the rest. I said the cops don't have a clue about art."

"They still care about value. What are we talking here?"

"A few grand, but they won't even notice that."

I almost shouted and caught myself. "Why would you kick a hornet's nest for a few grand? No way."

"Calm down for Christ's sake. The cops hired an outside expert to appraise the items so they'll know what to expect at auction."

The light started to come on. "And this expert—"

"Check out college boy!" Ryan cracked up. "Yeah, champ, he's with me. And the dude is as legit as they come in terms of bona fide knowledge of art, especially Central American antiquities. This was his idea! He and my police guy have pulled some side deals together here and there. But this is the big one. As we sit, the official auction listing includes some good stuff, properly valued, and also one set of high-quality replicas of three statues known as the Aztec Black Dogs."

Now my head was spinning. "So you are going to bid on fakes, but they are real?"

Ryan gave me a nod of admiration. "You'd make a great hustler if you put your mind to it." He shook his head. "A fine idea, but we already thought of it. The problem is we might have some competition."

"Who?"

"A certain party who has been watching this merchandise since the arrest knows they're real and wants them for himself."

"Hang on. How much are the real ones worth?"

"Retail? Over two million bucks for the set."

I could see what the fuss was about but also some huge holes in what he'd told me. "The cops don't realize what they have, but they still expect to find statues. I can still get locked up for swiping a few grand as easily as a pricier item."

Ryan was enjoying himself too much. "Our expert is also a frustrated but talented artist in his own right. He's crafted a set of replicas that match his appraisal description to perfection."

I let that thought sink in. "So the cops are expecting a set of fakes to go to auction and—."

"With your help, that's exactly what they'll have."

"So you're saying they'll never know they once had the real deal and won't realize anything is missing?"

Ryan nodded. "Like I said, victimless crime."

"Damn. That's pretty good."

"It doesn't get any better. The artist has been waiting years for a chance like this. Everybody wins." Ryan said.

"Wait. What are you going to do, take the statues to a pawnshop?"

"Really?" Ryan rolled his eyes, face going stony. "This is where I need your help most. Part one is making the switch. Should be simple. So is part two, but a little riskier."

"I'm still sitting here."

"I mentioned potential competition at the auction. We offered a chance for him to avoid a costly bidding war."

"Who is he?"

"You don't want to know. We're not dealing with him directly, anyway. Buying knockoffs at a cop auction is one thing. High profile art sales are a bit different. So we had to bring in some local talent with more wide reaching contacts, the kind with deep pockets."

"Local?"

"A blast from our past. Good news is that I think he trusts us."

"You *think* he trusts us? You know how to fill someone with confidence. Also, I don't know much in the way of local talent." I racked my brain trying to think who we'd both know who was shady. Didn't take long. "Wait a minute. You're not talking about Sheehan?"

"Shut up. You want the whole place to hear you?" Ryan looked around.

Danny "Iceballs" Sheehan went to high school with Ryan and me. I went the jock route and Ryan managed to hustle without pissing off either the Italians or the Irish. No mean trick. Meanwhile, Sheehan was hooked up with the Northeast Philly Irish mob.

"I don't *know* him," I said.

"You remember his cousin, Meg." Ryan smirked.

"We were getting along until you stole her from me."

"Excuse me, *you* broke up with her. Not my fault if she found comfort in my arms."

"Whatever." It hadn't been serious and I tried to let her down easy. She was nice, but there were lots of distractions in high school for a football player, particularly cheerleaders. Also I knew what her family was like. Danny was a mean mother when crossed.

I lost track of both by college. Apparently Ryan had kept in touch.

"This is getting heavy." I finished my beer. "How about I think about it?"

Ryan's face turned grim. He reached across the table and gripped my arm. "You haven't heard my offer."

"Whatever it is, it won't solve my problems." The words sounded strangely responsible coming out of my mouth. "I'm sure you know someone else."

"I already told you. The other driver is out. Sheehan's pissed about the switch and the only reason he calmed down enough to keep the meet was when I mentioned you."

I felt my teeth grind. "You had no right to do that."

"Kyle, I'm desperate. This thing is once in a lifetime and risk free." He paused. "We'll be even."

"You're not going there."

"Even and you still get what I promise."

He was. "That's not fair."

"I saved your life," he said.

"You did. And your own, don't forget that."

"Now who's being unfair? If I hadn't spotted the IED and noticed the way they forced that kid out into the road—"

QUICK FIX

"Stop." But it was enough. Now I saw the highlight reel of that truck ride in Iraq where we rolled through a hot zone and that kid jumped into our path. I swerved to miss him and yeah, it was Ryan who spotted the red gas can in the other lane and grabbed the wheel on pure instinct. The improvised bomb blast that ripped into the truck would have killed us both instead of just shredding my left knee and shattering my left eardrum. At least I didn't run over the kid. The explosion knocked him out of the way. In pieces.

"This is nothing. It's all set up and all you need to do is drive the truck. Not like it's a getaway car."

"How's it different than a bank heist?"

"You're serious? First off, no alarms and angry armed guards, and at the end of the day this so-called bank won't even know anything is missing."

That last thought stuck with me. "The state never even suspected these statues are valuable?"

Ryan must have sensed progress and he pounced. "The state goons don't know art! If you don't believe me, ask my guy inside." Ryan paused. "Okay don't, but trust me. That's what makes this perfect. The appraiser told them what they have and we'll make sure those expectations are met."

"I'm not saying yes to anything. But the buyer on the other end?" We were still just talking; I figured it couldn't hurt to have more info.

"They know about the statues and understand we have them. I don't want them getting the auction idea themselves. We deliver the goods and they hand over cash. Our friend from high school gets his fee as do you and my man on the inside."

"And my cut?"

"Fifty. And you get a favor."

"As in thousand?"

Ryan nodded. "That should get you out of that dinky room you're renting."

"And the favor?"

"Remember I asked about getting your job back?"

"I told you—"

Ryan held up his hand. "I know, but I heard about what happened and talked to my guy."

"You have a lot of guys."

"Maybe. This one is owed a big favor by a certain prosecutor who will be handling your assault case."

"What?"

Ryan flashed his teeth. "And that guy owes *me* a big favor, which I'll pass to you if you're in. He'll see to it that the charges get dropped."

"How?"

"Don't look a tossed case in the mouth. I try to focus on results. You said if the charges are resolved you get to work, right?"

"Yeah, I guess."

"Well, there you go."

I didn't see that one coming. On the one hand, I'd smacked Fenster all right. I hadn't known he had a glass jaw under his beard but still. And he provoked me, no two ways about it. Might be worth it all just to see his expression. "What about the lawsuit?"

"What lawsuit?"

"Fenster can still sue me in civil court."

Ryan shook his head. "One miracle at a time, huh? Work with me and after the criminal charges fall apart maybe he sees things in another light."

"All right. Let me think about it."

"Twenty-four hours."

Chapter 3

Outside Philadelphia

I sat at the rest stop inside my truck and drummed my fingers on the well-worn steering wheel. More than once I tried to tell my hands to start the thing and drive away. Who needed this crap?

I did. But it killed me to admit it. The rationalizations flew thick in my head. I'd gotten myself into a fair spot of trouble all on my own, so who was I to judge Ryan? And wasn't he coming along at the perfect time for me to do some, let's say questionable but, ultimately harmless, work? And wouldn't that work help me patch up my self–inflicted wounds?

It wasn't the first time Ryan had cut some corners at risk to himself, to help me out.

I remember Mom sat at the kitchen table when I came through the door after football practice. She held a letter and stared at it with this blank, numb expression.

"Mom, are you okay?"

She turned to me like she'd just noticed I'd entered the room. Usually I got a hug and then something to eat. Not today. "They cancelled me."

"Who? The insurance company?" Since her recent ovarian cancer diagnosis they'd fought tooth and nail over every treatment option. After the surgery, the chemo follow up had been helping, but it was expensive.

"Those bastards. Alternate regimen, my ass. They put Jeanie Davis on the same crap and she was gone in six months."

QUICK FIX

I hardly knew my mom's friend from high school, but after the diagnosis it seemed like everyone had a story. Too many with shitty endings.

She'd swatted away her tears like they were pesky flies, but she couldn't conceal her shaking when I held her.

"Don't worry. When Dad gets home we'll think of something. Maybe one of those lawyers...."

"We can't afford a lawyer. They know that."

"Maybe one of those free ones on TV?"

The next day I told Ryan about it. "The thing that scared me the most was when Dad did come home he got this defeated look in his eyes that I'd never seen before."

"What did he say?" Ryan asked.

"Oh, all the right things. We'd appeal and try one of those lawyers. Maybe we'd sue the pants off them."

"Yeah, and you might see a dime from them by the year 2000," Ryan scoffed.

"Mom said she wasn't interested in their pants, she just wanted her meds."

And that was when Ryan got his own look and it had nothing to do with defeat. "She said the meds she is taking are helping?"

"Definitely. But they're big bucks, you know?"

"You still got the scrip bottle? The good stuff?"

"Yeah, but it's almost empty," I said.

"She won't miss it for an hour will she?"

Ryan made a copy of the scrip and about a week later showed up at our house right after I got home from practice. She was already showing signs of being off the old medicine.

"Mrs. Logan, may I speak to you for a minute?" Ryan asked.

I saw the bottle in his hand and heard the rattle that told me it was full. When they came back into the kitchen my Mom still looked exhausted, but her eyes sparkled.

"What's in that?"

"My old medicine, bless him."

I took the bottle from her and saw it was the same old bottle but refilled as if by magic. For a second I thought he'd come up with a placebo or something and I was ready to knock him cold for playing games. But I looked inside and they were identical.

Ryan seemed to read my mind. "Yeah, they're the real thing. Not even generic. Nothing but the best for your mom." He grinned.

"Where—"

"Don't ask. The less you know the better," Ryan turned to my mother. "Mrs. Logan, stick with what it says on the label and don't forget to fill the scrips for that other garbage. Don't say anything to your doctor, okay?"

Mom got with the program and laughed at her doctor's surprise that she was responding well in the coming months. She always wanted to pay Ryan, but he shrugged it off every time.

QUICK FIX

Years later, after the cancer came back and there were no more miracles, Mom spoke to Ryan on her deathbed. "Tell me, do you also have connections on the other side?"

"No ma'am, but I could probably use some," he'd told her.

He could always make her laugh.

Ryan didn't charm everyone and sometimes his small size and appetite for hustles put him at odds with some burly, if gullible, servicemen. Over in Iraq I'd protected him from a couple of Marines who were ready to pound him flat for tricking them. I got a cracked rib and a chipped tooth for my trouble. Ryan hadn't even been bruised.

And now he needed my help again, but I needed his too, so I found myself waiting for him at a rest area while the normal people of the world prepared to start their day.

* * *

The A-1 Movers truck pulled up alongside my aging pickup. After my last trip to the Sandbox I'd been thinking about replacing it, but the financial horrors that come with divorce meant it'd have to wait. Then again, if things worked out on this deal....

I reminded myself not to count anything and focus on the task at hand.

Ryan hopped out of the truck, already dressed in white coveralls, and he carried a set for me. "Morning, sunshine."

"You remembered my size." Maybe I sounded more confident than I felt.

"Hop in back and get changed. We need to roll." Ryan tossed me the white uniform and dug through his pocket until he pulled out a set of keys. It made an echoing sound when he opened up the back. It was empty other than some canvas pads and bungee cords piled in the way back.

Sure enough, the clothes fit and I climbed down. The four ibuprofen I'd taken earlier kept the knee to a dull ache.

Ryan watched me walk. "Don't worry. Truck's automatic. You know where the Troop in Media is located?"

I shook my head and climbed into the cab on the driver's side. It was a basic white-box truck, no different from a U-Haul available for rent. Ryan joined me on the other side.

"It's near the Mint on Baltimore Pike."

"Got it." I knew the place. He handed me some cards, including my driver's license that I'd let him borrow.

"In case they ask. You're a new hire, but here are your bona fides. Doubt we'll need them."

I looked them over. "That's my real name."

"So you should be able to remember it." Ryan pointed to the ignition and I started the truck. "I told you. Nobody will be looking for anything when we leave."

"Keep telling me." I put the truck into gear and pulled out onto the road.

* * *

Delaware-Pennsylvania Border

"Take 202, it'll be on the left." Ryan guided me, turn-by-turn, to our first stop, a self-storage place just over the state line.

QUICK FIX

I pulled in the gate and this early it looked like we had the place to ourselves. Ryan got out and I noticed he wouldn't let me see the code he punched in. I didn't care. The gate rolled open and we drove to his spot. He unlocked the door and I left the truck to join him.

It was a large storage unit with some old furniture and a partially covered upright piano to one side. Toward the front sat a medium-sized crate, maybe double the size of a steamer trunk.

"There's our baby." Ryan unlocked the back of the truck and pulled down a dolly. The crate wasn't too hard for him to handle alone. "Can you pull out the ramp?"

I slid it out from under the truck, and together we got the crate loaded and secured.

"Good to go?"

"As good as I'm going to be," I said.

* * *

Troop K; Pennsylvania State Police

"Pull around the side. There should be some other trucks loading up the Diaz case property. Remember, our load is next to it, the Saxby case."

There were. The wheel felt slick and I gripped it tighter. I tried to focus by remembering how I'd block out danger in hot zones. Nobody was going to blow us up, anyway.

I saw several workers from Surefire Transport and Storage and for a weird moment worried I'd run into someone I knew. Nope, never saw those guys before, a pair of men carried a large boxed up painting into a long truck. I

23

pulled around and backed the truck up. I rolled the window down and strained my good ear in case I was about to roll over something expensive or living.

The back of the truck tapped to a rest on the rubber dock bumpers. "Now what?"

Ryan held a clipboard. "Wait a second. I'll get us signed in. You going to be okay to move some things?"

"Yeah. I can carry stuff. It's more the bending and speed work. I can run if I have to, but then I'm usually done for a week."

"Slow and steady. We get paid by the hour, remember?" Ryan jumped out.

A few minutes later he called me and I got out of the truck. Once I reached the dock I saw a middle-aged cop with a clipboard of his own. Several pieces of furniture sat on the dock along with a couple of crates.

When the cop turned away Ryan winked at me and we put the crate on the dolly. We got it onto the truck and put it next to the one we'd brought. A perfect match.

Twenty minutes later, after we'd put away most of the items from our assignments, the cop ambled over and peered at his clipboard. I read the name tag on his uniform: Bishop.

Bishop called over one of the other crew from the Diaz locker. Bishop jabbed a finger at one line on the sheet and the worker shook his head. Eventually the guy pointed in our direction.

"Hey!"

Ryan looked over. "Who? Us?"

QUICK FIX

Bishop walked over. "We're missing a crate. You guys grab it?" He read off the description.

"Was it sitting right there?" Ryan pointed to where the crate we'd taken once sat.

"Dumb ass. That's not on your manifest." Bishop flipped through some pages and jabbed a finger at the paper. "There. Do you see a crate that size anywhere on this list?"

"I guess not. We were told to hurry up and it was right next to the other stuff."

Bishop shook his head. "I don't give a crap. Put it back where you found it." He hooked a thumb at the crew who now stood off a ways in amusement. "They're in a hurry too."

"Relax! We'll put it back. Simple mistake." Ryan raised his voice.

"Two minutes." Bishop pointed at the dock. "I have better things to do than babysit you people."

I got the hint and started to move some items to clear the way. Ryan joined me and we off-loaded the crate with the fakes from the storage unit. He covered up the one we'd just taken off the loading dock with a tarp.

Bishop returned, scowling, and examined the crate then checked off the item and nodded to the other crew who whisked it away.

We'd reloaded everything and Bishop came over and looked over the back. My heart sped up, but he never set foot inside the box. "Sign here." He held out the clipboard to Ryan who scribbled away.

* * *

25

Back on the road, Ryan gave me directions to the auction house. Turned out it wasn't all that far from the storage place. Just over the state line still in Pennsylvania.

"I swear Bishop is a frustrated actor." Ryan laughed once we were clear of the police facility.

"I wasn't sure at first." An understatement. "Your guy?"

"He's been a fixture there. Bitter about his career until he figured out how to work the angles."

"What about on the other end? Should we get the crate moved first?"

"We've got our official inventory now. Everything on the manifest is in the truck. They won't worry about anything else we're carrying. They aren't cops."

"It felt too easy."

"Have a little faith." Ryan punched me in the shoulder.

* * *

After we dropped off the other property I drove the truck back to StoreMore storage where we off-loaded the crate and tucked it in back among the old furniture and an upright piano. I had to trust Ryan's judgment that it would be safer here than left overnight in the vehicle. Then again, for fifty grand I'd be willing to take a blanket and sleep next to it in the truck if necessary.

"Now what?"

Ryan locked the steel corrugated door. "Now we take you back to where you parked and I'll meet you back there tomorrow night. Then you and I take it to our meet-up and an hour after that, we get drunk."

"Just like that?"

"We stick by the numbers and it should go fine. Everybody wins."

"I appreciate your faith in my intimidating presence and all, but what if they plan a rip-off?"

Ryan feigned shock. "Hey, you're right. I never thought of that. Let's bring an army."

"You done?" I just wanted to get through the whole thing alive. "I might make a mugger think twice but professional gangsters?"

"You're going to be there because Sheehan trusts you and we shouldn't look like pushovers. You can handle yourself."

"Against Sheehan? And whoever he brings?"

"Against a curveball." Ryan held up his hand. "A very unlikely curveball, mind you. Plus, you can drive under pressure."

"You're not making this easier." The reality of what we were doing was sinking in. A little late, but the crate transfer earlier seemed like a game. Sheehan didn't play games.

"Sheehan has no reason to rip us off," Ryan said.

"Why not? And don't say because he likes me so much."

Ryan smiled. "Remember, he's the middleman. He's handing over someone else's cash in exchange for the statues."

"He could keep the cash and still make the delivery."

Ryan rubbed his chin. "He could, but he's trying to show that he's a player to his own organization. Robbing us would look bad."

"If we're around to say anything."

Chapter 4

The next day Ryan had me back the truck up close to the storage unit door. He had to squeeze his arm in to unlock the handle and roll it up. I understood. This way in the dark nobody would see what we were doing.

"I'll get the crate; you take care of the ramp."

He wheeled the dolly inside and I saw the flicker of a penlight after he banged into a couple chairs.

I pulled out the aluminum ramp, trying to do it slow and quiet though I couldn't tell you why. We were allowed in here. Just felt sneaky, I guess. There was just enough room to drop the ramp down and in place with the truck so close.

A minute later I heard Ryan grunt with effort and was about to offer to help when he rolled out from the back with a partially tarp-covered crate. Ryan's coveralls were coated in gray dust. The whole room smelled like my grandmother's attic, old wood and beeswax furniture polish.

"You know, you might think about doing this for real. You're pretty good with a dolly," I said as he struggled to push the crate up the steep ramp.

I let him struggle, his pride clamped his mouth shut. Fine by me. This was his show.

I spared a glance at my watch and we needed to get moving. "Forty five minutes," I reminded him.

"Give me a sec. One more tie-down. They may be stone, but they're real old and worthless if we swerve and bust them up."

"As long as the kids stay out of the road." I had meant it to be a lighthearted throwaway, but the remark sat on my chest like a brick.

* * *

In the cab Ryan handed me the fake IDs. "In case we get stopped." I tucked them away and tried not to think about it. My job was to drive smooth and safe and not to attract attention.

Ryan bent forward and reached into the canvas bag at his feet inside the cab of the truck. I rechecked the fuel and had already checked the tires before getting in. It was weird, the rituals both comforted me and keyed me up. My body knew we were on the job.

"Put this under your seat," he handed me a black Beretta 9mm. Just like what we carried in Iraq.

"Are you nuts?" I was glad the cab doors were closed. "Fake ID won't mean a thing if we get caught with those. And Sheehan would probably shoot first if he saw them."

"Don't worry about the cops. These are a precaution." Ryan put a twin to my gun under his own seat. "The last thing I want to worry about is getting jacked before or after. Okay?"

I stuck the pistol under the seat. I wasn't too relaxed about the idea of driving away with a case full of cash and I figured the exchange wouldn't be in the safest area of Philly.

* * *

"Stay on Richmond until you see the warehouse on the right."

QUICK FIX

"The one that used to be the plumbing supply company?" We weren't far from the old neighborhood.

"You remember that dump?" Ryan said.

"Smoked my first Lucky Strike there." I smiled. "And my last. Mom smelled it on me and I got whipped so bad I never touched them again."

"You always told me it was 'cause you were playing football."

"I thought I said it was for my health." I turned into the lot of the old building, now a *For Lease* empty storage site. I didn't see any other cars.

"Pull around back," Ryan said.

I saw some shadowy SUVs in the darkness beyond the security light, a half-assed effort to keep away thieves. My guess is burglars stayed away because there wasn't anything left to steal. Other than the limited spotlight, the back area was as dark as city places can get. The property backed onto an empty field and past that, the Delaware River.

"Now what?" I asked.

A large door rumbled open and fluorescent lights flickered on to reveal a bare concrete floor inside the warehouse. Then the SUVs came to life and our truck was awash in their headlights. One vehicle pulled into the building and a beefy arm stuck out of the driver's side and waved for us to enter.

"Follow him," Ryan said. The second SUV pulled in behind us. Once all three vehicles were inside, the door lumbered closed.

It was a big area inside, but I was conscious that we now had three engines spewing carbon monoxide into the space. Still, I was reluctant to turn off the motor.

Two men got out of the first SUV. One, the driver, looked like a washed-up nose tackle. He stood about six foot three with broad shoulders inside his black leather coat. He carried a pump shotgun with a pistol grip that looked like a toy in his hands.

The second man I recognized. Danny Sheehan. *Iceballs* to his enemies. Named after the snowball fight he picked with some of the bigger kids from the Italian mob when we were all a lot younger. They'd beaten Sheehan up the day before and the legend was that he challenged them to a rematch, only he used snow covered rocks instead.

"Cut the engine," the big guy said. The shotgun wasn't aimed at us. Didn't need to be. I was an educated man and got the idea.

I was conscious of the gun under my seat and the fact that Ryan was armed as well. "Go easy, here." I tried to speak without moving my lips.

"Everything's cool," he said.

"Toss the keys," the goon ordered.

I glanced at Ryan who shrugged. It sent a chill through my body because it seemed like he hadn't seen that coming, either. Now we were stuck.

I threw the keys out the window and put my hands on the dash.

Sheehan noticed that and grinned. He'd had dyed blonde hair for as long as I could remember and now that it was thinning it looked almost white in the harsh light. His cold, pale blue eyes locked onto my gaze.

Sheehan gestured for us both to come out.

"Just stay chill and follow my lead," Ryan whispered.

I stepped to the concrete floor and now all the engines switched off. Exhaust stench filled the air, but it was breathable enough. The place looked bigger on the inside.

I could hear the door open from the SUV behind us but didn't bother to look. We were covered. Nothing to do now but play out the hand.

Sheehan approached me. He was taller than Ryan, but so was almost everyone. I had a couple inches on him and maybe thirty pounds, some of it even muscle, but Sheehan was like a pit bull. Up closer I saw he'd never gotten his broken nose reset properly. The bridge canted to one side.

"Long time no see, Kyle. How you doing?"

I paused, unsure what to call him. We'd never been friends, but I wasn't about to call him Iceballs. "Just fine, Danny—"

The goon interrupted. "That's *Mister* Sheehan."

I shook my head. "That was his father."

Sheehan gave a little nod. "Yeah, it was. Danny is fine. You too, Ryan. We're all old buddies."

Despite the light tone, the goon still held the gun. Although not aimed at us, we were meant to see it. The easy banter bit never touched Sheehan's eyes.

"Sorry to hear about him," I said. The old man's death made the papers, and this deal might have been Sheehan's effort to step up to fill his shoes.

"He always smoked too much. But thanks." Sheehan looked at the truck. "So what have you fine hoodlums brought me today?"

Ryan found his tongue. He looked more nervous than I felt. Probably from playing in a bigger league. "No hoodlums, just a couple of middlemen, right?"

Sheehan's eyes narrowed and I didn't think he cared for that characterization. He moved to the back of the truck. "Let's see them."

I hadn't noticed any sign of payment yet, but decided to shut up about that and let Ryan play his part. Unless he started to piss Sheehan off.

It took a moment, and we had the crate sitting in the room. Still no sign of money. I fought the urge to look behind.

Sheehan glanced past us and said, "Brian."

I spared a glance and saw a second man with another shotgun wave toward the other SUV that was blocking the exit. A short man hopped out and approached the crate. He carried a pry bar about a foot long in one hand a notebook in the other.

"Who's he?" Ryan's voice quivered as he looked.

Sheehan answered for the man, who ignored Ryan and went to work with the bar to open the top of the wooden crate. The nails screeched in the quiet space. "He's with me, that's who he is. Our client wants to make sure he's getting what he's paying for, and I'm not an art expert."

34

QUICK FIX

"We aren't either, but our guy is and he swore," Ryan started and stopped when the weasely guy with the tanned bald head and stringy hair worn in a skullet reached in with two hands and extracted one of the statues.

I wasn't sure what to expect. The thing looked like a dog, black, polished stone. Once placed on the ground it stood about two feet high. I'm guessing it weighed about forty or fifty pounds. The whole crate packed up was almost two hundred pounds, so that seemed about right including the rest of the statues.

The guy thumbed through his notebook and mumbled to himself. He seemed to be comparing it to a photo.

"Height's good. Solid basalt stone. Okay." He shone a light on the figure and took a measuring tape out.

Ryan stood, and beads of perspiration covered his face. His anxiety was contagious, I fought to keep my composure.

Sheehan looked bored, except that his eyes kept shifting to the guy evaluating. He was plenty interested.

"Tool markings are the correct size and depth. Let's see the rest of them." The guy said.

When he took out the other two, the heads of the dogs were at different angles. One down, one up and the last looking straight ahead. Considering the pair of shotguns near us I hoped like hell that was what the buyer was expecting.

"I heard you got banged up over in Muzzieland," Sheehan spoke to me.

How'd he hear that? And why would he care? "Yeah? People exaggerate, I'm doing much better."

"I didn't know you pulled this sort of work. If you're feeling up to it and want something more interesting than being a bagman, give me a call."

"I don't do this sort of thing," I said without thinking.

Sheehan laughed. "Me either."

"He's getting his straight job back," Ryan said.

"Yeah." I said and hoped it was true. I wiped my sweaty hands on the coveralls, this was not my next career path.

The guy with the scraggly hair stood up. He posed the statues and held up the reference picture. They matched. Above the photo read, "ItzCuintli."

"What's that mean?" Sheehan said.

"Mythological guide dogs for the dead," the man said. "One looks at this world, one for the underworld, and one to the heavens."

"Before they get done with all the looking and take a piss on the floor, you going to tell me if they're real or not?" Sheehan said.

"Everything matches exactly, right down to the scuffmarks," the guy said.

Sheehan grinned. "Okay then, put them back, real careful." He looked at Ryan and me. "Step over here gentleman, I have something for you."

Ryan seemed relieved, but I figured this was the part where we either got paid or shot. I wasn't going to kid myself about all that happy chatter from Sheehan. He was dangerous on a good day.

QUICK FIX

Sheehan led us over to his SUV and he popped the rear hatch and leaned inside. I turned my head so my good ear might catch one of those goons coming up behind me. Not that it would help much.

Sheehan reached inside and pulled out a briefcase. He flicked it open and presented it to Ryan. "It's all there, but count it if you like."

I peered over and saw more cash than I'd ever seen in one place. Banded stacks of bills filled the case. Ben Franklin and his clones all but winked at me. Now I began to understand why Ryan was so tense. People got killed over a hundred bucks in this town. Less, even.

Ryan closed the case. "Not necessary. Thanks, Danny."

"Thank the client, it's his money," Sheehan said.

"I'll do just that. Hope he enjoys." Ryan backed up and we made our way toward the truck. I tried and failed to keep everyone in sight. No guns pointed at us and I took that as a good sign.

* * *

We sat in the truck and watched the goons load the resealed crate onto the back of one vehicle. Sheehan chewed on a toothpick and supervised.

When the metal door rattled up I began to think we might survive the transaction. The second SUV started up and backed out of our way. I reached for the ignition, the keys were missing.

Just then I felt a thump outside my door. I turned and Sheehan's grinning face was at the window. He held up the keys. "Thought you could use these."

"Shit, I forgot." I reached for them.

He closed his fist around the keys. "Think about my offer. You know how to reach me."

"Thanks. But you know...." I wanted to tell him I didn't have his number, but it didn't matter. Sheehan was as hard or easy to find as he wished. I knew where to ask around if it came to that.

He dropped the keys into my palm. "Yeah. I know."

* * *

"A couple more turns," Ryan said. We'd pulled away from the warehouse without incident, but both of us were wriggling in our seats like they were electrified.

"See anyone on your side?" I asked again. I felt like a looped recording, but we both were looking for signs anyone picked us up after we parted from the SUVs. Didn't mean another car wasn't waiting to make a move on us.

"No. Take the next right and head up a quarter mile. Pull into the strip mall on the left."

Now Ryan picked up a canvas backpack and unzipped it up like a giant mouth. He popped open the briefcase and shook it over the opening.

The stacked bills tumble into the pack until the briefcase was empty. I couldn't stand it anymore. "Is that as much as it looks like?"

"It is if it looks like a cool million." He blew his breath out. "That's the one. Pull close to the dumpster on the right side first."

QUICK FIX

I turned into the lit but vacant strip of stores all closed for the night. I eased the truck as close as possible while being careful to keep the side mirrors from scraping.

Ryan leaned out the window and tossed the now empty briefcase. "Park it. Leave the keys under the seat and grab the piece."

"What's this?" Now that I thought of it I hadn't focused much on what happened after we got out of there. Once we got clear and were watching for tails it had occurred to me that going straight to my truck might not be the smartest idea.

Apparently Ryan agreed. "The briefcase *this*, is on the off chance Sheehan has gone high tech and put a tracker on it."

"And the truck?"

"Say goodbye, it's not our concern anymore." He wiped down his side of the interior of the cab, opened the door, and stripped off the coveralls. I did the same and we added them to the dumpster. "Head for that blue Caprice."

I walked over to the lone car. Ryan unlocked it and tossed the backpack into the trunk before getting into the driver's seat. "Let's boogie."

I was glad he drove slow enough to avoid attention from any cops. We were both carrying guns, not to mention a hell of a chunk of hard-to-explain change in the back.

We headed into Center City and mingled with the thin late night traffic. All the while both of us looked for signs of a tail. When we were sure it was safe Ryan drove up Market Street and picked up I-95.

* * *

At the rest area Ryan parked and left the engine running. He grinned. "Told you it would be easy."

"That's why you could wring out your coveralls from all the sweat?" I asked.

He laughed too long for the joke. "Yeah."

"It's over. Now what?"

Ryan held out his hand like I was supposed to pay him or something and I realized that he wanted the pistol still tucked into my belt. I glanced around to make sure nobody was watching, took it out, dropped the magazine and cleared the chamber.

"Here you go."

"Hold that thought." Ryan took the pistol and used a sweatshirt to conceal it while he got out of the car and went to the trunk. He returned a minute later with same sweatshirt wadded up in his hands and gave it to me.

I felt the weight. "I don't want—" The contents shifted and I looked inside.

"Yeah, you do." Ryan said.

Yeah, I did. Five bundles of cash, each marked with a white band reading, "$10,000."

"Don't spend it all in one place." He didn't smile. "Really. That'll attract the wrong kind of attention."

I stared at him. "I'm not an idiot. What about the other thing?" The more important part of the deal, as nice as the money was.

Ryan nodded. "That'll take a little longer, but I'll get the wheels going. I'm going to lay low for a bit so don't look for me, okay?"

"I thought we were going to get drunk together," I said.

"We will, I just need to get this safe, you know?"

The way he said it, I knew I'd be drinking alone.

Chapter 5

Three days later; Fishtown

"Two hands on that ladder, son," Rollie Trent, my stubborn landlord, hollered down to me when I turned around at the sound of a car backfiring.

I was anchoring the aluminum extension ladder while Rollie finished cleaning out the gutters on the place. "Sorry. I wish you'd let me do this."

The man was seventy three and a Vietnam War veteran who'd served as a sniper with the Marines. He tried to do everything himself, and the surest way to get him to overdo something was to suggest that he should take it easy.

I still tried.

"Bullshit. With your knee? I'm too old to catch a load like you if you fall. Incoming!" I heard him cackle as leaves and muck plopped onto the sidewalk.

I bitched about the circumstances around why I was living there and even let people like Ryan refer to it as a dump, but the truth was that this widower couldn't help the state of the neighborhood, and as far as the place itself went, he kept everything ship-shape.

We'd hit it off the night I met him playing pool at Kelly's. When he heard I was out on my ass he offered me a room.

At first he wouldn't hear of payment, but we agreed on five hundred bucks a month when it was clear I wouldn't be moving out anytime soon.

"Coming down," He shouted while wiping his hands on his jeans. The silt and decayed leaves smeared the clean denim in long finger-streaks. Rollie was a short guy with a lean physique. He still kept his dyed-brown hair in a crew cut.

The ladder trembled under my hands, but I was careful to make sure the red rubber feet kept their grip on the sidewalk.

"Kind of nice having you around here," Rollie said.

"Hopefully I'll be out of your hair before too long." I'd been going stir crazy waiting for some movement on the case so I could get back to work.

Rollie dug his hand into his pocket. He pulled out a fold of bills. The same one I'd given him this morning.

I glanced around. The narrow street was quiet, but I didn't know who might be watching. Not too many secrets in a neighborhood this close.

"What are you doing? That's yours."

"I know, and it will be again. I've been around. This sort of thing can take time to work through. Goddamned lawyers drag it all out until everyone forgets what the issue was in the first place."

"It's okay, Rollie. It's my rainy day fund."

His steel-gray eyes looked right through me. He didn't believe a word. "You might need it more right now, that's all."

Rollie didn't stay in the place because his wife died here, I knew he wasn't rich. Most of his tools were older than me. To be fair, they were probably in better working order.

I held up my hands so he couldn't give it to me. "Tell you what. If I need it, I'll ask, but that's two month's rent fair and square."

"All right, kid." He re-pocketed it and went inside while I collapsed the ladder and put it back in the crawl space under the house.

* * *

I'd begun to wonder if it was a good idea to keep the rest of the fifty grand hidden in the tiny bedroom at the house. I mean, I wasn't going to open a bank account or anything dumb like that, but I couldn't imagine what it must be like for Ryan to mess with nearly a million in bills. Knowing him, he already had it figured out.

True to his word, Ryan had been quiet. I doubted he'd gone back into work but couldn't be sure. I was staying away from the place at least until I heard something about my assault charge.

I couldn't speed Ryan up, but I haven't been known for my patience. I had an idea about moving things in the right direction. I pulled out ten grand and stuck it in a large manila envelope then grabbed the keys to my truck.

"Be back in a while, Rollie," I yelled up the stairs. The off-white paint still smelled fresh from the touch-up work we'd done yesterday.

"Bring me back a brunette. Six feet or taller," his voice carried down the stairs.

* * *

It wouldn't take long to drive from Fishtown to the upscale neighborhood of Chestnut Hill. Just ten miles, but a whole world away. I'd take the highway today to make time, but sometimes I'd drive the old neighborhoods just to remember. That would take me right through Temple University where Beth and I first met.

QUICK FIX

From the first day we met I knew she was determined to make her way to something bigger, just like me. She'd grown up in Baltimore, in a working class neighborhood not unlike Fishtown. Over the years it turned out our ideas of success weren't as similar as we thought. Maybe it was like Ryan said, that we were just very young when we fell in love, but that was such a cheesy cop-out that the phrase made me sick.

The truth is we both changed. She always worked hard, but over time it seemed like she needed to make sure everyone could see her progress. Who knows, maybe the material stuff was her way of keeping score for herself. At any rate, designer knockoffs became the real thing. Costume jewelry graduated to fourteen-carat. A little engagement ring was replaced by a rock the size of a damn skating rink.

Getting blown half to hell in Iraq rearranged my priorities too, and that wasn't her fault. I'm the one who had to seek adventure. Can't blame her that I found it.

* * *

Once I reached Chestnut Hill I found Fenster's small, pricey house and parked a half block away. I pulled out my cell. It annoyed me to have to act this way, and it bugged me even more the way jealousy stabbed into my belly when I'd seen the name on the mailbox. Fenster.

Technically, Beth still lived in the house we'd bought together, but more and more she was here. We were selling the place and I remember Beth laid out a bunch of logical reasons why I shouldn't keep the house. All I could hear in my memory was Fenster in the background yelling, "He can't afford it on his salary."

That night I played pool and drank beer at Kelly's until the urge to burn the place down went away.

Now here I was skulking around Beth's new neighborhood unwilling to march up to the door. Actually, I was, but the last time we spoke Beth had suggested Fenster was muttering about restraining orders and I didn't need to be arrested again. Hopefully he'd change his mind after tonight.

"Hello?" Beth picked right up. My stomach clenched at the sound of her voice and I could picture the girl from Temple on the other end of the line. I wondered when that crap would stop happening.

"Hey. I'm here."

"Outside? What's up?"

"I won't keep you long."

"Where are you? I don't see you." She sounded confused.

"Just down the street, the same old truck."

"He's away for a conference, you can come in if you want." Her voice sounded cool but not unfriendly.

"Nah. The neighbors might think something's going on." My brain knew it was over. Sometimes my heart ran on muscle memory. "I'll wait out here."

* * *

"You cut your hair, I noticed it the other day." I could swear her smile even touched her eyes for a second. She wore a simple white blouse and jeans. The cut of the fabric showed off her curves. Her left hand glittered with that diamond that must have cost more than my entire share from the other night.

"Looks more professional, don't you think?"

"It suits you." I paused and the silence weighed my chest down.

"Are you okay?" She walked next to me as I headed toward my truck.

I never knew how to answer that. "Getting by."

"I'm sorry about your job. I doubt Richard will budge on the charges but...."

I reached the truck and opened the door. The creak it made sounded extra loud on the quiet street. I leaned inside and took the envelope off the worn bench seat. "I'm sorry about what I did, but that won't pay doctor bills. Take this and give it to him. Hopefully it'll carry more weight than my apology." I handed it to her before I changed my mind. The air here even smelled like money.

Maybe it was her perfume.

"What's this?" She peeked inside and her nose crinkled like I'd given her road kill.

"In the days before bottomless credit cards it was known as cash." She always hated when I used air quotes at her.

Now her dark eyes flashed and her gaze drilled into me. "This is a lot."

"Ten grand." I'd taken off the paper band so it would look less like I'd robbed a bank. I jammed my hands into my pockets so she wouldn't try to give it back to me. "If it isn't enough, I'll see what I can do."

"Where did you get this?"

"Working. Where do you think?" For a second her condescending tone pissed me off so much that I forgot about where it really had come from.

She just stared at me, giving me a withering look that settled my stomach right down but lit a fire in my chest.

Oh yeah, those *good old days.*

"I've been working odd jobs here and there."

"What does that even mean?" The old Beth would have just said, "Bullshit."

"Ryan needed help on some things."

She held up her hands. "I don't want to know what he's into. Kyle, we can't accept this. It's a big gesture but…."

I shook my head. "Tell him it's an out of court settlement offer. It's a lot of money to me and I deserve to get hit for what I did, but I need my life back. You have a new, fancy world to play in. Me? I'm still stuck where I came from. Losing my job won't get me out of there."

She moved closer to me and I thought I saw some sympathy in her eyes. "This is all a little fresh. Maybe he'll let up after the swelling has gone down."

"I doubt it. He pulled that stunt in the bar on purpose. Maybe he wanted me to swing so he could rub it in even more." I tried to keep my anger from spilling onto Beth.

"And you fell right into his trap? Come on Kyle, you know he's been wanting to move forward and you've been cleared medically for a while."

"Are you saying I was dragging my feet? I know we're over, it's just—"

"Just what?" Beth said.

"I don't know. Wondering when I'd feel different?" It sounded lame coming out of my mouth because I didn't want her to realize that I hated losing her to a puke like Fenster. Shit, we were already done, but I didn't need him to keep pushing.

"What would that really change? You weren't around. Not for a long time. Even before you got hurt. And you were just as far away when we slept in the same bed."

"Overseas pays more. Always will. That seemed so important before, for both of us," I said.

She lowered her voice, but it hit me harder than if she screamed or punched me in the chest. "I won't apologize for wanting to do better in life." Her right hand covered her left and her fingertips traced over her ring. "I'm a damn good paralegal. Richard thinks I'd do well in law school." Now she stepped close. "You're a hard worker too, but the draw of overseas wasn't all about the money."

She had me there. "I guess it's like everyone said. We grew apart." I pulled my hands from my pockets but skipped the air quotes, though I hated that pat phrase.

"You don't believe me, but I'm sorry. And how all this," she swept her hand in the direction of Fenster's place, "got started. But he's been so supportive and helped me see things I never thought possible."

"I could move on, if I had my job back." I pointed at the envelope clutched in her hand. "Isn't that what everybody wants now?"

Now she looked sad and cast her gaze toward the ground. "He's furious. You don't understand how stubborn he can be."

Under the street light she looked more perfect than I'd ever seen her but somehow less beautiful. I felt sorry for her. Despite all the crap we'd put each other through, I saw she'd traded a big piece of herself to get this new lifestyle. Maybe she loved the guy. I hoped so, for her sake, but that selfish ass would only love her back on his terms. He had to be in charge. His way, all the time.

And a pillowcase of cash wouldn't change his mind.

"Keep the money, or give it to a good cause. Whatever he chooses to do I understand it's between him and me."

My cell phone rang and I didn't recognize the number. I dumped the call to voicemail.

"Kyle…."

I got into the truck and drove off. I saw her in the rear view mirror watching me.

Chapter 6

Kelly's Korner

By the third beer I already knew I'd be leaving the truck parked and walking home. It wouldn't be the first time. Luckily, Rollie's place was close.

So was the old house. I could always go back there, except Beth had changed the locks. Now one of those realtor key boxes sat on the front door. I knew how to get in anyway, but the brief thought faded. We were really selling to get rid of the mortgage. After that, and other fees, there wouldn't be much left. Kind of like our old life.

I signaled for another and Dave brought it. He was busy tonight so we hadn't talked at length. There wasn't much I could say to him.

I thought about what to do with the rest of the cash and began to laugh. I dialed it back before people near me started staring. If Ryan wasn't able to get those charges dropped, I'd be handing every cent over to one of the lawyers Dave had mentioned.

Easy come, easy go.

My cell rang; it was the same unknown number again. Damn telemarketers. Dumped it again and clipped the phone back to my belt.

I tried to watch the Phillies game on the TV over the bar, but I couldn't get into it despite the cheering section of old timers glued to their stools at the corner. I pulled out some cash and left it on the bar. Dave saw it and gave a little wave. Outside, the air had turned chilly. I thought about driving after all, but the walk would clear my head. I left my truck parked in a spot behind the bar where it would be safe.

* * *

A car slowed down when I was just leaving and my hackles came up. The car moved along and since nobody piled out and rushed me I figured it was nothing. It wasn't the best neighborhood, but I knew as long as I was careful I shouldn't worry. I don't start crap and certainly try not to look like an easy target.

The phone rang again and this time there was a message after I ignored that same number. This may not have been a great area to walk alone in the dark, and it was certainly not the place to hold a conversation. Might as well have a "Kick me!" sign on my back.

It could wait. I was only half a block away.

* * *

The glow from the lights in Center City illuminated the night sky between the boxy houses. I reached the door when I heard a low whistle from around the side of the house.

"Rollie?" He was usually in bed by now.

The same whistle again. Weird. I stepped around the corner and a blinding light stabbed out of the darkness. My hand flew up to shield my eyes and I couldn't see anything for a moment.

I took a step backward right into something solid that wasn't there a second ago. I tried to pivot and swing an elbow hoping it wasn't a misunderstanding with the cops.

Then a rough canvas sack popped over my head. Much worse than cops.

QUICK FIX

In an instant, the guy behind me knocked me to the ground. I heard a car engine roar then tires squeal to a stop. I yelled out and began kicking hard while trying to get that damn bag off my head. I felt a moment of satisfaction when one heel mashed into something soft and I heard a choked curse.

"Shut up and shut *him* up." I knew that voice. Danny Sheehan.

Fists and boots pummeled my body and then they rolled me onto my back and the bastards stood on my arms. I got ready to kick them away now that I knew where they were.

Then Sheehan hissed into my ear. "Quiet. You wake the old man up and he's dead. Got that?"

They knew about Rollie. Of course they did.

A second later I heard tape tearing and my legs and arms were bound up and then someone picked me up like I was a little kid. "No," I whispered.

Whoever had me must have been a professional wrestler. The next thing I knew it felt like was in a vice and I could barely breathe, let alone make any more noise.

The crusher threw me into an open van, judging by the sound of the thud and rocking while all the musclemen jumped in after me. The door closed and we were off.

"Danny. If you're there, this has to be a mistake. Whatever you think—" Someone punched me in the gut and knocked the rest of my breath out of my mouth. His fist buried so deep it felt like he could have grabbed my spine.

Gray and black dots swam across my eyes and I think I blacked out for a second. It felt like I might never get air into my lungs again.

"Don't kill him. Not yet." Sheehan's voice sounded a mile away.

* * *

I gave up trying to count the right and left turns. They were taking me somewhere and at least for now if I kept my mouth shut, they didn't beat on me.

Finally I heard an automatic door open and my mind's eye pictured the warehouse where the deal went down the other night. This place was quieter, more like a house somewhere.

The van pulled inside and seconds later the door rattled closed.

Out of sight.

They carried me out of the van and slammed me onto a hard chair. With the bag still over my head they strapped me to the seat with more heavy tape. I imagined I looked like something a huge spider captured, wrapped into a tasty package.

I could smell damp mildew and insect spray along with one of the goon's cheap aftershave.

"That's enough." Sheehan spoke to the guy with the roll of tape.

He snatched the bag off my head so quick the canvas gave my bad ear a rug-burn. The light made me blink. We were in an unfinished basement.

QUICK FIX

Sheehan smiled at me, then snapped a hard jab into my nose. The pain exploded into my brain just behind my eyes, which watered like mad.

I tried to speak, but Sheehan worked my midsection like I was a boxer in the ring.

The attack took me off guard and the gut punches knocked the wind out of me again. When Sheehan let up, my face felt wet and sticky, my nose throbbed and sent blood down my lip.

Sheehan paced in front of me. He wore a dark leather jacket and held what I thought was a pistol. As my vision cleared I saw it was a phone. My phone.

"Danny, what the fuck?" I said, when I got my breath back.

"Shut up. Little bastard brought you in on purpose. That was slick." Sheehan breathed fast and his voice came out in a snarl.

Sheehan's usual pasty complexion was flushed red. I remember even in high school that color meant someone was going to get bloody.

"Do I get to know why?" I couldn't stand the suspense.

Sheehan ignored my question and smiled. "Now boyo," he affected an Irish brogue, "Where's the cash?"

"*I* don't have it. I was just the driver. And why rip us off now?"

Sheehan backhanded me and wrenched my nose until a fresh stream of blood poured out like a faucet. "Rip off?

Coming from you, that's a good one. What is it, Kyle? You remember me as a mark?"

"Danny, I don't know what you think I did." It sounded like, "Thig I did."

"I don't *think* anything, you piece of shit. I *know*. You palmed off fakes on me like some crappy bobo sneakers."

"Fake?" What did Sheehan have to do with the stuff we planted at the auction house? Unless. "Oh no. Son of a bitch."

"Excuse me?" Sheehan cocked his fist.

"Sorry, not you. Those things were fake?"

"You're a shitty actor, Kyle."

I shook my head and it hurt, but the mists in my brain had cleared. "Not acting. Why do you think they're bogus?" I said. "Your expert confirmed them."

One of the goons smiled. He had hockey player teeth.

"Didn't you catch the news?" Sheehan asked. "He's not anybody's expert anymore."

"What are you talking about?"

"Terrible robbery gone wrong at the Fishtown Pawn shop. Some mutt bashed his brains out. I think it was a junkie, Brian here says it was gang banger."

"We'll never know for sure," Brian, the hockey player, said.

Sheehan leaned in. "You and that little fucker made me look like a thief and a liar, not just to the buyer, but to *my* people."

"I thought they were real, so did Ryan. It sounds like we all listened to the wrong experts." The words just came out and I hated how I sounded like I was about to beg. But I also wanted to know what really had happened. I'd be damned if I was going to be the fall guy.

"Oh no, your little shit friend set me up. Diaz had the real hounds, the real hounds went into police lockup and fakes came to me. Now, if you really didn't know, this is your chance to prove it." He got so close I could feel the heat off his face and smell peppermint over sour milk on his breath. "Where is he?"

"I wish I knew. If he did this, I had no idea." My mind was racing, bouncing between thinking about where he might have gone and how I was going to leave this room alive.

"Not good enough." He waggled the phone. "You have his number?"

"He told me he was going to lie low," I stalled. "You caught me easy enough. Shouldn't that tell you something?"

"That you're an idiot?" Sheehan said. He held out my phone. "Your message light is blinking. Play it."

I told him my passcode as my arms were still welded to the chair by all that tape.

Sheehan keyed in the code and set the phone to speaker. We all heard a panicked sounding Ryan on the voicemail. "Chrissake Kyle, pick up. You see the news? I'll try to find you next few days. Watch your back, man."

"Oops." Sheehan said.

Sheehan hit redial and held the phone up to my good ear. While the number rang he whispered. "Set up a meet and make it count."

A computerized phone company voice asked me to leave a message. I asked Ryan to call me back and Sheehan hung up before I could say more.

"Now what? We're not just going to sit and wait for him to call, are we?"

"Oh, no. You're going to make it your mission in life to find this prick for me or bring the money back yourself."

"But what if I can't?" I thought I knew the answer.

Wrong again.

* * *

They kept me waiting so long my fingers felt numb from the tight tape strapping them down. I sounded like I had a bad cold when I spoke, but my nose wasn't bleeding anymore. The hockey player watched me in silence.

I could hear people yelling upstairs, but it was impossible to make out the words. When Sheehan came back into the room he had his own phone in hand. He glanced over to Brian.

"No callbacks from Buckley," Brian said. He held my phone in one of his big paws.

As if on cue, my phone rang. Sheehan nodded to Brian who held the phone out to me. I wasn't sure what to say to Ryan, but knew I better make it count.

I looked down expecting to see the number that had been calling earlier.

Instead the face icon on the screen made my blood freeze. It was Beth.

"It's not him." I tried to sound casual.

"I know. You want to take this, Kyle," Sheehan said.

Brian touched the answer button and put it on speaker.

"Hey. This isn't the best time, can I call you back?"

"Kyle." I knew that voice. She was terrified.

Sheehan grinned.

"Are you okay?"

There was a long pause, and I felt the adrenaline surge through my body. Then another voice on the end growled. "Answer him, bitch."

Beth yelped and it took a lot to get her to admit something hurt. "Who are these people, Kyle?"

"It's a misunderstanding." I looked right at Sheehan and would've popped his eyeballs like grapes if I could reach him. "Nothing to do with you. They wanted to get my attention."

"They won't even tell me what they want. Why are they doing this?"

"Beth—" I stopped when Brian broke the connection and put the phone in his pocket.

"You motherfucker!" I tried to get up but only managed to tip over in the chair. I tried to wriggle closer to Sheehan, but Brian stepped on my head and ground my skull into the cold cement floor. "This is between us."

"I never had much use for coaches back in high school. But it did always amaze me how they could get you mutts all riled up for games." Sheehan squatted down and spoke to me. "I think now you understand the stakes and have found some fresh motivation."

"If you hurt her…."

"If she gets hurt, it means you fucked up. You want her safe? Don't fuck up."

"But I don't know where he is."

Sheehan stood and gestured to Brian who took his foot off my head and sat me up. "That, I believe. But I also think you can find him."

"What can I do that you can't?"

"Don't flatter yourself. We won't stop looking. Ever. But you know him, and he has been calling you, so that should give you an edge." He handed me a cheap cell phone. "Use this when you have news," he paused, "and don't even think about going to the cops. We'll know before they're done taking your statement and that'll be the last you ever see of her."

"Let her go. All I did was drive for the guy. She knows nothing and I had no idea he was planning all this or I would never—"

"Shut it. This falls on you because I say so. You want out? Fix it."

Chapter 7

Fishtown

They'd blindfolded me and dropped me off like a mafia car service.

It was still dark out and I slipped inside before anyone else decided to take a shot at me. The house was quiet and I padded upstairs. I looked in on Rollie who was asleep in his room. I felt like a parent checking on a kid.

The image jolted me as hard as one of Sheehan's punches and regret knifed through my chest. Beth and I never had children. Neither of us wanted them when we first married. She was all about her career, and so was I until that boy stepped in front of the truck. I gripped the doorframe and squeezed my eyes shut despite the pain from my whole face.

I crept upstairs to my room.

The last sliver of rational thought forced me to take a breath and think about my next steps.

What if I tipped the cops? Would Danny really know that fast? It was likely. He must have a bunch of cops on his payroll. At best, it'd be like playing Russian roulette with Beth's life.

I flicked on the bathroom light and hissed through my teeth at the mess that stared back at me. My nose looked like I'd stashed a roll of quarters up one nostril. My eyes were both starting to blacken. The bottom of the bridge of my nose hurt like hell to touch, and I was sure it was broken. Not my first. I'd live.

I washed the blood off my face and blotted it dry taking care not to restart any bleeding. I checked the medicine cabinet for Advil and gulped down four.

I left the bathroom and sat on the bed. Who was I kidding? Even if I called the most honest officer in Philly nothing could happen right away other than they might just arrest me for being involved in the scam that set Sheehan off in the first place.

So what, then? Do what Danny said. He held the cards right now. I wasn't sure what else to do so I lay back and closed my eyes.

* * *

Two years earlier; the Green Zone, Iraq

I lay on the cot still dripping with sweat from my most recent session of physical therapy. The brace on my knee dug into the still swollen scar tissue and I wondered if the effort to get me back on my feet was going to finish the job that damn bomb started.

"Hey, hey, hey! Look who's going to be ready for the marathon soon." Ryan let the door to the hut bang closed behind him.

I waved him over and sat up. "I'm just glad to be faster than a speeding bedpan," I said.

"I hear you," Ryan said. "Rumor has it you have to go stateside before you can resume work?"

While I couldn't wait to see Beth, this felt like going home defeated. "Yeah, but I'll be back." I failed to put much conviction behind that. I hadn't been off the compound since the explosion.

QUICK FIX

Ryan gazed at me. "You need to get back on the horse and all that, man."

"You know I can't drive even if they'd let me, which—"

"Not talking about that, Slim. This isn't about driving, this is you needing to get out of the bubble, right here. I'm not worried about your driving skills," he said.

"Then what are you saying?"

Ryan pulled me to my feet and handed me my crutches. "It's time to play hooky from feeling sorry for yourself."

He led me outside, where the heat rekindled my sweating so it was hard to hold on to the crutches. But I didn't have to go far. There was a dust-coated car nearby and Ryan jumped in the passenger seat. I didn't recognize the driver, who looked like a local, but he wore Delivergistics coveralls.

"This is Ali," Ryan said while we headed toward the nearest gate. The guy had his credentials out and we were out of the green zone a few minutes later.

"If this is a kidnapping, I'm not worth much on the open market," I said. "Where are we going?"

"Keep low." Ryan scrunched down in the seat and put on a baseball cap.

"What is this?"

"Just a little errand," Ryan said

It didn't take long for me to figure where we were headed. "Sadr City? Are we bait to see if the peace will hold?"

The odor of garbage and urine wafted in with the fine dust like it was powdered sewage.

"Immersion therapy, bud. If you can not get blown up here, you can not get blown up anywhere." He grinned at me. "Seriously, you'll want to see this place."

We turned down a dirt-covered street barely wider than an alley and I felt my hands turn clammy. This was a perfect ambush spot.

Ali spoke. "We are here." He turned to Ryan. "One hour?"

Ryan nodded, "That should be plenty."

Except that it wasn't.

Ryan had brought me to an orphanage. The director, an exhausted-looking woman named Nadia, spoke broken English, but between that and my smattering of Arabic, I understood that this place served children of both victims of terror and also the children of dead terrorist parents. "We heal through these young," she pointed to several children who couldn't be more than two years old playing on the floor with a ragged doll and some blocks.

They looked up at me with big dark eyes and I saw none of the fear (or raw hatred) I saw from kids when I was behind the wheel of my rig in an armed convoy. It hit me that the last kid I'd seen was that boy right before he was blown to bits. Hearing these little ones laugh and seeing their smiles didn't dim that memory, but it did fill some small space inside me.

Ryan had brought a couple boxes of candy as well what appeared to be some much needed medical supplies. Nadia allowed us to hand out the treats and it seemed like we'd only just gotten there when Ali returned and it was time to go.

* * *

The light through the worn shade told me I'd slept later than I had in years.

"Shit!" I rolled over and staggered into the bathroom. Almost ten o'clock. I was usually awake before dawn.

Despite the rest I still looked like an extra in a zombie movie. The flesh from my forehead to chin throbbed with pain.

I took some more Advil and drank from the tap. I thought of Beth and stopped feeling sorry for myself. Then I thought of Ryan and put on some clothes.

Dreaming about that orphanage trip always left me feeling drained. I hadn't realized how much it had affected me until I'd come home to Beth. We'd always agreed we didn't want children, but that experience changed my thinking. I'd tried to explain it to her and was more than hoping she'd feel the same way. She'd made it clear that she wasn't interested in children. I thought I understood, but it hurt to see all the ways we'd drifted apart.

I could smell the fresh coffee Rollie always brewed and fought the urge to grab a cup. Better to slip out and get to work. At the bottom of the steps Rollie came out of the kitchen with a steaming mug in his hand.

Crap.

"Hey kid, that must have been a big night. Thought you might want some… holy shit! What the hell happened to you?" The mug wavered slightly in his hand and he spilled some.

Now that I was caught, I accepted the coffee and held up a hand while I took a big sip. Top shelf beans, fresh ground. For a guy on a fixed-income, the man had his priorities straight. "Looks worse than it feels."

"The last guy I saw that looked as bad was on a slab in the morgue." He waved me into the kitchen.

I followed and plunked into the wood chair by an old wood table. "I'm in a rush, but I had a few too many last night at Kelly's and these guys came in with Bruins jerseys. It was stupid, but we went back and forth and next thing we were throwing punches and I forgot to duck."

Rollie banged down his mug and spoke through clenched teeth. "You know what isn't stupid?"

"Huh?" I'd never seen him like this before.

"Me. You want to insult me after I took you in, you can get your stuff and get out."

"Wait."

"No, *you* wait. I'll help you out and give you a chance to get back on your feet, but I'm too old to put up with bullshit. Whatever problem did that to your face might look for me next. I can either help you or you can tell me what I need to watch out for, but I won't stand for a goddamned sneak under my roof."

"Rollie, thanks, but it has nothing to do with you and I want to keep it that way."

He folded his arms across his chest. "I stick by my friends. If we're friends, I want to know what happened. I might surprise you. If we're not friends, get the fuck out."

The stress of the last couple days must have built up because that hit me hard. "All right. I'll tell you, but it will have to wait. I need to find someone and if I do it might clear things up fast."

"And if it doesn't?"

"I'll tell you either way. Deal? Just don't throw my stuff in the street and change the locks on me, huh?"

Rollie looked embarrassed. "I didn't mean that." He pointed at my face. "Mary left some of her makeup shit in our bathroom. I don't know the expiration dates, but you might want to slap something on your face or you're liable to scare little kids."

When I realized he wasn't joking, either about the makeup or the desire to help, I trudged upstairs and found a jar of foundation that didn't cover up the bruises but at least faded them.

* * *

When I stepped outside for a second I thought my truck had been stolen, then I remembered that I'd walked home from Kelly's. I hoped the hoodie I was wearing would hide the worst of the bruising.

I got about half a block away when I heard the whoomp of a big V8 engine start up. I glanced back and saw a black Mustang with dark tinted windows pulling from the curb. It was the sort of car I'd notice in the neighborhood, mostly because I wanted one. I'd definitely never seen this one before.

It rolled by me slow but never stopped. I got a quick look at the driver. He was a white guy with shoulder length blonde hair.

Call out the sketch artist.

At least it wasn't Sheehan. I walked toward Kelly's and watched the car turn to the right. Maybe just my nerves, which felt nice and taut. About a block from Kelly's I heard that rumble and the same car rolled by again.

I didn't get the plate, but it was clear it was the same ride. By the time I reached my truck I was using every car mirror and window I passed to scan the area around me for threats.

I pulled the sweatshirt hood down so I could see better and looked under my truck out of old reflex before getting inside. Dummy. Sheehan wasn't going to plant a bomb in my truck. He wanted me to do his dirty work, at least the hard part of finding Ryan. After I'd finished being useful, then I might have a problem.

Who was I kidding? Every roll of the dice lately was coming back to bite me.

The truck started and nothing blew up, so I eased it onto the street.

There was that damn Mustang again. I drove east down Girard Ave and watched the black car pull into the two-lane road. When I slowed down he never caught up so my guess was that the guy thought he was being discreet tailing me. He might as well have been a string band captain at the Mummers Parade.

After the IED, my awareness was honed to an excruciating degree when I first started driving stateside again. Every bit of roadside debris was a potential bomb, and even short drives drained me mentally. After a time, the jitters faded but never fully left. As for surveillance and ambushes, that was something Ryan and I watched for automatically.

QUICK FIX

Some of the terrorists were experts and they'd shadow us for miles during delivery runs.

This oaf was pure amateur. I was willing to bet it was his personal testosterone mobile. I considered losing him. I had plenty of tricks that had nothing to do with horsepower, but they could wait.

I was headed to Ryan's and I figured two things. First they already knew where he lived, and two that didn't help because Ryan wouldn't be caught dead there, literally, now that he knew Sheehan was on the warpath.

It didn't take me long to get to Ryan's place, a small townhouse on the north corner of Fishtown. It had two stories and window unit air conditioners for the upstairs rooms. There were bars on the ground-floor windows, and the rust on the bolts said they weren't going anywhere without a fight. The shades were drawn with no sign of activity. No surprise.

With all his hustles, I suspected that Ryan could afford to move to fancier digs, but I think he liked to keep the pulse of the neighborhood.

My buddy in the Mustang hung back and before I looked for a parking spot he'd pulled into one that gave him a view of the entrance, like they knew where I'd be going.

* * *

I walked around to the back of the house and the peeling paint on the wood siding fit the area. This sort of block held a mix of people. Some were long-time residents who would die in their homes but couldn't afford to fix things when they broke. Others were gentrifiers who landed an affordable fixer-upper after the old timers died.

Then there was Ryan, who grew up in the small house, and after his parents died he kept the place. I knew where he hid a key and looked over where the Mustang was parked and confirmed that the guy's view would be obscured by wood fencing.

I squatted near the rock and found the key with my fingers while watching for the driver. I stood and slipped the cool metal into my pocket. As soon as I reached the back door I saw the key wouldn't be necessary after all. The old wood of the doorframe near the lock bore fresh splinters, and I could even see the gray smudge of a boot print from where it had been kicked.

When I stepped inside dust motes danced in a ray of sun coming through the window over the sink. No dishes or any other sign of recent use, not unless all the silverware and other odds and ends dumped on the floor at the far end of the kitchen counted.

Damn. Sheehan must have sent his best tweakers to search the place. I decided to look further, not like I was going to mess the place up.

I walked into the living room, and the dust here was thicker along with a familiar musty odor. I didn't get to know Ryan well until later in high school so I hadn't been to the house all that often. I think I met his folks once or twice about a year before they both died.

Amazingly the furniture was mostly unchanged, same with the pictures on the walls. Many were on the floor along with seat cushions, but the sun-faded wall paper showed the outlines of the frames.

What struck me about the place, aside from the recent upheaval, was that the house looked like a snapshot of the life Ryan used to have. For a guy who enjoyed wild times and wilder women he was always subdued when I saw him here with his parents. In high school he'd find other places to hang out. He was popular with girls and at parties, but I don't think he ever brought anyone home.

Ryan rarely spoke directly about his folks. He said they were strict, and whenever we went places in high school it seemed he always had to sneak out and meet me, usually just around the corner.

I knew they worked hard, everyone in the old neighborhood did, but unlike my folks and other neighbors Ryan's parents reminded me more of people who grew up in the Great Depression when frivolous expenditures were unimaginable. Maybe they never could break the old habits.

I sometimes wondered if Ryan's outsized personality was to make up for the holes left behind by his parents. Standing in the house it was a mystery to me why Ryan, who was outwardly nothing like them, would keep the house like some sort of dusty shrine after they were gone.

When we were both home from Iraq one time I gave him a lift home from Kelly's. That night he'd been on a mission of drunk. He drank shots to my beers and by the end was trying to pace me two to one. I'd been surprised that he was still awake when I walked him in the house to put him to bed. Before I could get him upstairs he led me over to the kitchen and opened the cellar door.

I walked over to the door now and remembered thinking he'd fall, and saying so.

"Not me," Ryan had said. "Dad. Ten years ago today. He fell down these steps and broke his neck."

"Sorry." I hadn't known what else to say.

"When Mom saw him she called the ambulance, sat on the bottom step, then keeled over with a heart attack."

To this day Ryan and I never directly talked about their death again, and for a while I thought he'd been so drunk he'd forgotten telling me. But he hadn't. He referenced it one other time when I tried to lecture him about taking too many risks over in Iraq.

"I don't worry about Death and I damn sure won't wait around for him. When he's ready, he'll come find me. You remember, he even makes house calls."

Now I stared down those steps and gripped the rail on the way down. The basement was unfinished with a washer dryer plugged in and a cement floor with a drain in the center. Detergent and other items littered the floor including a broken mason jar that had been filled with assorted sized nails.

I returned to the ground floor and made my way to the stairs leading to the bedrooms. I peered out the front window and could just make out the fender of the Mustang. I couldn't see if the driver was inside.

Hell. What difference did it make? He knew I was in here and for that matter it was obvious that they had searched the place. A check of the two small bedrooms and the single bathroom told much the same story.

In Ryan's bedroom the mattress was slashed to ribbons and the drawers were scattered along with what I could see were not too many clothes. The closet held more hangers than anything else.

I also didn't see among the scattered luggage pieces the familiar black case on rollers that he always travelled with. They were crazy if they thought he was coming back anytime soon.

QUICK FIX

I sat on the edge of Ryan's bed and looked at the yearbook I'd found on the floor. It was from high school, the year we graduated. Ryan had used a chinstrap from a football helmet as a book mark. Inside the chinstrap I saw in clear black marker Ryan's last name, Buckley. Weird. Ryan never played football, but I had. I flipped to the marked page and there was the team picture. I was there and so was Danny Sheehan, looking younger but mean enough to punch the photographer.

Seeing him snapped me back to the task at hand. Which was what? What was I expecting to find? Not Ryan, but maybe a clue where he'd gone. But if he left an obvious indication I wasn't seeing it and the goon squad had already been here.

For that matter if Danny had found a clue on how to get Ryan I'd be out of the conversation.

No, you'd probably be dead.

That sounded about right.

What if they realized I didn't know any more than they did?

Beth and *you will be dead.*

And that sounded *exactly* right.

Maybe this was the wrong approach. What did they know about the deal? They worked with Ryan and they knew me, unfortunately. Did they know the cop, Bishop, at the loading dock? Maybe, I wasn't sure. Who else?

I looked again at the writing on the chinstrap. The ink looked fresh, not all smudged and dirty like a real kid's would have if it had been used. I flipped to the senior pictures section and found Ryan's page. His hair was long and he looked like a baby, as we all did. But there was an inscription below his picture.

Hey, Man! We're gonna party like it's 1999! Remember, true art is found in the strangest places. You never know what the future has in store. —Kyle L.

My name and last initial, but I never wrote that. It wasn't even my handwriting, it was Ryan's.

Then it hit me. Even with the disruption of the searches, of all the books to be sitting in his bedroom why would he have out a stupid yearbook?

It was a message.

Why not just call or text me? I thought about how Danny made me play the message back on my phone. I wondered how sophisticated Danny's people were, but I had to agree with the thought that Ryan was being careful. But this was more or less out in the open.

Really? Danny or his people would know this scribble wasn't more than fifteen years old?

Okay, probably not. But would he know I'd ever see it?

Because he knows you're a sentimental sucker.

Not so sure about that one, but it stood to reason that I might start at this place looking for clues.

Okay, but was it supposed to help me find the son of a bitch? If I caught him the only thing keeping him alive would be my need to turn him over to Danny to get Beth released.

I cut off the internal debate which wouldn't solve a damn thing if I couldn't figure out the message itself. I memorized the lines and returned the book. If I got searched by Mr. Mustang on the way out, the last thing I needed was to call attention to this book.

The part about partying and 1999 had to be a red herring as it was the year we graduated. It sounded like something we might say to each other at the time. Everybody else did. No, it was the other. Neither of us cared one rip about art back then.

True art. As in real art? Genuine art? Had to mean the statues. This confirms he has them. Unless he messed up and left the real ones with the cops by accident?

No, couldn't be. I was there for the switch and the boxes, while very similar, had enough distinctive scuffs and scrapes to ensure against such a rookie mistake. That meant the ones the cops had were fake and the ones Sheehan picked up were also phony.

They made *two* fake sets, unless the ones the cops had were never real. But Danny seemed to know real ones had existed at some point.

If there were real ones, why keep them? What would he do? Or did the artist want them for himself? Then the case full of money dropped onto my brain.

"Dumbass! They're going to sell them again." I checked the volume of my voice, but the words popped out of my mouth.

How could I be so stupid? They'd planned it all along. And left Stupid Kyle to play the chump and take the hit from Sheehan.

I'd kill him and turn any cash I found over to Sheehan along with the body.

Felt like a plan.

I took a deep breath. Ryan screwed up all right, but why reach out if he'd intended to leave me holding the bag?

I thought again about the inscription. *Found in the strangest places?*

Shit. Did he bury the things in the basement? Impossible. That was old concrete. Even Danny's goons would have seen fresh cement or digging. And that took time. No.

Damn. It could mean anything. What was a strange place?

I stopped pacing the room and sat back down. Not in the house. Ryan knew they'd search it and they had. Plus, he'd be taking a risk coming back.

What would Ryan think I'd guess?

It hit me. "What the future has *in store.*" Where had I last seen the statues? Well, the box anyway? Assuming he didn't mean the police station, the storage unit at StoreMore Self Storage.

So wouldn't Danny know that, too?

Not necessarily? Not at all. If Danny didn't know the artist or the arrangement with Ryan why would he? Once the buyer was convinced the goods were real and the cop, Bishop and Ryan worked together, the rest was detail. Danny might not care about that.

He damn sure cares now.

Yes, he does.

QUICK FIX

Whatever was on Ryan's mind, at least I had a starting point. But I had to get rid of my company.

Chapter 8

Fishtown

Mustang Sally, as I'd come to think of the goon in the black muscle car, had resumed his surveillance. I had no idea if he bought it when I left Ryan's place feigning frustration.

At least I had a place to begin. But I'd need help if this was going to work, so I let Sally tail me during the short ride back to Rollie's place. My aggravation wasn't an act and every time I thought about Beth it threatened to boil over and cloud all rational thought. That kind of thinking would get people killed, and I clung to that knowledge and remained what passed for cool in my life.

The Mustang took up a post near the house. I had to circle several times, but there were two dirty plastic chairs guarding his space. I noticed a guy leaning against a wall staring at his phone. Small for a leg breaker, but he had a tough-guy slouch and red hair that told me I shouldn't believe in coincidences.

They had Rollie's place staked out. That cemented my resolve.

* * *

"Rollie, you home?" I hollered once I got inside the front door.

"Kitchen," came the muffled reply.

At first all I saw were legs on the floor and my heart did a summersault. Even as I ran down the hall, trying not to jack my knee in the process, I pictured him beat up and bloody.

QUICK FIX

He was under the sink. A box of tools lay next to him and his hand emerged from the wood frame and felt around the tools.

"Jeeze, you scared me."

"Got a fear of plumbers, kid? Where's the damn crescent?"

"Here." I placed it into his waiting palm.

"Thanks." I heard it rap against the pipe. "C'mon, you bitch. One more turn." His hand popped out and put the wrench onto the floor. "Gimmie a hand here. The cabinet frame's digging into my ribs."

I helped extract him from under the sink. "Thanks." Rollie pulled himself up by the counter edge. The back of his t-shirt was smudged with dust. He had a fading anchor tattoo over one bicep.

He reached over to a switch by the sink and a disposal growled to life. Rollie grinned. "Don't she purr? No more scraps drawing flies."

"Speaking of maggots, you ready to hear what really happened to my face?"

He wiped off his hands and packed the tool box. "If you're ready to tell me."

"I should have this morning. Everything is moving so fast."

"Start from the beginning and go slow. I'm older than I look." Rollie sat at the kitchen table.

I took a seat across from him and did as he asked. I started from when Ryan walked into the bar right up through this morning. His face barely changed expression except for when he winced at the part where I described them putting Beth on the phone to prove they had her.

"So that's it. And I can't tell you how sorry I am that you're dragged into this, but they're out there and know who you are."

Rollie sat so still I thought he might not have heard me. Then he took a deep breath. "They don't know shit about me." I was about to argue, but he held up a finger. "Kid, never mess with a person who has nothing left to lose."

"Are you saying you'll help me?"

Rollie didn't miss a beat. "Thought you'd never ask. What do you need me to do?" I could have kissed the guy.

* * *

Five minutes after Rollie left the house in my truck, wearing my leather bomber jacket and Flyers cap. Sure enough, there went Mustang Sally right after. The tinted windows were too dark to let me see the driver.

I put on Rollie's old fedora and tan raincoat and checked myself in the mirror. I looked ridiculous but at least a *different* ridiculous. If I kept my head down I might get away without too much notice.

I moved at what I thought was Rollie's walking speed and headed to his car. The kid guarding the plastic chairs was busy with his phone and never noticed me. I reached Rollie's immaculate 1980 Oldsmobile Delta 88. Powder blue and about as far from my kind of car as I could imagine, the thing was spotless and fired right up when I turned the key.

I almost lit the tires when I pulled away from the curb. I had to smile at that. The thing was a sleeper. It may have looked like a granny mobile from the outside, but it had one beast of a motor.

I tried not to draw attention while leaving the city and I kept my head on a swivel looking out for tails, but it appeared we'd drawn the flies away after all. I'd told Rollie to give me an hour and then sneak home. If all went well, these assholes would have no reason to bother him or me again.

If it was possible to wear out a rear view mirror from looking into it I would have gone through two. I made it to the storage facility by dusk without any sign of being followed.

* * *

StoreMore Self Storage

Now what? Ryan wasn't sitting at the entrance waiting for me, not that I was surprised. I wasn't sure exactly what to expect, but it had to be at the unit itself.

My first problem was figuring how to get into the facility without bringing the cops down on my head. Ryan hid the access code for the keypad lock the last time we were here and I wondered if he forgot that detail while penning his little scavenger hunt clue in the yearbook. I hoped Ryan hadn't overestimated my intelligence, but on a hunch I tried *1999* even though this was the access to the whole facility. Nope. What else could I try?

A beat up Camry passed me and pulled up to the gate. That gave me an idea. I tore a scrap of paper from the owner's manual in the glove box.

I pulled up behind the guy before he entered the code. An older guy, he looked annoyed and a bit frightened.

I got out of the car and waved the scrap of paper as I approached the driver side.

"Can I help you?" I heard the guy say in a tone that really said, "Get away from me."

I let my shoulders sag and hung my head like the world was coming to end. "If I didn't have bad luck I wouldn't have any at all."

Now I had his attention. The guy, had to be in his seventies, remained in the car, but at least he didn't roll up the window or jump on his phone.

I pointed to my battered face. "First I wreck my car, then my father-in-law lends me his," I hooked a thumb towards the Olds, "then he tells me while I'm out to pick up his baseball card collection."

Progress. I hadn't asked for money. The guy looked less apprehensive.

"No problem, I tell him. I can do that. Just tell me where." I pointed to the facility, as if the guy hadn't guessed.

"I don't...."

I nodded like I got his point and plowed right on. "But here's the thing. He's not exactly a young man and his memory isn't what it used to be."

Now the guy looked bored and impatient. "I'm in a bit of a rush. Don't mean to be rude, but could you move back so I can get in?"

"Oh, right. Sorry. See, he wrote the number down to get in and would you believe it's wrong? I'd call him, but once he takes his ears out he won't answer the phone, so now I have to drive all the back and hope he gets it right this time."

QUICK FIX

"You need to get in, is that it?"

"Would you mind?" I started back to the car.

"Whatever. Gate opens for you when you have to leave. I can't wait around."

"That's great." I jumped in and let the guy punch in the code.

I tailgated all the way in and smiled when he zipped around the corner.

Luckily the guy's spot was in the opposite direction. I pulled up to the steel door and let the headlights wash over the surface.

No sign of notes or mysterious runes to lead me to Ryan. But I did see one thing different. A fresh padlock. This one was blue and I remember the last one was plain chrome, I was sure of it. Fortunately, I had a skeleton key. Of sorts.

I pulled out the long red-handled bolt cutters and held the tool close to my body. I didn't want any witnesses to get the idea I was breaking in to the place.

The lock offered little resistance, and I pocketed the pieces and rolled up the door. I had a small penlight and shone it around the dusty space. I could see where we'd taken the crates and disturbed the dust, but otherwise it looked much the same.

There was the old piano and the wooden chairs stacked on a drop-leaf kitchen table.

No yearbooks.

I glanced over my shoulder, all clear, then moved deeper inside the unit.

When I got around the back of the piano I saw the crate and my heart pounded. Couldn't be. Looked just like what we pulled out of the police warehouse. I reached out and tugged on the corner and the familiar weight made me grin.

Whatever Ryan wanted no longer mattered. I pulled out the small pry bar I'd borrowed from Rollie. I pushed down slowly to keep the nails from screeching, but they lifted easily enough.

He must not have expected me to come out this soon or he didn't know to watch for this car. Too bad. As soon as I confirmed the contents, they were coming with me. Screw Ryan, his turn was long overdue and all that mattered was that I had a chip to get Beth back. Anything else was between Ryan and Danny Sheehan. As for the artist who made the things? He too, could suck it.

I got the last nail up and took off the lid. I shone the light and under the wood wool packing material I saw the deep black stone. It was cool to the touch. Which dog was it? Heaven, Hell or good old Earth?

I pulled out a fistful of the material and shone the light on a rectangular block of stone. Unsculpted.

Then the door rolled down.

Chapter 9

StoreMore Self-Storage

I'd left the overhead lights off to avoid attracting attention so with the door now shut all I had was my penlight. The beam danced and jumped around while I hustled to the door.

I heard a lock rattle and click shut right before I reached the door and yanked up on the handle. No good.

Damn.

I pounded the metal with my fist. "Hey, there's someone in here!"

"I know." I heard Ryan's muffled voice on the other side. Part of me wanted that Beretta back so I could fire through the door at the sound.

I drew in a breath so I could scream at him, but a rational thread penetrated my rage and I managed to speak in measured tones. "What are you doing? I thought you wanted me out here?"

"I did, but I need you calm." Ryan answered.

"I am calm."

"Like hell."

The idea of counting to ten while Beth sat trapped in some room snapped the last thread. I hammered the door with both fists and managed to bruise my hands and break the flashlight in the process.

The room plunged into darkness and I tried to remember where the fucking light switch was. Ryan probably cut the power anyway.

Now I heard him speaking from a distance, and I put my good ear to the door.

"No. It's okay. I locked him in as a joke and misplaced the key."

A pause and a voice too distant to decipher replied.

"That's all right. I went home and got a spare set. I think he thought I forgot about him."

More chatter and Ryan's laugh. "Yup. You have a good night too."

"You with me?" Ryan spoke through the door.

"Yeah." Nothing was getting solved with me caged.

"Security is watching to make sure I have the right keys. He was about ready to call the cops."

"Open the goddamned door." Just as well. Sheehan never said dead or alive. All he wanted was his money.

"Be nice." I heard the key in the lock and I stepped back. The door rolled open. I kept my head down but saw Ryan wave to a guy leaning out his car window. There was a rent-a-cop shield decal on the white door.

I waved too and the guy pulled away.

Ryan walked past me toward the light switch. "We need to talk."

While the overhead fluorescents flickered to life, I stepped forward and spun Ryan around and clamped my hand around his throat. "Oh, we'll talk." I glanced toward the road to confirm the guard was gone.

QUICK FIX

Ryan pawed at my arm, but his feeble efforts weren't going to matter. I dragged him toward the back where we'd have some privacy. The choked sounds he made were like music and I could feel the blood running hot in my face.

I had some tape with me, but it was in the car. I needed answers first and if I had to choke him out to secure him that was okay by me. I took a final look at the wide open door and decided not to chance closing it first.

Then I felt the barrel in my belly.

Ryan *had* brought his pistol. I relaxed the grip on his throat but only a little. I could probably snap his neck, but what was the point? He'd still get a shot off and I'd bleed out here and Sheehan would have no reason to keep Beth alive.

Ryan's color returned to normal and he stared at me with an infuriating, calm expression.

"You'd do it, wouldn't you? You fucking weasel." I kept my voice down.

He shrugged and I released him. "Better than dying alone." He stared at my face. "What the hell happened to you?"

Fatigue washed over me. "Don't look so surprised. Sheehan. What did you expect?"

Ryan kept the gun on me. "It's not what you think. He wasn't supposed to figure it out. I didn't mean for you to get hurt. That's why I tried to warn you."

"With a note in your yearbook?"

Ryan actually smiled at that. "So it worked. I wanted you out here. I was hoping you'd see it before he got to you. Once I saw what happened to the pawnshop guy I tried to call and then came up with that in case they were watching you."

"Of course they were."

"I had to slip past that lump they had covering my place, but those leg breakers aren't exactly operators. Looks like they did more than watch you." Ryan paused. "But he let you live. I saw you pull up. No sign of a tail?"

"I made sure of that." I saw Ryan look more relaxed. "So, where's the money?"

"The money?"

"You need to give it back to Sheehan. All of it."

Ryan shook his head. "Not that simple."

"Yeah, it is." I picked up the pry bar. We were close, tucked in back of the unit. He'd have to kill me to get past. "Think I can't brain you before I bleed to death? Or take that from you?"

Ryan looked at the gun and like an old west gunfighter, spun it around and handed it to me with the muzzle pointed at himself. "Shoot me, if that helps. Won't solve the problem."

I took the gun and lowered it. "I don't care what Sheehan does to me. He has Beth."

Ryan frowned in confusion. "How?"

"They want you. Or the money. When you disappeared they followed me and grabbed her after I went to see her."

"Fuck. I didn't know."

"Lot of that going around. Clock's ticking. She didn't ask for this."

"You still love her, don't you?"

"Doesn't matter, she's innocent! I was stupid enough to listen to you, but she didn't do anything." I lowered my voice. "And yeah, I do."

"I get it. Can we settle that later? We have bigger problems."

"We have only one problem and we can solve it right now," I said.

"Wish that were true. Even if I wanted to give you the money, I only have about half. Think that'll satisfy him?"

I got an idea. "It might, if we also gave him the real statues. You were going to sell them to someone else, weren't you?"

"Very good. And I swear, we were sure the fakes would fool Sheehan."

"They did. You were there. But not the buyer."

"He promised me that guy would never know either." Ryan said.

"Who promised that?" I said. "Never mind, where'd you put the real ones?"

Ryan pointed to the box. "They were supposed to be right there."

"I checked, those are uncarved blocks." I said.

"Yeah, I found that out when I came here to move forward with the second sale."

"So you sold them twice. Then you have more than enough cash to fix your fuck up."

Ryan shook his head. "If I did, I would. I was beaten to the punch. The artist double-crossed us all. They were gone and this shit was all that was left."

"Where can we find *him*?"

"That is literally the million-dollar question. And it is why I've been here. I keep hoping that the dirt bag will come back for his stone, maybe try to make a third set."

"The artist, right? What is his name?"

"Tom Ratigan, and when he isn't playing footsie with the PA state police property cops he works teaching Art History and sculpture."

"Does Sheehan know about him?" I asked.

"Not from me."

"Where's his house?"

"Not far. But I already checked there. He's gone."

"How do you know?"

"He packed his gear. And it's probably a waste of time staking out his work, he'd taken a sabbatical to study something, but it was really so he could work full time making the statues."

A stakeout implied long waits anyway, that was out of the question. "How'd his place look?"

Ryan looked puzzled. "Arty? I dunno, pictures of sculptures, selfies at pyramids."

"No, was it trashed like your place?"

"Oh, I gotcha. It wasn't. And no sign of anyone covering it."

"Then maybe Sheehan doesn't know about him," I said.

"We shouldn't assume that."

"But if he caught Ratigan, wouldn't he have learned about this place? Maybe if he tried to give you up?"

"I'm beginning to feel unpopular here." Ryan tugged his lips into a fake smile.

I didn't return it. This shit wasn't funny. "Or what if Ratigan got spooked by the news and decided to take the real statues right to Sheehan? Make a deal?"

Ryan shook his head. "If he had, the deal would have ended up being Ratigan and you dead and me still with a price on my head."

Made sense. "How well do you know this guy?"

"Considering he stabbed me in the back? Not well," Ryan said.

"I thought I knew *you* well." I couldn't help myself.

It stung.

"I told you, I fucked up! And I'm still around, aren't I?" He yelled and looked out the unit door.

"Whatever." True, he could have disappeared and never looked back. "Any idea who Ratigan knows well, who might help him hide?"

Ryan answered right away. "Just one. Bishop."

"The cop?"

"Yeah. Remember this was their baby to begin with. They were tight and worked small stuff before I was brought in." Ryan said.

"Is Bishop working tonight? We need to talk to him." I didn't like sticking around here. Felt like pressing our luck.

"Easy there, cowboy. Sheehan definitely knows about Bishop. Even if he hasn't talked to him, there's a good chance he is watching the place."

"Pretty ballsy to stake out a police station," I pointed out.

"We can't trust Bishop, but you can still get information and, since you're already working for Sheehan, it won't freak him out if you show up. You're just doing your job," Ryan said.

"I don't work for him." I felt my jaw tense.

"As long as Sheehan thinks you're doing what he wants, call it what you like. But we better move fast."

"No shit. Beth—"

Ryan cut me off. "Beth will be fine unless Sheehan thinks he won't get his money. Bishop works nights, but don't try to go through the gate with those cameras. You look memorable, you know?"

"So, when?"

"He usually leaves around seven in the morning. He stops at that diner on Route One. Like clockwork. Catch him there."

QUICK FIX

I fought to hold down my impatience. "All right. But you better come with me."

"No way. Unless you still plan on capping me, I'm not about to be spotted with you. You should know how dangerous that'd be for both of us." He paused. "And Beth."

"I wasn't followed." But my heart wasn't in my argument. I thought what Sheehan might do if he thought I was teamed back up with Ryan.

"Your goofy outfit and that old car told me how you gave them the slip. But don't tell me they aren't outside that guy Rollie's place."

At the mention of his name I felt a mixture of guilt and fear for the old man. He'd done more than I had any reason to ask, but this was getting dangerous. "They are."

Ryan pulled out a prepaid cell phone. "Use this to call me. When I pick up I won't speak. Say my name and who you are. If you're being forced, just say 'Hello? Hello?' and I'll dump my phone on the spot."

"You've given this some thought." I wondered if I'd have to label all these damn burner phones.

"See? I'm as motivated as you are to get this fixed, okay? My ass is on the line too. We're up against the clock and I can't run away on chickenfeed. If we don't catch Ratigan before he makes the second deal, we all lose."

Chapter 10

Fishtown

It wasn't too late in the evening and I got lucky with a parking place. I checked myself in the old rear view mirror and pulled the fedora lower. Under the brim a faint odor of ammonia lingered. I recognized it from Rollie's hair dye, his one concession to vanity.

The kid guarding the parking spot was gone and the Mustang sat there, brooding and black. I hoped the jerkoff inside was bored out of his skull.

Then I imagined him telling Sheehan all I did was sit inside the house all afternoon.

I shuffled past the entrance, knowing I was being watched, and hoped my slouch and tentative stride would throw the guy off.

Once I got around the corner I made my way to the back yard and scaled the fence. Some little dogs barked over at the neighbor's house. They seemed to do that from the moment they woke up, so I didn't worry about it. I reached the back door and tapped on it wondering how hard I'd have to bang on the thing before Rollie heard me. I could see by the flicker of light off interior walls that he was watching TV.

To my surprise he came into the kitchen moments after my first knock. "Get in, kid. You okay?"

Rollie looked ten years younger, and hair color had nothing to do with it. His eyes were dancing, he looked over my shoulder and closed and locked the door.

"Fine. Rollie, are you all right? Anything happen?"

He practically dragged me into the living room and I noticed the shades were drawn, only sealed might be a better word. I doubted any light was getting out and I thought about stories of WW II-era families using blackout curtains to try to foil enemy aircraft. "Hell, yeah. Lots!"

I didn't like the sound of that. "But you're not hurt?"

He looked confused. "Course not. He took his hat back and placed it on the wood rack perched by the front door. I saw a new deadbolt and chain was in place along with a baseball bat leaning by the door.

"Sit down." Rollie paced the floor. "I saw your friend behind me the whole way in that tarted-up pony car."

"Worked like a charm. Thanks. Where did you go?"

"Well, you told me you were looking for statues, so I went and looked at some."

"Huh?"

"I led him to the Philly art museum. Don't worry, I didn't think it'd be like you to do the Rocky Balboa run up the steps thing." Rollie chuckled. "While he waited for me I checked out the suits of armor. Great stuff."

"He didn't follow you in?"

"Nah. Bet that knuckle-dragger is allergic to culture. I let him cool his heels for about an hour and then headed out."

"Back here?" I felt awful dragging him deeper into the weeds on this.

"Hell no. I gave him the slip a couple times just to remind him he was a mope. Thought he'd lost me for good once until I double parked so long I was sure you'd get a ticket." Rollie grinned. "He was busy all afternoon. I stopped by a couple stores and the library. The guy's not much of a reader either, by the way."

"Why so many places?"

Rollie chuckled. "C'mon, kid, let an old man have some fun." But I saw iron in his jaw that told me this wasn't a game to him. "Just tell me that burning up most of your gas was worth it."

I thought about how much to tell him and felt another pang of guilt. "We'll see. I'm going to ask you to do something, but I hope when I'm done you'll understand."

He stopped pacing and took a seat and nodded for me to begin.

I told him about connecting with Ryan and after we tussled and he filled me in what we were up against. Ryan probably would have been pissed that I spilled so much to a guy I'd only known for a short time, but I couldn't care less about Ryan's idea of operational security.

"So you'll need another distraction in the morning?" Rollie said.

"No, I'll shake the guy on my own tomorrow. I need to see this cop without a goon on my ass, but while he's chasing me I have to ask you to take off somewhere safe until we get this solved. A few days, but maybe longer."

"Nope." Rollie said without hesitation.

"I have money for you, but pick a place Sheehan would never guess."

"I appreciate the offer, but I'm in." Rollie folded his arms across his chest.

"Rollie, this isn't your fight. You've already—"

"Beg to differ, son."

"I appreciate how you've taken me in, but my problem isn't yours."

"Who said it was for you? Damn, but you kids are self-centered these days."

"You lost me."

"You know my wife died several years ago?" Rollie said.

"Yes. She passed from cancer, isn't that right?"

Rollie nodded. "The love of my life, just like you read about. We lived in this house for more than fifty years. Bought it after I got out of the service. This is a big city, but Fishtown is a small neighborhood. Everybody knew everybody even if we weren't all pals."

"I get it." I'd grown up here too and while I'd never met Rollie, I did remember seeing his face around.

"And I knew Sheehan's dad."

"Big Dan." He'd been a hard man to ignore.

"Yeah. I never wanted any part of what he was involved in, but I also steered clear of his bad side."

I nodded. Not aggravating the local mafia was a good practice, one I hoped to return to pronto. Then I thought about Beth, and cold anger kicked that idea to the curb.

"Back in the early eighties," Rollie continued, "the Feds got a hard-on for the Irish mobs. They'd been running

97

meth and for a while it was all hands on deck to intercept shipments."

"But you weren't."

"I already had a job, and didn't want another. Turns out he felt otherwise. They were feeling the squeeze and Dan's reputation was suffering. All his runners were stuck. They couldn't get a cheesesteak without a Fed on their ass. So Big Dan decided to outsource."

I could see the way Rollie's face had gone pale that the memory made him sick, but he was determined to tell me everything.

"He liked my car, the one you drove. It was new back then, called it the blue bomber. She was fast for the time. And so, with my squeaky reputation and on nobody's radar, I was a perfect candidate. Big Dan let me know I could make what he called my Christmas fund in one day if I took a package to Pittsburgh."

"Did you do it?"

He stared at me, and for a moment I thought he was going to shut down. "It's important you believe me here. I said no. I tried to be as humble and respectful as I could stomach, but he just looked at me like I was some sort of dog."

"That's it?" I knew it wasn't, but wanted him to continue before he changed his mind.

"It's never *it* with these people. You better learn that quick or you'll be sorry. That bastard left, and before he did he said, 'If you change your mind, you know how to reach me.'"

QUICK FIX

I got a chill because I could hear those exact words in Sheehan's voice directed at me. "They messed with you?"

"No. They messed with Mary."

I heard a groan before I realized it came from me. All I could see was Beth's face. The Beth before everything turned to shit.

"She came home one day. I'd never seen her so shook up." Rollie's chin quivered then snapped back to iron. "I never saw her so brave."

"Rollie, it's okay, you don't have to get into it."

"Yeah, kid, I do." Rollie looked into the distance. "She told me some guys, bunch of micks, grabbed her on the way home from work. They pulled her into an alley and surrounded her. Real subtle, just said 'Tell him to take the job. Last warning.'"

I exhaled when I realized I'd been holding my breath. "Shit. I guess it could have been worse."

"I thought the same thing. For a long time. But I took the damn job. Drove a big box of I-didn't-give-a-crap-what to Pittsburgh and met some dirt bags up there. Never did see what it was."

"How long did you drive for him?" I hoped I hadn't overstepped my bounds.

"That was it. Funny, he never even asked again. The heat seemed to drop off, and he was back in business with his regulars. I never knew why, but I worried that I delivered enough whatever to frustrate the Fed's efforts."

"You didn't have any choice," I said.

"We always have choices. Just not always good ones."

I could relate to that. "That doesn't explain why you're so set on helping me now."

"She never kissed me the same." Rollie stared into space. "The rest of our marriage. She was different in bed, don't want to be too specific, but there was always a detachment that hadn't been there before."

"I'm sorry."

"I blamed myself. I thought she'd lost respect for me or something because I'd caved into Big Dan."

"Did you ever ask her?"

"She always denied it, but every time I did, that… chill would be even worse for a while." Rollie took in a shaky breath. "Mary died and life went on, such as it is. Then Big Dan made the news because he was dying and everything changed."

"Why?"

"Apparently all the glowing news and tributes hit the national wires. Pillar of the community, scion to a hard-nosed business family in Fishtown and all that. I didn't see any mention of the mob." Rollie wiped his hands along his jeans. "Out of the blue I got a call from Mary's sister who lives out west. That was unusual enough, but she told me that a letter from her was on the way and I needed to tear it up without reading it."

I waited for him to continue, not daring to speak in case it would break the spell.

"She told me she was drunk when she wrote it and didn't mean what it said. I had to guarantee that I'd tear it up and burn it just to get her off the phone."

Rollie smiled, but it barely touched his lips. "I kept my promise, more or less."

He met my gaze. "Well, what would you have done?"

"Same as you I'm guessing. Read it, then destroyed it."

"Yup. Part of me wishes I'd done just what the sister asked." Rollie sniffed and rubbed his nose like he'd caught allergies all at once. "Mary's sister said the news glorifying Big Dan got her so angry she broke a vow of silence she'd made to my wife and kept ever since her death."

Rollie took in a deep breath. "Mary had confided to her something about that day in the alley but made her sister swear she'd keep it from me."

My heart sank.

Rollie stared at the floor while he spoke. "She'd told Katherine that the gang did more than warn her in that alley."

"Oh, no."

"They didn't want to leave a mark so they forced her on her knees and made her…."

"I get it." I didn't need him to finish.

"Mary knew that if I ever found out, that I'd kill Big Dan."

"I would too, or die trying," I said.

Rollie looked at me. "That's what she was afraid of. All those years." He smiled and his eyes grew watery. "Mary's sister said in her drunken letter that she didn't want me to die thinking I'd done something wrong."

"That must have been hard to hear."

"I didn't see the point of trying to go see the man on his deathbed, but after the bastard kicked the bucket, I did make it to the funeral," Rollie said.

"Big Dan's?"

"I watched their ceremony from my car and drank a twelve pack of Pabst Blue Ribbon and ate a pound of steamed asparagus."

I began to wonder what he'd been drinking before I arrived.

"When they all left to go get drunk again, I went over to pay my respects. After I zipped up my pants you better believe it didn't smell like roses anymore."

"You know they would have killed you if you got caught?" I didn't think I'd be eating asparagus again for a while.

"Still would've been worth it."

"So this is why you're helping me?"

Rollie shook his head. "No. I've never been one to believe in all that sins-of-the-father crap. I know I'd never figure out all the mutts who were in the alley and in the end it didn't matter because none of that would have happened without Dan's say so. Most of them were dead or retired anyway."

"I'm confused, then why?"

"Weren't you listening? I said sins of the *father*. But now it looks like Dan's boy is a chip off the old block in how he treats women. And this time I'm not too late to do something about it."

Chapter 11

Fishtown

The next morning Rollie had woken up before me and the coffee was ready by the time I came downstairs. It was still dark out, and I'd barely slept thinking about Beth in light of what Rollie had told me.

"Got an idea, kid."

"What?" I'd accepted Rollie was going to help no matter what, and I had to admit it was nice to have someone I could trust. At the same time, the last thing I wanted was to steer him into danger.

"We don't need to lead that mope on another wild chase."

"No?"

"I was thinking. In case he's not as stupid as he looks, this time he just sees me go out."

"He isn't following you."

"Exactly. And you slip out back. I'll pick you up in the Bomber. If he's following me I won't stop."

"He might be covering the back."

"Nobody in sight back there until you get to the streets. Wear this." Rollie tossed me a gray hoodie. "Cut through the neighbors' yards and head north on the sidewalk."

* * *

It was more like fifteen minutes and I'd walked several blocks fighting the urge to look over my shoulder.

The traffic was just starting picking up with the early commuters moving out and I heard a rumble and was sure it'd be that damn Mustang.

Then Rollie passed by and pulled over ahead of me. I looked and saw no sign of our tail.

"Told you." Rollie said.

"Where were you?"

"Kid, when you borrow someone's car, fill it up next time," Rollie said. "He saw me go by, and I hope he was awake all night, the bastard. He followed me to the gas station and filled up right next to me."

"What happened?"

"It turns out he's not as dumb as he looks. He guessed our move and while he pretended to be interested in the Bomber he checked inside. He may look like a reject from a pulp romance cover, but he knows his engines, I'll give him that."

"Did he say anything about me?"

"No, but when he asked to look at the trunk I think he expected to see you hiding there."

"What did you do?"

"I showed him, but before I opened it I did my best to talk his ear off." Rollie grinned. "Once I opened the trunk he must have figured I was trying to stall him and he left in a big damn hurry. He's gonna be pissed when he finds your truck still sitting there."

"I hope this lead pans out." I wasn't even sure what to expect from Bishop.

QUICK FIX

"One step at a time."

* * *

Thirty minutes later we parked near the Route One Diner where Ryan had promised we'd find Bishop.

An unmarked Crown Victoria pulled in at five after seven. The sky was brightening enough that I'd see who got out before he went inside.

I got out of the car and approached from the front. I didn't see the point of sneaking up on the guy. If he was nervous, it might get me shot.

"Remember me?" I spoke. Bishop looked up, his hand moved to his waistband. He was in a sweatshirt and jeans. I barely noticed because all I could see was the swollen and blackened eyes.

It was like looking into a battered mirror.

"Who're you?" Bishop was more than jumpy and I was certain the hand under his sweatshirt now clasped a pistol.

"Looks like we use the same makeup artist. Friend of Ryan's, remember?"

Bishop took his hand off the gun and turned back toward the car. "Wrong guy. I don't know you." Then he whispered, "What the fuck are you doing here?"

I followed a bit behind him and kept my voice quiet. "We need to talk. Buy you a cup of coffee?"

"Bullshit. Meet me up the road. Follow my car." He jumped in before I could respond, but Rollie had been watching and pulled up.

I got back into the Bomber. "He looks worse than you. I guess we know he's talked to Sheehan." Rollie slid the car behind the Ford and followed it into traffic.

I was sure the guy would try to shake us, but he kept to the speed limit and led us on a meandering trip through an adjacent neighborhood.

"What the hell is he doing?" Rollie said.

"I don't know." My instincts screamed trap, but what else could we do? Sheehan already knew how to reach me.

Finally the guy pulled into an empty parking at the far end of one quiet street. The sign said Puzzle Tree Swim Club. It was closed at this hour.

"I guess he wants privacy." Rollie parked a short distance away and kept the car running. "I'll leave the window open. Jump in if it gets hairy."

I doubted I'd get the chance if it came to that. I got out.

Bishop emerged, and I saw his gun was cradled in his arm so a casual observer wouldn't notice. Right now I saw no observers of any kind except Rollie.

"Who's that?"

"A friend."

"Answer the question."

"Sheehan knows him, that's good enough."

I could see the way the guy tensed that he hated evasive responses. But he moved on. "What do you want?"

"We're on the same team here."

"I don't have a team," he said.

I pointed to my battered face. "Looks like neither of us are exactly volunteers. But we have the same source for our problems."

"So what?"

"If you help me out, maybe we get our lives back."

"You got something to say, spit it out," Bishop bit off the words.

"I'm looking for Ryan. Maybe you are too."

He shrugged. "I don't know where he is. If I did, this mess would be over."

"Same for me, but I'm wondering, did he say anything that would give you a clue as to what he had planned?"

"Why are you wasting my time? Whatever I had to say I told him already." It was clear Bishop meant Sheehan. "I'm just a working man who got caught in the middle of a misunderstanding. You're nobody to me and whoever your friend is, he's even less."

Heat crawled up my face. I wanted to snatch him up, but the guy had a gun on me. Seemed I was making a habit of picking fights with people packing weapons. "I'm not a snitch, dumbass! Our problem isn't the law in case you hadn't figured that out. Sheehan wants what he wants and will burn everyone in his way."

"Wrong. He won't burn down a cop."

All at once I got it. Sheehan tuned the guy up, no question, and I didn't doubt that if necessary Bishop could disappear. But even Iceballs Sheehan would think hard before killing a police officer. That didn't mean he wouldn't, but now Sheehan owned a corrupt cop and that carried weight.

"Keep thinking that. And know that he grabbed someone close to me just to make sure I play ball."

"That's not my problem." For the first time I saw the hard look in his eyes waver.

"I guess your duty to protect and serve doesn't get much exercise outside yourself anymore huh?"

"Fuck you. You're nobody to judge me."

"For what it's worth, the person in question doesn't even know why she's being held."

"She?" Another crack in the armor.

"Yeah."

"So what do you want from me? Not like I can arrest him. You haven't gone to the Feds, that's obvious."

"I want her safe. Best way is to keep our guy happy. Right now both our faces make for a pretty good mood indicator, wouldn't you say?" Now it wasn't a guilty conscience I saw but anger and, for the first time since we met, not directed at me.

"You got any ideas?"

"We know who screwed us over and put us in this position. Ryan was a friend, but he put me and mine in harm's way and you, too." Time to go for it. "Now that I think of it, you know the artist? Maybe he could help."

"If you mean the guy who does the appraisals, I think he's in the wind."

The way he phrased it, he wasn't completely convinced I was on the level. That was okay, he was giving me information. "You sure? I'd hate for Sheehan to catch him off guard. I bet he couldn't take a punch the way we did."

There was that flare of anger again. "I think he figured that out. You should worry about yourself."

"I am. But if you knew how to reach him and he had any tips for finding Ryan we might all breathe easier."

"Sheehan won't find him and neither will Ryan."

"You sure?" Bishop must have warned his friend. If Sheehan was all over Bishop, it meant we could rule out finding the artist staying at the cop's place. Ratigan had to be somewhere else. "Did you check his house?"

"Yeah, I'm sure."

Might as well push a little harder while I had Bishop's attention.

"If we don't help, Sheehan's going to get desperate and even more pissed off. I'd hate to be the guy then. I hope for your sake you aren't helping him hide."

"What's that supposed to mean?" Hit a nerve there. "The one who should be worried is Ryan. Have *you* heard from him?" Bishop's face flushed.

"He knows he burned bridges with me." I'd pass the lie detector on that one.

Just then my cell phone rang. It was one of the burner phones. Sheehan.

Bishop must have reached out to him during our driving tour of the neighborhood. "You going to take that?

109

And keep any crazy theories to yourself or we're going to have a problem."

I picked up.

Sheehan dispensed with the pleasantries. "What the fuck are you doing?"

"Exactly what we talked about."

"We talked about you getting that old fart involved? Are you out of your mind?"

"How's Beth?"

"No. I want answers now. Why are you bringing him into this?"

I felt the pressure in my chest. I was both glad I wasn't in front of Sheehan and wishing I had him by the throat at the same time. "You brought him in when you threatened him that night you grabbed me. But we're all on the same page. Sooner you have what you want, the better. He understands."

"Get me some results and call me on the new phone that I'll leave at the old man's place."

"Let me talk to Beth, first."

"Kiss my ass."

Chapter 12

The Blue Bomber

"Hell of a crowd you're running with, kid. Now you have the cops on your ass." Rollie drove us back to his place.

"Bishop stopped being a real cop a long time ago."

"Not my point. He has the badge and more importantly he can tap their resources."

"I wish Sheehan thought that was enough."

Rollie's jaw tightened. "Until he gets what he wants, nothing is enough."

I pulled out the phone Ryan had given me. I hit the autodial and almost forgot his little code. It rang several times then I thought I heard it click. "Ryan? Ryan you there? It's Kyle."

A pause and I was sure I'd gotten the system backwards. "Where are you, man?" I heard Ryan's voice.

"Going to Rollie's, just getting back from meeting Bishop."

"And?"

"Sheehan used his face like a piñata, same as mine. But he's working with him for sure."

"Okay, at least we know. What about Ratigan?"

"I got the impression Bishop warned him, but I can't be sure he knew anything about the rest of his plans," I said.

"Probably not. I'm learning firsthand the punk doesn't want to share. Plus he's scared shitless of Sheehan and wants enough dough to stay gone."

"Sounds familiar."

"You want to wage a one-man war against the Irish mob, be my guest. I'm a pragmatist, not a coward." Ryan said.

"Semantics. What's next then? Think we should hit Ratigan's place?"

"I already did, remember?"

"You said the guy left in a hurry. Scared people make mistakes," I said.

Ryan paused long enough for me to check the connection. "Maybe."

"C'mon, before Sheehan figures the same thing. We're in a car now, where's his house?" I said. We were almost back to Rollie's place, but I figured there was no time like the present.

"I got it, you sit tight," Ryan said.

* * *

When we parked at Rollie's the Mustang wasn't just gone, but the kid guarding the spot was nowhere to be seen either. Was that good or bad?

Didn't have to wonder long.

Rollie started swearing the moment we walked through the door. I saw why a second later. The place was trashed. It made the inside of Ryan's place a model home by comparison.

QUICK FIX

The couch cushions were slashed open and the stuffing lay strewn over the inverted rugs. Anything with a drawer now resembled a cartoon version of itself with the gaping space a mouth wide-open in surprise.

Contents littered the floors. There were photos, letters, playing cards, old coins, batteries and enough odd and ends to make it look like a flea market in a blender.

"What were they looking for?" The second that question left my mouth I thought of the bag with my payoff from Ryan. "My money. Shit, it was…."

Rollie turned to me, his face looking like he'd fallen asleep in the sun. "I found it. I figured you must have something left over after you flashed the cash to me the other morning."

I waved my hand to encompass the mess. "They must have it now."

He shook his head. "I'm not as foggy as I look. I put the cash in the Bomber, in the spare tire well. Which reminds me," he ducked out the back door.

I wandered through the place, taking in the rage. This was more than a search, it was a full-on violation. Paintings slashed, wedding pictures stomped and gouges in the plaster walls. I wondered how many must have been in here. We weren't gone that long.

I made my way into the kitchen. Right away I noticed the only thing not disrupted was the kitchen table. On it sat a new phone.

I picked it up and saw a folded piece of paper underneath. I could hear Rollie rummaging around his large shed he'd converted it to a workshop.

I opened the paper and saw handwriting I couldn't read because I couldn't take my eyes off the hank of hair. Chestnut brown and tied up with a green twist tie. I forced myself to read the words on the paper.

Clock is ticking. Next time it'll be something that won't grow back.

Rollie stomped up the steps and snatched open the door, muttering as he came inside. "They must have been in a hurry, didn't have much time in the workshop, didn't find my hidden footlocker, bastards… what's that?" He saw me holding the message.

I held the hair out to him, "It's her color."

"Motherfuckers." He looked at the note. "We gotta find her."

I was shaking with fury, but my mind felt clear. "We will. The fastest way is find what Sheehan wants. Beth could be anywhere."

"Maybe it's time we turned the tables. See how they like it for once." Rollie spoke as much to himself as me, but before I could ask him what he meant by that I heard the phone ring.

I thought it must be Ryan but realized that it was the new phone. I jammed my thumb on the button. "What?"

Sheehan's calm voice jabbed at my self-control. "Good afternoon, sir or ma'am, can I interest you in our award-winning cleaning service for a low introductory rate?"

I screamed into the tiny phone. "You didn't have to do that. And I swear, if you hurt her."

"Stick it, asshole. She gets hurt, it's on you. I'm not fucking around anymore. This was your last friendly reminder."

"I need time," I started.

"You're getting some help," Sheehan said.

I was sure he meant Rollie. "No, he just gave me a lift, he's not in this."

"Shut up and listen," Sheehan growled. "I'm putting him in it. But that's not the help I'm talking about. You're going for a ride. Leave the old man there. Bishop is waiting outside." Sheehan hung up.

Rollie studied my face and followed me when I walked to the front window and saw Bishop's car double parked.

He waved.

I stepped out of the guy's line of sight. "I guess I gotta go."

"Where?" Rollie asked.

"Not sure."

"Wait." Rollie scanned the floor and picked up a small folding knife. "I don't have time to get anything better."

I reached for it and then imagined Bishop searching me. I kept the knife but handed the phone from Ryan to Rollie. "Take this one. Don't dare let them get it."

We both heard the horn.

* * *

After he told me we were going to Ratigan's, I rode with Bishop in silence. It didn't take the cop long to pull into an alley. "Out."

For a moment that seemed to stretch out forever, I was sure that Sheehan had found Ryan or otherwise reached his goal and I was about to become another unsolved homicide, my body stuffed into a trash can. I thought about Beth and what he might do to her and then figured maybe I could at least jam the pocketknife somewhere important first.

"Doesn't look like an artist's crib." My mouth tasted sour and dry.

"Quiet." Bishop was holding his gun with discretion, but he made sure I could see it. "Turn around."

I wanted to pull the blade but doubted I'd get it out of my pocket, let alone opened, before he could put two slugs into my skull. "Sheehan called off the search?"

Bishop spun me round and leaned me over the hood of the car.

"No dinner first?" Sometimes shit just came out of my mouth.

What began as a frisk turned to a quick jab in the kidneys that took away my breath. He resumed frisking and I decided to take him up on the being quiet.

He found the Buck knife of course, and the cell from the kitchen table, but I was glad about leaving the other phone with Rollie and by the time he opened the door again the knife was the only thing tossed into a trash can.

When I thought it was safe to speak without getting pistol whipped, I said, "Why'd you change your mind? You could search the guy's place all on your own, couldn't you?"

"I didn't change anything. This was his idea. He figured you're going to go anyway, so kill two birds."

"Don't you mean babysit?"

"Sheehan might not, but I sure do." We were headed in the direction of the storage center which would have worried me, but I did remember that Ryan said the place wasn't far from where Ratigan lived.

"You certainly got with the program in a hurry." I'd probably get hit again but couldn't help myself.

But he didn't, he looked like the words scalded him. "I'm with the same program you are. Find the double-crossing asshole friend of yours and get this Irish psycho off our backs. We may not be on the same team, but we should be on the same page."

"He doesn't have your ex-wife hostage," I said.

"I wish he did. I'd spit in his face to seal the deal." Bishop laughed. "But my nuts are in a vise all the same. Sooner we figure this out the better."

We passed the storage area, and he didn't so much as turn his head. We took a left and soon the landscape shifted into a mix of developments and old farm houses. Had to be getting warm.

"What were you guys thinking?" Bishop looked at me long enough for me to worry about the approaching truck flashing his headlights on the two lane road. Bishop turned at the last moment. "Couldn't you find any drug dealers to hold up?"

"Wasn't my idea." I pointed to him. "Yours either, considering we're the ones in Sheehan's vise, as you say."

"You mean we're the two dumbasses with nowhere to sit when the music stopped."

Chapter 13

Ratigan's Farmhouse

There was a red barn facing a stone two-story house. An old place, a bit run down, but it looked comfortable, the kind of home I used to imagine living in with Beth someday. Now I'd settle for mobsters not trying to kill me and everyone around me.

"Who the hell is that?" Bishop muttered as we pulled up the driveway.

I saw a gold Cavalier parked facing out just on the edge of the grass. The same car Ryan was driving the other night. My heart pounded.

"Not Ratigan's, I take it?" I tried to sound calm.

"He drives an old Jeep SUV, or did. C'mon." Bishop drew his pistol and approached the vehicle. I followed behind him and hoped any random loud noise wouldn't cause him to spin around and start blasting.

I didn't see anyone and could imagine Ryan trapped inside the house. My leg gave its usual protests after being cooped up in a car. "Wait up, my leg's killing me." I made sure to speak loud enough that someone inside might hear me.

Bishop whipped around and I thought he'd fire at me after all. "Shut up," he hissed.

I lowered my voice and pointed at my bad ear. "Sorry, this messes up my volume control sometimes."

He just shook his head and I could see he was busy committing the license plate to memory. That didn't worry me. I was sure it had to be stolen anyway. Ryan never said where the car came from, but he was good at covering his tracks.

Except now.

"Want to wait and call Sheehan? Might be one of his."

Bishop waved me off. "It's not." He crept to the front door. "It's open."

I hobbled to the door, feeling the knee begin to loosen up. I wanted to stay close enough to grab Bishop if he got the drop on Ryan.

Bishop popped inside and I saw his gun swing right and left while he cleared the room. I followed, being careful to stay right in his view. Despite the extra weight and sedentary duty Bishop moved like he must have been a decent cop at one time.

Inside the house I saw low ceilings and exposed beams. One direction led to a living room area with a red pattered antique rug over hardwood floors. A stone fireplace marked one end of the room and I could smell damp soot in the air that told me it was a real wood-burning hearth.

Ratigan favored wood antique furniture. Prints and paintings adorned the walls, all with a Mexican or South American motif. A large one of an adobe village at sunset hung over the fireplace.

Bishop moved to the dining room, a misnomer as the rectangular wood table seemed to hold about a file cabinet's worth of papers.

I glanced at some, they appeared to be largely stacks of research or student paperwork.

QUICK FIX

Bishop moved to the small kitchen and it looked far tidier. It didn't smell like there'd been any cooking here recently, which made sense.

Actually what I had expected was that the place would be turned upside down. It wasn't, it looked lived in, comfortable and homey.

Bishop cocked his head and listened while he crept toward the stairs. Again I was reminded that he moved well for a guy who looked like a fat, over the hill, cop on the take. I could still feel that kidney punch too.

We went upstairs and on the wall I saw some of the pictures Ryan had described. There was a thin guy with gray hair looking tan and fit while he posed for vacation shot atop Mayan pyramids. Another one showed him wearing a poncho and sitting on a burro trying and failing to look fierce.

All the while Bishop moved and covered, stopped, listened, and moved again. There were a couple of bedrooms up here. One was the master and Bishop was especially careful when he checked the closet.

I held my breath, knowing if something went down suddenly that I'd be too late to help anyone.

But still no sign of Ryan and I began to wonder where he could be. I looked under the bed. No monsters, including Ryan.

Bishop did a cursory sweep of the master bath which was small with no hiding places. The guest bedroom held old clothes with enough dust in the rumpled folds that it told me Ratigan hadn't had too many guests lately.

The remaining bedroom was Ratigan's converted office. No bed here, and a computer sat on a nice old antique mahogany desk. A small table held a printer and on the floor was a paper shredder.

"No basement, so the house is clear. We'll look in the barn next, but I want to check something first." Bishop holstered his pistol and plopped into the chair. I noticed he sounded winded and his body seemed to sag while he fumbled for the power switch.

The computer whirred to life and the printer, which must have been on the same power strip, clunked through its warm-up exercises.

Bishop pawed through some of the papers he found and cast them aside with little interest. We both watched the screen and saw simple text appear instead of some sort of desktop or password prompt.

No Operating System Found

"Damn."

"Wiped?" I asked. I wasn't an expert, but it seemed a good guess.

"Maybe, maybe not. It'll take time to figure out. I know some people." Bishop looked at some of the papers. "Nothing here." Then he glanced at the shredder.

He reached inside the waste bin and pulled out a rat's nest of confetti. A bunch of inch long strips littered the floor. "So much for that, unless you think you can piece it together." He tossed the mess aside and kicked the shredder over.

Then we heard a car engine start.

"Son of a bitch!" Bishop raced to the small window. "It's Ryan! C'mon."

QUICK FIX

"Go! I'll slow you down," I barely finished the thought when he bolted from the room, gun already in hand, and thundered down the stairs.

I hoped Ryan had enough of a jump as that Cavalier didn't exactly look race-ready. Meanwhile, I noticed something about the shredder. The top had been knocked off from the trash can underneath. I could see the bottom part of the shredder had some larger chunks of paper stuck. I'd jammed my share of these things, usually when I was in a hurry and trying to feed too many pages at once.

I heard Bishop slam his car door followed by a loud bout of swearing. He should have been spitting gravel in hot pursuit by now.

It was hard not to yank on the paper, but by the sound of Bishop stomping back to the house I'd only have one chance. I tugged gently at the pieces and was able to slowly work free a few dog-bite sized hunks of paper.

The front door slammed open. "Get down here."

"Coming." I saw some ink on the pages, but it would have to wait. I stuffed them down my shorts, didn't think he'd search me there. Might be a lead. Might be nothing.

Bishop's face was almost purple. "That piece of shit."

"What happened?" I exaggerated the limp and came down the stairs.

"Hurry up, dammit. I need your help."

"For what?"

"To change the fucking tire, that's what. The cocksucker slashed it."

I fought the urge to grin and took another look at Bishop's face. He looked capable of murder. "Bastard must have seen us coming," I offered.

"Oh, you really think so? Wasn't just some bad luck?" Taut cords radiated around Bishop's neck.

"I didn't slice your damn tire. I'll help you change it, but do you really think we can pit crew it fast enough to catch that junker? Considering you don't know which direction he went?" Purple rage or not I was only going to put up with so many tantrums.

He took a deep breath. "Maybe not, but we can be the first on the scene after I call in that tag as a hit and run."

Shit, that could work. "Sure you want to do that? That's a lot of official trails that lead back to you."

"I'm not going to shoot the guy. Sheehan might, but that's on him."

"I just want to strangle him." I felt better, because the longer we talked the more I knew he must realize I had a point. "We could try it that way if you think it'll work fast or we could search the barn before anyone else shows up."

He saw it my way. We changed the tire, and he went inside the barn with me. The place was an impressive studio, and I could see the spot where he'd worked the statues. Under a worktable leg was some black dust the same shade as the basalt stone.

The size of the barn and amount of costly lathes and drills and power saws told me one thing for sure. It would take a lot to abandon it. Mortal fear, for one, but also the prospect of a substantial payoff would help.

Another good thing was the size of the place gave me a chance to glance at the paper chunks I'd found in the shredder while Bishop wasn't looking. Most were blank. The last one I saw had a fragment of a search string from a website.

We didn't find anything else in the barn, but I no longer cared. Back at the house we confirmed it looked like Ratigan had grabbed a bunch of clothes from his bedroom closet, taken his car and disappeared, leaving his home and stocked studio behind.

Bishop was livid, and I tried to sound just as pissed. I was ready to get out of there.

"Think you'll have any luck with that computer?" I hoped not.

"We'll see. All right, strip."

"Excuse me?"

Bishop placed the computer onto the floor. "I know one of your damn ears works. I said strip, down to your shorts."

"For what?"

"'Cause I don't trust you and neither does Sheehan. I'm not telling him we found nothing unless I know it's true. Now empty your pockets."

I put my regular cell and the one from Sheehan on the kitchen table. A thick stack of takeout menus rested under porcelain salt and pepper shakers shaped like pigs.

I stripped out of my shirt and left my jeans on the floor. "Happy?" How far was he going to take it?

"Jeeze, you did get caught in the blast, didn't you?" Bishop whistled. It was always awkward when people saw all the scars for the first time. Maybe it would distract him.

"Good times," I deadpanned.

"I used to do intake for the graveyard shift lockup a long time ago and you never knew what all people had going on. You're right up there. Lift your arms."

I did. Felt like a bug on a pin, but if it put him at ease it would be worth it.

"Almost done. Drop your drawers."

"You gotta be kidding. This isn't intake at the jail, bud."

"Not going to ask again."

"If I don't? You had your free shot. Next time I hit back."

"I tell Sheehan you're an obstacle. He'll take it from there." He pulled out a phone.

"Fine. If you get jealous, it's not my fault." I dropped them and gave him a quick turn. "Want me to cough?"

"Nah, we're good. Put 'em back. Nothing personal." Bishop said.

I didn't trust him either, which is why I'd eaten the paper scraps once I'd skimmed them.

Chapter 14

Bishop's Car

I kept my mouth shut the whole drive back. Bishop had his head on a swivel as if he'd expected to catch a glimpse of Ryan in his car. He called in to Sheehan and judging from this side of the conversation, Bishop was getting an earful when he explained how the guy had slipped right past him.

"He doesn't sound like the most understanding boss," I said.

"If that asshole is so brilliant, why hasn't he caught Ryan?"

"He knows the guy's as slippery as we do," I said.

"And what do you think Ryan was looking for at the house?"

"Same as us, I guess." I knew that was a mistake the instant the words left my mouth by the way Bishop glanced sideways at me.

"Yeah? How so?"

I forced my tone to sound casual, if not bored. "Hell, I don't know. I thought I had Ryan pegged, but then he pulls this stunt. Maybe he was trying to find out what Ratigan knew."

"About what?"

"What Sheehan knows? How pissed he is? How far to run? Or maybe he was looking for money."

"We've been looking for Ratigan to find Ryan. This little stunt tells me maybe we have it backwards," Bishop said.

Damn. Bishop hadn't just moved like a real cop back at Ratigan's, he still thought like one. "You tell me. Ratigan was your friend."

"Operative word, was. You weren't the only one stabbed in the back. Think they cut me in for a fat piece of the action?"

"Don't need a detective badge to guess that the two left holding the bag weren't the ones rolling in the big bucks." I didn't need to hedge my words there, that was the simple truth.

Bishop didn't say more, but I noticed he sped up enough to make me think about the safety of the spare tire we'd put on.

* * *

Fishtown

"It's been real. Stay in touch." Bishop practically shoved me out of the car in front of Rollie's place. I'd already figured he was eager to get someone on that computer.

I knocked on Rollie's door instead of just coming in because I thought he might be jumpy.

"Who is it?" He sounded like he was yelling from deep inside the house.

"Me. Can I come in?"

"You live here, don't you?"

I put in the key and opened the door. Where the hell was he? The hair on my neck stood up and I realized Rollie was lying on the floor in the front hallway. He wasn't hurt, he was sighting down an old pump shotgun. "Jeeze, Rollie don't shoot me."

He raised his head and set the gun aside. "Sorry." I could see his hands were shaking.

I looked around. The place was still a mess but only by Rollie standards. "You've been busy."

"Gave me something to do." He climbed to his feet and looked me over. "You all right? I wasn't sure what to expect."

We didn't have time to waste. "I think we have a lead. Are you up to driving?"

Rollie pulled the keys to the bomber out of his pocket. "Where to?"

"I'll need that phone, we have to get together with Ryan."

Rollie took it out of another pocket. "It rang a couple of times, I didn't think it would be a good idea to answer."

I saw the message light blink. I hit the redial.

Ryan picked up before the second ring. "Yeah?"

"It's me." I thought that would be enough.

"Thanks for the fucking warning!"

"Hey, dickhead. I got grabbed and he freaking strip-searched me twice." More or less.

There was a pause and Ryan actually chuckled. "Seriously? That's a hell of an image, son."

"Listen up. Dump that gold beater. I tried to talk Bishop out of it, but for all I know there's a BOLO on it."

"The license plate is swiped, but you're probably right." I could hear he was still in the car. "That was too close."

"Did you hear me yelling? I almost got shot for it."

"I heard you. Thanks for that. Think I have time to ditch the car close to another dealer? I have a place that sells for cash."

"Careful, Bishop might be tapped in to any transactions." I was trying to figure out how he might be looking. Cyber stuff wasn't my strong suit.

"They don't ask many questions, and I haven't been flying under my own name since I dropped out of sight."

"I keep forgetting you had this all planned out." I let that sink in for a second. "Except for where you didn't."

"You told me so, okay? And I came up with shit at Ratigan's anyway."

"I didn't."

Ryan had sounded like he was about to continue speaking. "What did you say?"

"I think I know where to find him."

"Where?"

"No. In person and don't freak, I'm coming with Rollie." I looked at him with a questioning expression and he nodded without hesitation.

Good. I felt better with him in sight after all that had gone on. Plus I needed as many friends as I could get.

"You're killing me."

"Wrong. At the moment I'm one of the few who isn't trying to do just that, and that's just because I need you to help me get the statues or the money. We need to do this smart and you'd try to go cowboy."

"I wouldn't... maybe." Ryan let out a breath. "All right, boss, where and when?"

"Get some clean wheels and meet us at the rest area, same as before. If we get tailed or burned there I'll call. They know Rollie's car, so we need to get clear soon. And hurry, Bishop has the computer."

"Computer is a bust. I already checked. What did you find?"

"We saw the computer, but they're going to be busy trying to restore files. Do you know what Ratigan used to wipe it?"

"Nope. You sure you don't want to tell me what you found?"

"See you in a couple hours."

* * *

I-95 Rest Area

"Over there. By the dumpster. You won't be as visible from the road." I told Rollie. We'd doubled back a couple times when I thought a car was following. One was a guy who wanted to give thumbs up on the Bomber. There weren't many like it on the road. But it was fast, and Rollie drove it like he was trying to qualify for the pole at Dover International.

To his credit, Rollie hadn't asked me what I knew, but I could see he was curious. His lips would move like they were about to form a question then they'd press together.

I watched the two prepaid phones. I was praying that Sheehan was busy pestering Bishop for results and that had them occupied. I jumped when one phone rang.

It was Ryan. "Kyle here."

"I see you."

"You're here?"

"No, dummy I hacked a spy satellite," Ryan said. "If the coast is clear, get ready."

"As far as I know we're good."

"I'll have to take that. I'm rolling by in a silver minivan."

I passed the description to Rollie who got out of the car and popped the trunk on the Bomber. He shouldered a large, heavy, olive-drab canvas duffle bag.

A moment later a dirty silver van pulled up. There was one of those dopey stick-figure families on the back window. The sliding door opened and I saw Ryan at the wheel.

"You bought this?"

"I think I passed the mutts that traded it in. Dumbasses even forgot to take off their plates."

We climbed in. It smelled like apple juice and stale cookies.

It was perfect.

"Where to?" Ryan asked. He smiled like we were off to take in a ball game, but the dark circles around his eyes told a different story.

"Valley Forge," I said.

Chapter 15

Ryan's Van

Ryan laughed hard and offered me a soda when I told him how I'd disposed of the evidence. Then he turned serious. "You're sure that's what it said?"

"Yeah. It was a webpage address from a printout. Based on the way it was stuck in the shredder it was one of the last things he searched before bugging out."

"Who prints out directions and leaves them?" Ryan asked.

"This was the web address that's on the top of every page. This was probably an extra sheet with ads or something," I said.

Rollie interrupted. "If you have a better place to look I'd like to hear it. He's got people in harm's way."

"I let you tag along for Kyle, I don't work for you," Ryan said.

"Kyle?" Rollie deferred.

"*Do* you have a better idea?" I asked.

"Why do you think we're heading up there now?" Ryan said. "And I don't want anyone to get hurt either, but if we blow this chance we'll never see Ratigan again, then we're all screwed."

"So we start with the Residence Inn?" I said.

"Seems logical. Thing is, if he's smart, he won't use his own name and will have a different car. But he's improvising and took off in a hurry." Ryan swigged the cola and stifled a belch. "I'm not so sure the covert stuff is his thing, so keep your eye out for his car, a beat up blue Jeep Cherokee."

"That's too much to hope for, isn't it?"

"Who knows? We were supposed to do the second sale in Camden, Jersey, so he really switched things up."

"Do you know these buyers?" I asked.

"Not any more than the first group. This part was going to be much more Ratigan's bit. He said these guys were from Colombia and the main guy was an aficionado with deep pockets. The guy was with one of the Nickel Exporting Groups and is nuts for Aztec artwork, especially statues."

"How's that different from the first bunch?"

"For one, Ratigan said the art had to be the real thing. He never hesitated, and you better believe he was cocky about his replicas."

Rollie shook his head. "If this guy is so legitimate, what's with the cloak and dagger? He can afford to buy the real thing."

Ryan answered. "No, these statues are extremely rare. Most are assumed lost or destroyed. To have a complete set of Black Dogs pop up on a legit auction would trigger a bidding war. Our guy is rich by our standards, but from what Ratigan said would get squeezed out by bigger collectors, or museums."

"Sounds rather convenient, how can we trust that?" Rollie said.

Ryan smiled. "We don't need to trust him on that."

"Why?" I asked.

"Think about it. Is Ratigan going to act this way and place his own life at risk if he wasn't convinced of a genuine payoff?"

"I suppose not," Rollie said. "What happens when we find him?"

"Let's find him first," I said.

* * *

Residence Inn; Valley Forge

We arrived right at the beginning of rush hour so while there were plenty of cars in the parking lot there were also quite a few empty slots. Our van blended in well with all the commuter cars. We saw plenty of stickers indicating vehicles from a rental fleet. Not a big surprise, lots of businessmen as clientele mixed in with some tourists.

It'd be dark soon. Good and bad for our purposes. We'd be harder to spot, but so would Ratigan.

"What do you think?" Ryan asked. "Once more around the place?"

It was just small enough for us to drive by all the guest parking spots in a matter of minutes. So far we'd seen no sign of Ratigan's Jeep, but that didn't mean he wasn't here.

"Maybe we should park near the entrance and keep an eye out," I said.

"Which entrance?" Rollie asked.

Damn. He was right. There was a small outlet leading to the road in addition to the main entrance. Ratigan might use either one. Maybe that side road was more likely, but if we left the front uncovered we were still out of luck. "Wish we had two cars again."

"There's nowhere obvious to park to see the entrance anyway," Ryan said.

"What about right in front of the manager's building? They're not even reserved," Rollie said.

I saw what Ryan meant. "If we're there for more than a few minutes some staffer is liable to notice and wonder why we don't come in to talk to them or something."

"So why don't I talk to them about a room?" Rollie asked. "That way we could have a parking card and everything."

"That could work, though hopefully we won't be here that long," I said. But it gave me another idea. "Ryan, you figure the change and speedup of the sale to the Colombians still would take a couple days, right?"

"From when this crap started, definitely. We're already a couple in, though. What are you thinking?" he replied.

"You knew Ratigan, was he much of a cook?"

Ryan thought for a minute. "I don't think so. When we were planning the whole thing, way back at the beginning, he invited me over to his house. We got Indian and when we cleaned up I noticed his kitchen trash was full of takeout boxes and stunk of curry."

I pictured being in Ratigan's kitchen earlier today. "He had a fat stack of takeout menus."

"So what? You guy's getting hungry?" Rollie said.

"There's a strip mall just down the road. Several places to eat, including Indian," I said.

Ryan grinned. "You are beautiful, man."

* * *

The strip mall was just far enough down the road that Ratigan would probably drive unless he wanted to walk for exercise. But who wanted cold takeout?

As soon as Ryan parked the van he scrunched down in the seat and stared at a smartphone just like every other person seemed to these days. Rollie sat in the passenger seat, but not for long.

"Stakeout can be hungry work. What do you guys want?"

"If he sees us we blow the whole thing," Ryan said.

Rollie stared at him. "If he sees me it won't matter. We don't know each other, remember?"

"Good points, excellent even on an empty stomach," I said. We could see the three eateries line up along the small strip mall. Ratigan wouldn't get by as long we were paying attention.

We all told Rollie what we wanted to order and he marched off to the Tandoori Palace.

"What are we doing here?" Ryan asked.

"Being sneaky to catch a sneak?" I said.

"No, what if he doesn't show up?"

As weird as it sounds, it hadn't occurred to me that we wouldn't catch up to Ratigan. Maybe it was because I didn't want to consider the alternative. "He has to."

"He's smarter than I thought. He may realize he left tracks and could have already changed up his game plan."

"Including the buy? Don't you think he'd have to be concerned with spooking his buyers, especially if they are supposedly legitimate?"

"Don't go crazy here," Ryan said. "I never said legitimate, exactly. Just not professional crooks is all." He took off the Phillies baseball cap he'd been wearing and wiped his forehead. "But you have a point. All this business is touchy and the fewer disruptions, the better."

Now I was thinking about what if we missed our chance and Ratigan got away clean. "If we blow this, he's going to kill Beth."

"You don't know that."

"Yeah, I do. And then he won't have to worry about finding me."

* * *

"That guy's got a good gig there. Plenty of customers even out here in the sticks." Rollie handed back the food packed in fragrant Styrofoam boxes. Curry and cumin odors filled the van.

"No sign of our boy?" Ryan said. He'd shown Rollie a faculty picture he'd called up from a University website.

"Nope." Rollie dispensed napkins. "A cold beer would go great now."

"Who's that?" Ryan said and scrunched down in his seat. I drew back in the back seat. We watched a red Ford Explorer roll past. One of a dozens of similar vehicles that buzzed in and out of the hive.

This one parked, and a lanky guy got out and scanned the parking lot with his eyes shaded. He wore a painter's cap and with his hand in the way it was hard to see his face.

Ryan never hesitated. "That's him."

Rollie placed the food on the floor and remained calm, looking in another direction. "What do you want to do?"

"Wait until he goes inside," Ryan said.

"We can't make a scene out here and even if we could, we need the statues more than him. He might not be in a talking mood," I said.

"He will be," Rollie said in a gravelly voice that made both Ryan and me look at the old guy.

* * *

"You're following too close, he's gonna see us," Rollie said from the passenger seat as we tailed the Explorer back to the Residence Inn.

"Shut up," Ryan said, but he did back off a bit. Any slower and cars behind us would start honking. "No point following the guy if we don't see which unit."

We rolled up the road and Ratigan did turn into the Residence Inn.

"Looks like he'll be eating at his room," I said. We pulled in soon after and watched the direction he turned.

Ryan tugged the cap low on his head and we drove past. I peered out the back window and watched him get out with his food. He did look around before crossing the driveway but our van might as well have been invisible for all the attention he gave us.

"Pull in. I can still see him through the back window."

Ryan parked.

"Got it. He's in a ground floor suite," I said.

"Makes sense. That crate full of statues would be heavy for him," Ryan said.

"I don't think he'll have much appetite in a few minutes," Rollie said. "I have an idea."

"Who made you Chief?" Ryan said.

"Hear me out, for Chrissakes. I'm not trying to bruise your tootsies."

I held out my arm between them. "Ryan, let him talk. If your idea is better we'll go with that." Unless, I thought it sucked too and then I'd have to think of something.

Rollie took the hint to continue, "We got surprise on our hands and the fact he doesn't know me. Why don't I go to the door with one of you," he stared right at me to let me know his preference, "close and out of sight?"

"And then?" Ryan asked. I could tell he was listening, at least. We sure didn't have time to argue.

Rollie was warming to his topic and his eyes got a crinkle like he was about to grin. "And then I go into my confused old man routine and knock on the door to yell at Maude that she locked me out."

"Who's Maude?" Ryan said.

"Dunno," Rollie did grin now. "But neither does he, and I'll make a fuss until he opens the door to tell me just that."

I'd had visions of how we were going to get in the room without busting down the door and what would we do if Ratigan had refused to open the door, or worse, picked up a weapon.

Ryan shook his head and smiled. "You know, that's not bad."

"So how long should we give the guy to eat?" Rollie asked.

Ryan didn't respond. I followed his gaze to the vehicle he was watching. My heart jumped into my throat. "Get down, you guys."

"What? Oh, fuck." Rollie saw the same thing.

It could have been one of a million gray Crown Vics pulling into the slot by Ratigan's room. Of course it wasn't.

It was Bishop.

Chapter 16

Ryan's Van

"How did he find him so fast?" Ryan interrupted his nonstop cursing in hushed tones.

I could feel my mind shift into overdrive. I'd come to call it battle-think. Where some froze and died under fire, I functioned effectively. Afterward was a different matter.

"Never mind, we have to call an audible here, quick." I crouched on the bench seat and peered at Ratigan's door.

Bishop approached the room and took a casual look around. I was grateful he didn't give our van more than a passing glance. By now we were all hunkered down.

"Check his hands, see? The son of a bitch pulled his piece," Ryan said.

I was glad to see Ryan regain composure. As for Rollie, he could have been waiting for a bus for all the excitement he showed.

"We can rule out him coming in as a friend," I said. Bishop held the gun low and close to his body, nearly concealing it from view.

Rollie spoke up, "What's that in his other hand? I can't see."

"A passkey. He must have pulled his badge on the manager," Ryan said.

"Without a warrant? Managers were tougher in my day," Rollie said.

Bishop took another look around and slipped the key into the lock.

"Yeah," I said. "Figure he means to secure Ratigan, then what? Sweat him for the meet? Steal the statues for himself, or call Sheehan and end it?"

Ryan scanned the area. "He might have already called him."

"It's possible, but I figure he'll at least wait until he knows he has Ratigan and the statues in hand." I said.

"He's right," Rollie said. "Sheehans don't do well with bad news. So what's our move?"

I thought about it. "Ryan, what if we let Bishop take the statues back to Sheehan? Can we call him, let him know we allowed it, and maybe offer him some cash for his trouble if he lets Beth go and backs off?"

Ryan made a face like I'd just farted. "Are you insane? Beth is a tiger by the tail for Sheehan. If he gets what he wants without having to release her to us, what do you think is the safest and easiest course of action for him?"

Rollie processed that and nodded. I didn't like thinking about it, but Ryan had a good point. "He'd kill her, disappear her body, and deny any involvement." Might as well say it out loud.

"Exactly," Ryan said. "And even if by some miracle we could trust him, who's to say any amount of money I could scrape together would satisfy him? We have to deal with him from our strongest position and that's statues in hand."

"Back to cops and robbers." I put my brain back into tactical mode. "I'll go with Rollie behind me. Ryan, why don't you hang back and make sure Sheehan doesn't show up. If we can get to Bishop and reason with him we might be able to salvage the situation."

"Or you'll startle him and he'll put one through your head," Ryan said.

"He might. But he'd grab you up on sight." I could see Ryan agreed.

"There he goes," Rollie said as we watched Bishop turn the key and move inside in one fluid motion.

"He didn't lock the door behind him," I noticed the door slightly ajar.

"That's our cue, I'm right behind you, kid." Rollie opened his windbreaker and I saw the butt of a 1911-style .45.

"You know how to use that?" Ryan asked.

"The hollow end goes toward assholes."

* * *

I tried to shake the stiffness out of my knee in case I had to run. Rollie moved like the younger man and strode across the road. He stayed out of sight of the door, which was still slightly ajar.

I imagined Bishop was busy, and part of me expected to hear a rapid exchange of gunfire. When I didn't, I pictured Ratigan trussed up like a pig.

Okay with me.

I reached the door and Rollie strolled up beyond the sightline of the room like he owned the place.

I wasn't sure how I felt about him with a gun behind me, but the guy had turned out to be stand up all the way. I also knew the last thing I wanted to do was startle Bishop, especially without a weapon in my own hand.

I got to the door hoping for a brilliant flash of insight, but instead heard a muted conversation. I thought it was just Bishop's voice. Worse, it was a real possibility Bishop was on the phone. That would not do.

I gave Rollie a *here goes nothing* shrug and knocked on the door to let Bishop know I was coming. "Room service!"

I opened the door and showed my empty hands first.

"We didn't order... what the hell?" As soon as I cleared the door I saw Bishop right next to the door with his gun in hand. I also got a glimpse of a figure handcuffed to the metal handlebar of a folded sofa bed. One cushion had been tossed to the floor.

He snatched me by the wrist and yanked me inside, the gun pointed at my face, finger on the trigger.

"We need to talk."

"Shut up. On the floor." He spun me around and smacked the back of my knees with the sole of his foot while yanking on the back of my collar. It forced me to my knees, facing the still open door. The cold steel of the barrel pressed against my neck.

"Gonna get that door? Lots of people around," I said.

He hesitated, but I could tell he was thinking the same thing. "Down." He shoved me and I caught myself with my arms.

Bishop kept the gun aimed at me, backed toward the door, and began to close it.

Just before it closed all the way I saw Rollie's booted foot stop the door and his blocky pistol slid through the gap, aimed right at Bishop's head.

I thought the surprise would get me capped for sure, but Bishop released the door and took his own gun in two handed grip, aimed at my skull.

"You going to shoot a cop?"

"Up to you." Rollie squeezed his body into the room and closed the door himself. His .45 never wavered.

"You fire that thing and your friend is gone."

"But you'd still be dead," Rollie said. "Why don't you put it down and then nobody gets shot?"

"What do you want?"

"I just told you."

I got to my feet slowly, betting Bishop wouldn't pull the trigger. My legs felt shakier than I wanted to admit. "Bishop, I said we need to talk."

"I don't talk with a gun to my head." Bishop was sweating now. "Put it down and I'll listen."

"Don't think so," Rollie said.

"This is going to be a problem," Bishop said.

"Looks like we have an old fashioned Mexican standoff." I looked over at the terrified sculptor. "Or maybe that would be an Aztec standoff, huh Ratigan?"

He didn't answer. He was probably still trying to process how his evening had gone so sideways.

"Listen carefully," Bishop spoke in a deep cop authoritative tone. "You've both just committed enough felonies to get locked up for a long time. Nothing is worth that. You aren't career criminals, I know that. Let's do the right thing here."

"Jail doesn't scare me and neither do you." I leaned my face in closer to the gun so he had no chance of missing.

Bishop watched me and kept his composure. "What about you, old man? Is that how you want to be remembered? As a cop killer? Why are you doing this, anyway?"

Rollie's cool façade cracked and I saw real anger turn his face crimson. "I'm a Marine. We storm beaches."

I took a deep breath. "Look. None of us got into this situation to be part of a bloodbath. How about we stop trying to kill each other and work this out?"

"How about we just wait until reinforcements arrive and see how your standoff looks then?"

My stomach churned. "You called him?"

"You're wasting time asking. I won't shoot if you are going out the door," Bishop said.

But he was still sweating. A bluff?

"A get out of jail free card? What do you think, Rollie?"

"Maybe we should ask the guy locked to the couch. Hey, buddy, can we trust your friend here?"

I held back the smile I felt and glanced over at Ratigan. He looked like the trapped animal he was. "Get these cuffs off me, Bishop."

"Nope. You're a hard man to find," Bishop said, and made a point of checking his watch.

Overselling.

Ratigan made a strangled sound that I took to be a laugh. "Sure as shit doesn't seem like it."

Bishop pressed his lips together. "How did you find this place?"

"I think I know how *you* did. I never thought Sheehan was such a techie. You recovered the drive, didn't you?" I saw Ratigan go pale.

"I'm a detective."

"You're a corrupt security guard at a glorified junkyard for the state," Rollie said.

Bishop absorbed the insult. "Not anymore, thanks to this cock-up. I'm retiring after this so you two get the fuck out of here and forget about it. He and I have business. You're nobody to me, but that offer is closing fast."

I picked up the change in tone and whatever Ratigan made of this conversation scared the crap out of him. His voice came out in a squeak. "Wait! He didn't call anyone. He jumped me and barely locked me to this before you showed up."

I thought Bishop was going to spin around and shoot Ratigan after that. "Stupid motherfucker."

"So the cavalry is delayed? Can we stand down here and talk?" I asked.

"What's there to say?" Bishop growled. "We all want the same thing, don't we?"

"To get out of this alive? Yeah. But how about we all put down the guns and see if there isn't a better way?"

"If I say no?"

"I suppose we can stay like this until his buyers figure out there's no deal. How about that?"

Bishop wasn't used to losing. That was clear. "Then your ex will get it."

"And that's fine with you? Isn't any part of you still a cop?"

I was just spouting off, but I saw a glimmer in his eyes. "I don't want to kill anyone." He paused realizing he was still pointing his pistol at my face. "Unless I'm forced."

"I'd like to meet my wife at the right side of the pearly gates when my time comes, if that means anything to you," Rollie said.

Bishop let out a breath. "Everyone, let's walk easy to that table and on the count of three we both place our guns on the table."

"Then what?" I asked.

"Then we talk and if it gets ugly neither of us can use our weapon before the other can get a shot off too, right?"

I didn't trust Bishop and thought he was up to something, but if he'd been trying to bait Rollie's pride one look at the guy told me it worked. "Dead man's ten seconds? Yer on."

The men counted down and tension cinched the muscles in my shoulders.

They made it past one without ventilating each other and like a weird reflection shadowed each other's movements while they placed the pistols onto the white Formica table

150

top. Each man kept his gun hand near his weapon. They remained standing.

"It's a start." I sounded calmer than I felt.

"What's on your mind? For your sake, and your lady's, I hope it's better than what I'm working with already." Bishop gestured toward Ratigan.

"I want to check outside to make sure the coast is really clear," I said.

"Ratigan told you, I didn't call him yet," Bishop said. "And I like you in here where I can see you." His hand twitched.

"I'm not going anywhere." I waited a moment before giving in. "You keep me in sight, but I just want to get a look out the door. Okay?"

I got the sense that Bishop didn't really mind me taking a look. He probably wanted to make sure he hadn't been followed or something as well.

"First, tell me how you got here before me."

"Yeah, I want to know that too," Ratigan said.

I didn't see the harm so I let them know about the scrap in the shredder.

Bishop looked impressed.

Ratigan looked like he might cry.

Bishop nodded. "Hurry up and you try more than a quick look and I'll use my last seconds to put a whole magazine into you."

"Fine." I moved over to the door and opened it. I kept one hand on the inside doorknob so Bishop would know I hadn't gone anywhere. I stretched the rest of my body far enough to get a look at the parking lot. It was quiet and I could almost feel Ryan's gaze on me through the tinted glass of the van.

I used my free hand to motion to Ryan to come over, making sure Bishop couldn't see the gesture.

I pulled myself back into the room and closed the door. "We're good."

Bishop returned his attention to Rollie but spoke to me, "So, what are you thinking?"

"This all got started with each of us, except for Rollie, expecting to get a nice payday for little risk."

"Thanks for the history lesson." Bishop's jaw muscles worked as he clenched his teeth.

"Some of us, not mentioning names," I stared at Ratigan, "got greedy and it's turned into a shit storm we'll be lucky to survive."

"Speak for yourself," Bishop said.

"I'm speaking for more than myself," I inched toward Bishop like I was trying to emphasize a point.

Just as he began to notice how close I was getting and looked like he was going to react, someone pounded on the door.

Ratigan let out a squawk and even Rollie jumped.

"What?" Bishop began to reach for his gun. I leaped at the table trying to wedge my body between him and the table.

I slammed into him. The side of the table jammed me in the ribs but not seriously. The table absorbed enough of my weight to save Bishop's arm from being broken.

We both crashed to the floor and I saw his pistol slide off the table onto the carpet. I tried to untangle myself from him to reach the gun first when I realized he was rolling away and not contesting me for the fallen weapon.

He was reaching for his pant leg and pulling up the cuff.

Shit!

Still on the floor, I swung my arm around and grabbed enough of one of the dining room chairs to flip it onto Bishop. In the moment he had to push the wooden chair off his body, I lunged in and latched onto his wrist.

He'd managed to get a small, stainless steel backup revolver out of an ankle holster. I held the wrist with both hands to keep the muzzle pointed toward the ceiling.

In a moment he'd either use a maneuver to break my grip and shoot me or begin to bombard me with kicks and punches while my hands were occupied.

"Drop it." Rollie made sure he never got the chance.

Bishop and I looked up to see the old guy aiming the .45. From here the muzzle looked as big as the Holland Tunnel.

"Fuck." Bishop relaxed his grip and I took the revolver and stood up.

The knocking continued. "Rollie, keep him right there. We'll need to search him. I'll get the door." I snatched up Bishop's other gun on the way.

"Backstabber," Bishop started.

"Don't tell me, tell him," I opened the door and Ryan stepped inside. He'd also pulled his Beretta.

He took one look at me with guns in my hands and smiled. "You starting a collection?"

Ratigan stared and Bishop turned shades of red that may not have been named yet. "You son of a bitch."

"Fair enough." Ryan strolled in like he owned the place, and straddled one of the dining room chairs backwards. "But we're here to try and fix this."

I put the guns on the table and frisked Bishop, more thoroughly than I would normally be comfortable touching a man, but the guy wasn't dumb. I let him keep his clothes on, at least. No more guns, but I did find a folding knife and handcuff keys.

"I had it fixed," Bishop said.

"Not for me, you didn't," I said. "Now that we have all the interested parties we need to figure out how we all get to move on with our lives without making the Irish Mob's most wanted list."

"Good luck with that," Bishop said.

Chapter 17

"You're delusional." Bishop said. "Mind if I get up off the floor?"

"I prefer visionary," Ryan said.

"It's Kyle, right?" Ratigan spoke to me.

"Yeah." I said. We'd never actually met.

"I saw you have the keys, can you unlock me?"

I saw Rollie give a tiny shake of his head and already knew what Ryan would say if asked.

"Sure." I walked over to him and pointed to my face. "I'm surprised you knew who I was, I usually don't look like this." I unlocked the cuff around the sofa bed bar.

Ratigan stood up and held out his arm for me to free the shackle on his wrist.

Instead I yanked on the free cuff and when the skinny guy was off balance slammed him to the floor next to Bishop. I was careful not to bruise his face, but didn't bother being gentle when I grabbed his wrist and locked him to Bishop's arm.

"What the fuck, Kyle?" Bishop reached in vain for the keys.

"Let's practice a little teamwork, shall we?"

"Who put you in charge, asshole?" Bishop asked while the two struggled to their feet.

"Same guy that has you by the balls, got it?" I said.

"You still don't get it," Bishop said. "Maybe this could have gone smooth like we planned, but obviously these two pricks decided to get cute and go for two bites at the same apple. And it backfired on all of us."

"We didn't know—" Ratigan started and Bishop smacked him in the gut mid-sentence with his cuffed hand.

It looked like an older brother making a sibling hit himself with his own hand.

"You could have asked me," Bishop said. He glared at Ryan. "You too, Buckley. I would have told you the risk wasn't worth it."

"Thanks, Professor Hindsight," Ryan said. "It was worth the risk and we almost pulled it off."

"Bullshit."

"It was the Cartel who figured it out," Ryan said.

"And that makes it better?" Bishop asked. "Because they are known for just letting stuff go?"

"No." Ryan didn't have a snappy comeback to that one.

"Here's how the shit rolls downhill," Bishop said. "The Cartel boys spotted the fakes and gave Sheehan a life or death ultimatum. He could pay the cash back with interest or they could have a little war on the streets of Philly."

"We know Sheehan did something to calm them down," I said.

"You don't know shit," Bishop shook his head at me. "You punks have been too busy running all over town, but I happen to know that Sheehan doesn't have that kind of cash on hand. He had to borrow it. Any guesses? Wasn't Wells Fargo."

Rollie spoke up. "The real bosses, obviously?"

"Yup. This was Sheehan's play to break into the big time, and thanks to you wonderful people, he fucked it up royally."

All I could see in my mind's eye was that look on a young Sheehan's face when he got angry. "So they're all after us?"

Bishop gave a little laugh. "Oh no. Not yet, anyway. They put all of it on Sheehan to fix the mess he created. But they're plenty pissed. This deal was supposed to help increase their business with Mexico. Not so much now."

"Damn," was all Ryan said. I could have strangled him.

"So they gave Sheehan carte blanche to get the dough back? I thought they wanted to be lower profile since the old man kicked the bucket," Rollie said.

"What's low profile about kidnapping civilians?" I asked.

Bishop hesitated. "Nothing. And I don't know for sure, but I don't think the big Bosses had that in mind."

"So Sheehan's gone rogue?" I asked.

"You aren't hearing me at all, are you?" Bishop frowned at me. "It means Sheehan is so pissed off, or desperate, or both, that he'll do anything to get this back."

"And if we give it to him?" I asked, wondering if we could salvage things with a unified front toward Sheehan.

"Yeah. Let him have the Black Dogs and the money. We'll call it a push." Ratigan's sense of self-preservation appeared to have eclipsed his greed.

"We thought about that. Sheehans don't push, they hit," Rollie said.

Ryan stepped back, and I noticed his gun was stuck in his belt, ready for a fast draw. "That's not going to happen."

"Why not?" Ratigan asked.

"We may have hit some bumps here, big ones I admit," Ryan said. "But I'll be damned if I leave that much cash on the table and walk out of here with nothing to show for it."

"Sorry it's inconvenient. We need to end this," I said.

"And I think we can." Ryan was getting that look in his eye.

"I told you, Sheehan needs to pay back his bosses," Bishop said.

"So let him," Ryan pointed at Ratigan. "You have a deal with the Colombians to fulfill, do you not?"

Ratigan squirmed in his seat.

"No more secrets here," Ryan said. "We're all partners now."

"Since when?" Ratigan asked.

"Since we gathered you back into the flock, O wayward sheep." Ryan set his jaw and turned serious. "You'll live up to the new terms or Sheehan will be the least of your problems. "When are you meeting the Colombians?"

"I can't."

"Dumbass. We're not going to steal the deal. They'll bail if it isn't you, am I right?"

Ratigan brightened. "Yeah. They would."

"Exactly. So when is it?"

Another pause.

"Dammit. I need to know when for the plan. Sheehan's ass must be getting itchy as it is. Don't tell me where, okay? I know it must be nearby, but that can wait."

Ratigan was a better sculptor than a wheeler-dealer. "Tomorrow night."

"Okay. Good." Now Ryan was pacing which meant his brain was buzzing so hard it tickled his hair.

"You're going to keep your appointment and trade the statues for the cash, just like you planned."

Ratigan stared at Ryan. "And?"

"And you and I are going to take the cut from the first deal and this one to make up the million for Sheehan. We'll also kick in an extra hundred grand each for Sheehan to forget the whole thing ever happened."

I didn't like how this was going. "And? No way I let him pocket that cash until after he lets Beth go."

Ryan shot me a quizzical look. "How would you stop him, Kyle?"

"We hold out as a condition of release."

Bishop spoke, "No offense, but we don't all share that priority."

"I forgot, that's only for real cops," I snapped.

"Said the guy talking about swindling another million. I thought you wanted to save your ex not get in this deeper," Bishop fired back.

He had a point, but for now I ignored it and pointed to the crate. "You're saying these are another set of fakes?"

Ratigan shook his head. "Not that you'd ever be able to tell, but the Colombians would. These buyers are some of the most sophisticated connoisseurs on the planet. Those are the real Black Dogs."

"I'm glad they'll appreciate it." I looked at Bishop. "At least someone isn't getting swindled."

Ryan stepped closer. "Guys, can I finish here?"

We all shut up.

"Okay, this only works if we all get something and come out safely."

I waited.

"Ratigan, you can split what is left of your share with Bishop and he can act as a middleman to give Sheehan the payoff."

"Why me?" Bishop asked.

"Because you're already working for him, and I'm sure he'd kill me on general principles, probably you, too, Ratigan," Ryan said.

"Why not have your boy here do it? He's the one all fired up about the hostage," Ratigan said.

My gut tensed at the word. "I'll be around for that," I said. Ryan shot me a look.

"Hold that thought," Ryan said. "Bishop, you also need to string Sheehan along while we wait to complete the deal. Any chance you can work him to think we're using you as a messenger only?"

"I don't know." The way Bishop said the words made clear his doubt about everything so far.

"You only have to fool him until he gets the money and the hostage is free."

I wasn't about to go along with her survival depending on this dirt bag, but I held further objections until Ryan finished.

"Why don't you share your part with Bishop too?" Ratigan asked.

"Two reasons. First, this is my idea," Ryan said. "Second, Bishop's payoff is your insurance that he will help you instead of turning you over to Sheehan."

"I wouldn't do that," Bishop said, but it was clear to all is us he'd do it in a minute if it suited him.

"Of course not. Besides I'm covering costs on my end." Ryan pointed to Rollie and me. Rollie kept his mouth shut and so did I. We'd never discussed any money past the original deal. Rollie could have anything I got, as far as that went. Ryan knew what I wanted.

Bishop shook his head. "So we complete the deal and you just meet us later with your cut for Sheehan's payoff? Just like that?"

"Pretty much," Ryan said.

"If you trust us that much, how are we supposed to do all that locked to each other?" Bishop asked.

Ryan smiled. "That's the great part of the plan. I don't trust either of you. Kyle?"

"Yeah?"

"Be a lamb and fetch the hammer and pry bar from the van. There are some blankets in there as well."

I thought I understood what he meant and I had to give Ryan credit. "Will do."

Chapter 18

When I returned with the items and with the coast still clear I began to feel the first ray of hope in what seemed a long time.

"Great. Open 'er up," Ryan pointed to the crate.

"Wait! Those are packed carefully. Don't mess with them," Ratigan said.

"Sure thing, Boss," I said, as I jammed the bar under the wooden lid. The nails shrieked when they came out of the wood. I half-expected Ratigan to shriek along with them.

"Don't touch them," Ratigan shouted.

"They've been around a long time. I'm sure they can take it." I dug through the first layer of wood shaving packing material. My hand hit smooth basalt stone and I traced my fingers around the edges of the first statue. I could feel the carved teeth and ears.

"Which doggie do we have here?" Despite my cavalier tone, I made sure I had the dog in both hands before I lifted it out. The head was pointed downwards.

"The underworld. Fitting enough," Ryan said.

Ratigan cringed when I removed it and placed it on the floor. "If you're taking them why not leave them packed?"

Ryan smiled. "We only need one."

"They're only valuable as a complete set. The buyers won't accept any of them if they can't have the complete set." Ratigan trailed off as he began to understand.

Bishop spoke up. "Getting the picture, Junior?"

Ryan stepped close to Ratigan. "Now we all have our priorities in order. You'll let us know where to bring Underdog here and you keep the other two. We'll give it back just before your meet so you don't get any fresh ideas about a double-cross."

Ratigan simply nodded.

"Bishop, you can be close by when it goes down, but out of sight as I don't think a cop appearing at the last minute would enthuse our Colombian friends."

"I'm sure it wouldn't," Bishop said. "Then I'm the bag man?"

"Nope," Ryan said, and pointed to me. "That's for Kyle. Ratigan and you hand over the million from the Colombians, and I'll take the remaining two hundred from my share of the first deal."

"Then what?" Ratigan asked. "That leaves you with a smaller share."

"Will it? You and Bishop work out whatever you want and go your separate ways. I'll hook up with Kyle and complete the full one point two million. Kyle will hand it over once Beth is free."

"Whoa, whoa, whoa. Just like that? You already make a deal with Sheehan or something?" Bishop asked.

"Not yet," Ryan said and the flicker of doubt that crossed his face made me shiver.

"Let's call him now and make the offer. That way we can be sure," I said.

Ryan didn't blow me off right away. He pursed lips in thought. When he spoke it sounded like it was as much to

164

himself as us. "If we reach out after the Colombian deal and he says no, then we have the same problem as now but a million bucks in hand. If we call him first, and he says yes, we still have to do the deal to hold up our end. If he says no, we can still do the deal and we're stronger no matter what because of the money," he said.

"You're forgetting Beth?" I asked.

"I'm not. He's not going to kill her over another day unless we do something stupid to force him. We could just offer him the statues and some cash like you said before, but what's he going to do to her if that isn't good enough?"

"But the statues *are* the value. I mean isn't that why all this got started?" I asked.

"Now you are assuming the cartel still wants them," Ryan said.

"And at the same price," Bishop added. I could see Ryan was persuading him.

Ryan continued. "And how many other buyers do you think Sheehan has lined up? We don't know how the cartel would respond, but right now they are calm, at least no threat to Sheehan. If we can make him whole financially, even ahead, I think we have a chance."

"But shouldn't we at least ask first?" I felt like I was losing ground, but hated the idea of Beth in danger a moment longer than necessary. "If we're just speculating, maybe he'd prefer the statues. That's what he expects Bishop to deliver."

Ryan looked at me. "Fair point. We could reach out and give him the option."

"If we are respectful, it shouldn't piss him off any more than he is," Rollie said.

"All right, But however it goes when we get a yes out of him, we need to move as fast as possible. We can't afford to give him time to think of a way to screw us over, or Beth," Ryan said.

"Anyone have any better ideas?" Rollie asked. "Speak now, and all that."

None seemed to, including me, damn it.

"That's the plan, but don't make it sound so simple. I'm going to vanish, and it looks like retirement will have to wait, but I don't plan on sticking around right under Sheehan's nose, that's for sure," Ryan said.

"For someone who said he doesn't trust us," Bishop rattled the cuff on his wrist, "you're being cavalier with a whole lot of dough."

Ryan shrugged. "No choice, really. But remember, if either of you run off with it you are stealing Sheehan's money. And you know that really means the rest of the Irish bosses' money, because Sheehan will not be able to pay them back. Think they'll forget about it?"

Nobody had to answer that one.

"Ryan, what's your big plan if Sheehan says no deal either way?"

"He's still a business man. How's he going to say no, coming out far ahead?"

"Say that after he catches up to you and works you over," Bishop said.

"Let's see how he responds first," Ryan said.

"You going to unlock us now?" Bishop asked.

"In a minute," Ryan said. He wrapped the one statue in the blanket I'd brought.

I held up the handcuff key. "I'll leave this on the hood of Ratigan's car. Bishop, you can reach Ryan by phone, right?"

"Yeah."

Ryan nodded. "Cool. We'll talk more after we're clear. Better to remove temptation and all that."

"And my guns?"

"Sure." I still had both. I unloaded them, dumped the loose ammo into my pocket and placed the weapons on the dining room table. "Here you go."

"And don't call Sheehan until we say." We backed out of the room.

Chapter 19

Ryan's Van.

"You got balls, I'll give you that," Rollie said to Ryan, once we'd loaded the wrapped statue into the van and reached the road.

"Just trying to salvage something out this mess." Ryan scanned the rear view mirror. "Thanks for your help."

"Wasn't trying to help you." Rollie didn't hesitate.

"I appreciate you backing our play." Ryan sounded impatient.

"Whatever. Who's going to talk to Sheehan?" Rollie asked.

"Kyle, you up to it? I might not be the best one, given how pissed he is at me."

"I don't see any way to present our offer without him knowing we all got together to screw him."

"If we were really going to do that, we'd all vanish with the cash."

"That's not funny. Then he'd start with Beth, then make it around to the rest of us."

"He'd try." Ryan agreed.

I pictured leaving the task to Bishop. No way, and I wasn't going to trust Ryan with this either. "I'll do it."

Rollie put his hand on my arm. "Are you sure we shouldn't we make sure the other deal goes through first? I know I don't have enough in the petty cash drawer to cover this."

Ryan shook his head. "This ain't your deal. If he doesn't agree we need to be able to figure something else out before this other thing goes through, and before Bishop gets any ideas of his own."

I wondered if Ryan had read my mind. "It's okay, Rollie." I took out the burner phone Sheehan gave me and turned it on. The message light started blinking as soon as it had booted up. "Seventeen missed calls. All from him, of course."

"More like seventeen pissed calls," Rollie said.

My heart thudded as I looked at the log of calls from what was undoubtedly another burner cell. The intervals between calls went from hours to minutes apart.

There were no messages, but that didn't surprise me. Sheehan would ditch the phone and didn't want to leave any evidence behind with his voice on it.

I hit the call-back number.

It didn't ring twice.

"Where the fuck have you been?" Sheehan's yell made the earpiece squeal with distortion.

I closed my eyes and concentrated. "Keeping my phone from ringing. Thought you would have gotten that by now."

"Answer my question."

"I was following a lead, and where I was would have been disaster if the thing had rung."

"Is Bishop there with you?"

I prayed that they hadn't spoken already. "I don't know where he is. Haven't seen him since earlier today."

"Never mind. You've got a problem."

I forced myself not to exhale with relief then realized what he'd said. "Lately that's all I've got."

"First of all you tell her to cut the shit or I'll have to punish her again. And her boyfriend is going to get himself popped."

My body felt plunged in ice water. "What did you say?"

"You heard me."

"What did you do to her?" I felt Rollie's hand on my arm again and it was like he was touching someone else I felt so disconnected.

"A tickle compared to what's next. You're going to get a call in a minute and she'll be on the line. Pick up and straighten her out. Then call me right back and fill me in on what is going on. This in the dark shit ends now."

He hung up.

I began to shake and waved off Rollie and Ryan when they started to ask what happened.

The phone rang. I almost hit the wrong button my hands were trembling so much. "Hello?"

"Kyle?"

"Beth? It's me, are you okay?"

"I'm sorry." She was crying. I once saw her roll an ankle and she never shed a tear.

"For what? You didn't do anything for this. It's my fault, but I'm going to make it right."

"I couldn't wait."

Uh oh. She was also stubborn and smart. Raw fear would only piss her off after a while. "What happened?"

"I tried to get away, but they caught me. They made me call to say I was on a work trip and ...."

She was sobbing now.

"Who did you call?"

"You have to stop him."

Rage poured hot through my chest. "I will."

"Not him. Richard. He's suspicious."

"Richard?" Confusion diluted my anger. What was Fenster doing?

"That guy said Richard went to the police. How could he know that? Do you owe these people money? I said we could pay, but that only made him angrier."

I was beginning to understand. "I'm handling it. I think this can be over very soon. You have to trust me. Don't try to escape again, Okay? Promise."

"All right." She never agreed with me so quickly, but I believed her and what must have happened made me all the more enraged.

"I'll find him, Beth, and make him understand. Just stay cool, okay?"

Whoever had the phone hung up. I never heard her reply.

"Fuck!" I screamed inside the van. Then I slapped my own face, hard, and focused on the sting. Fury wasn't going to help Beth.

I did a fast recap for Ryan and Rollie.

"Quiet now, I have to call right back." I had an idea and there wasn't time for Ryan to talk me out of it.

Sheehan picked up. "See what you miss when you disappear like that?"

"You're going to bully yourself right out of the biggest score of your life, you low-rent fraud wise guy." A sharp intake of breath told me he wasn't used to being hit like that.

"I'll remember you said that."

"Just listen for once. You couldn't reach me because I'm close to getting your money back."

"You found Ryan?"

"Better. I found Ratigan *and* Ryan, and can get close to the final exchange."

"Where and when?"

I figured he'd be interested. "I can't tell you."

"You forgetting something?"

"What I'm remembering is how clumsy some of your people can be when the job calls for a covert operation."

He paused and that either meant he took my point or he was so pissed he'd make me listen to him torture Beth right over the phone.

"I have Bishop."

I cut him off. "Let's get real. He still can act like a cop, but he's not exactly a SWAT member is he?"

"I can get—"

"This isn't a raid and a big shootout is going to draw attention all over. Not good. I've done under the radar transfers, and I know how Ryan thinks. I don't need help, but we're only going to get one chance. Ryan already has a bunch of cash. He wants more, but if we spook him he's gone. Ratigan too."

"What are you going to do?"

"No details. Just hang on until tomorrow night without killing anyone. I have a great chance to get you your money and more."

"Why should I believe you?" Sheehan spoke without thinking apparently.

"Same reason you keep shoving in my face, what else?"

"Tell me the details and I'll hold back. I don't want to see Ryan get away, or that piece of shit hack sculptor, either."

I almost played my trump card. I could see Ryan and Rollie trying to follow the conversation from my side. "Ryan will smell it out. He's scary that way. Look, you went to a lot of trouble to get me to help. I'm helping, and you have to let me finish the job. Otherwise you're going to lose them and the money."

"We still have another problem."

"I talked to her. She said no more escapes."

"Not worried about that. The weasel boyfriend. That bitch signaled him."

"What do you expect me to do? He hates me." As soon as the words left my mouth I realized I was the one not thinking.

"Never mind, I'll handle it. You get that money. This is *your* marker now." Sheehan hung up.

I guess it was good I'd raised his hopes. At the same time he'd just told me I did indeed owe *those gangsters* a ton of money, as Beth would say.

"Well?" Ryan asked.

"This better work." I told them about Fenster.

"You know he's going to whack the guy, don't you?" Rollie said.

"Why? I thought he'd grab him if he could find him."

"He'll find him, all right, and that'll be the last anyone sees of him. Be amazed if there's ever a body found."

"Crap. You sure?"

"You told me yourself Beth said the guy is looking for her, and he now thinks she was kidnapped. Possibly by you, but where do you go when you suspect kidnapping?" Rollie asked.

Now Ryan, who'd shown little interest in Fenster's plight, spun around in the driver's seat. If we hadn't been parked he'd probably have crashed the van. "First he went to the cops, and that got intercepted by one of Sheehan's men on the take, but that's temporary."

"Kyle, is this Fenster character a patient guy?" Rollie asked.

I began to see his point. "He's the most demanding, self-important jackass I ever met. Shit, you're, right, he'll pester the cops and go to the supervisor or even the Chief and call in every lawyer, judge, and politician he knows to follow the case."

"Exactly." Rollie said. "Sheehan's dumber than I thought but not that stupid. Remember what I told you, the Irish bosses don't want that kind of attention. It leads to the Feds coming in and they'd love to have another shot at making a case against them."

"Damn. Sheehan will do anything to prevent that and if Fenster has to disappear, what of it?" I didn't say what that meant for other key witnesses, including all of us in the van.

"Not the way I meant to get your charges dropped," Ryan read my expression. "Bad joke. We gotta find him or he's dead. Where does he live?"

I gave him the address.

Chapter 20

"Think he'll be home?" Ryan asked while we headed back toward Philly.

"Hard to say. I just hope we aren't too late."

We left the highway and were on course to reach Fenster's Chestnut Hill neighborhood in a few minutes.

I pulled out my regular smartphone and powered it up. It had a couple of messages from a number I recognized as Fenster's. "Maybe I'm being too paranoid, but is it possible Sheehan served this on a platter to jump me when I try save him?"

"A wise man once said, 'When everyone's out to get you, paranoid's just good thinking,'" Rollie said. "Wish I could remember who it was."

Ryan slowed the van, as if my words added pressure to the brake pedal. "They were right. Beth mentioned Fenster too, didn't she?"

"They could have forced her to say it." I swallowed hard thinking what it would take to get her to do that. "I see he tried to call."

"Or someone did from his phone," Rollie added.

The van began to feel closed in.

"No messages. Just the calls." I noted.

"How about you call back and see if he answers?" Rollie suggested.

Made sense. I hit the button to call back. It began to ring and I thought it would roll to voicemail. I heard a click. "Richard?"

There was a long pause and I began to wonder if there was some sort of trace on the line to pin down our location.

"Where is she?" It was Fenster, but he sounded hoarse.

"I don't know."

"You're going to jail and if you hurt her, you'll never breathe free air again."

"Stop. Listen carefully—"

He cut me off. "Threats now? What happened to you in Iraq? Is this some sort of psychotic PTSD? You lost her. It's over."

"Shut up! You're in danger. Understand?"

"I understand plenty, and you don't scare me," Fenster screamed into the phone.

"I'm not trying to scare you." The van rolled ahead and I recognized the neighborhood. We were a couple blocks from Fenster's street. "I haven't done anything to Beth."

"Bullshit."

"But I know who has her."

"Yeah, who?"

"I'd rather do this in person."

"I agree. Meet me at the station house. Precinct 14, Haines and Germantown."

"I can't do that."

"That's what I thought. They're going to find you soon enough, and I'll be happy to pick you out of a lineup."

One more block. "Keep him talking," Ryan whispered.

I didn't think I'd be able to get him to stop.

"Richard. Where are you now?"

"Never mind where I am. You have one chance to get ahead of this. Tell me where Beth is."

I was about to cut loose on the obstinate bastard when Ryan turned at the head of Fenster's street.

I saw a souped-up black Mustang parked down the street. Right across from Fenster's place.

"Aw crap," Rollie whispered. "Go past, go past," he said to Ryan while he ducked down in his seat.

Ryan didn't question it and never slowed while we went by the car. I saw two figures inside, but their attention was fixed in the direction of Fenster's house. The driver had blonde hair.

Thank God they didn't know our vehicle.

"Still there, chickenshit?" Fenster asked.

"Richard. The kidnappers know you went to the cops. They work for them. Get it?"

"You're delusional."

We parked around the corner and if I pressed against the back window I could just see that Mustang.

"Are you at home?"

"I'm not telling you where I am, but I'll give the cops this number. You might as well let her go and turn yourself in."

"Goddamnit you stupid asshole! I'm trying to save her, and you too, if you'll listen. You are screwing with Irish mobsters and they aren't going to let you run your mouth."

"You can get help. There are doctors…." Fenster had stopped yelling and switched to a faux-soothing tone that curled my fingers into a fist.

The driver's side door to the Mustang opened and I recognized the goon. Mustang Sally. He wore a bad tweed jacket over jeans. He must have figured that passed for plainclothes cop wear. A second guy I didn't recognize joined him and they began to cross the street.

"Look out your window and you'll see two of them coming. They aren't cops. The blonde one has been trying to tail me for the last couple days."

"This fantasy has to stop." I heard some doubt creep into his voice. There was a pause and I pictured him moving to peek out a window. "How did you… are you stalking me now?"

"Richard," I spoke in an even, low tone to force him to listen to me. I'd get one chance. "I am here and do you think these men work for me? Of course not. Did you call the police just now?"

"No, but they might have information about Beth."

I cut him off. "They'd call first. If you answer the door, you're a dead man. Don't believe me? Try not responding and see if they break in. Real cops wouldn't do that for a courtesy visit."

"They must know I'm home." For the first time I'd gotten through.

"Don't open the door." I covered the mouthpiece. "Ryan, turn us around. This is bad." I gestured for Rollie's gun. He gave it to me without hesitation.

It only took a moment to get a better view of the front of the house. It was a quiet evening and Fenster's porch light was out. The two stood at the door, but I didn't think they'd knocked.

"What should I do?" The first signs of real fear crept into Fenster's voice. Good, but not if it paralyzed him.

What were those two waiting for? They just stood in front of the door and seemed to be whispering to each other. Ryan had the headlights off and the van rolled to a stop about a hundred yards away. The men took no notice of us.

"Can you make it upstairs? Turn on a light or something and they'll see you are home, Then hide. I'm coming."

"You're crazy." He spoke in hushed tones that put the lie to his comment.

"I see them at the door and not knocking. That make sense?"

"Maybe they'll call first, like you said." I could tell Fenster wasn't buying his own rationalizations. Better late than never. I hoped.

Now the second goon, the one with dark hair stepped off the porch and worked his way around toward the back.

"Are you upstairs? One is covering your back door."

"Holy shit, you're right. I saw him go by. He was peering in the windows."

"Did he see you?"

"I don't think so."

"When you can, get upstairs and switch a light, on or off doesn't matter, as long as they see the change. Then get out of sight and be ready to move fast."

"I'm no threat to them. Maybe I can talk to…."

Now "Sally" reached into his coat and pulled out a slim pistol with a long extension on the barrel.

"Suppressed .22." Ryan saw the same thing. He eased the van forward. "As soon as he goes in I'll hit it."

Rollie was rummaging in his big green duffel bag.

"Richard, they're not here to talk. Get up there now."

I saw a light go on in his bedroom. Sally saw it too. He rang the doorbell. His gun arm dangled at his side and the weapon slid under the fabric of his jacket.

"Now what?"

"Got a weapon? Shotgun, pistol, rifle, anything?" I wasn't sure if that would have been good or not.

"I hate guns," he said.

"Then hide and stay put or they'll hate you back," I said.

"Okay." Fenster sounded like a little kid.

Things happened fast.

Sally put a shoulder to the door. Most front doors even in nice neighborhoods tended to be sturdy. The first few hits simply made noise and the door held up.

I saw the guy step back to give his legs a shot at kicking it in.

"They're breaking in!" Fenster squeaked over the phone.

Now I heard a faint tinkle of glass from the back yard. Back doors were a mixed bag and I'd bet Fenster's was flimsy.

"One is inside!"

"Shut up!" I spoke into the phone but doubted Fenster could even hear me. I smacked Ryan on the shoulder. "Skip the Ninja routine."

"Got an idea," Ryan said. He gunned the gas and left the headlights off. "Hang on."

We covered the hundred yards in no time. Ryan swerved the van and sideswiped the Mustang hard enough to blow out the driver's side windows, and the sheet metal puckered with an awful screech. He stopped. "Oh shit, where'd that car come from?" Ryan yelled. Our windows had survived, but I'd bet there was now a long black scrape down the side.

The goon whipped around and stared at the violation of his precious car. I would have laughed at his expression in other circumstances.

He looked befuddled what to do next. I only hoped that his friend breaking in or already inside had heard the crash as well. Ryan got out on the driver's side so the goon couldn't see him. Rollie and I stayed inside, out of sight.

QUICK FIX

"Who parks in the middle of the street like that?" Ryan yelled in a passable drunk voice.

Still at the door, I saw that Sally had hidden the gun and now the front door opened. I thought for a second Fenster had doubled-down on stupid. A moment later I saw it was the second thug.

They conferred for a moment and my heart pounded when Sally ran toward us, but the other one ducked back inside.

"Shit. Make this quick," I said.

Fortunately, Sally wanted a piece of the witness who'd trashed his car.

"Oh man, this ain't my fault," Ryan wailed. Now more lights came on in the neighboring houses.

"What did you do to my car?" The guy reached the back of the van and ran around the side. "You!"

At the same time I slid the side door open. I'd seen what Rollie'd dug out of his bag. It was perfect.

The instant the guy got to the driver's side of the van where he could see Ryan, we jumped in front of him. Rollie switched on a portable spotlight, the kind perfect for jacklighting deer and the guy was blinded with a thousand lumens right in the face. His arms flew up to his eyes and he nearly ran into me. I gripped the gun arm with one hand and put all my strength into burying my fist into his midsection. The big dude folded in half and he fell into the damaged side of his car. His gun clattered to the pavement and I picked it up and pressed the barrel into the guy's forehead.

Ryan came over and borrowed the spotlight. He began shining it at the upstairs windows of Fenster's House.

From inside it must have looked like the SWAT teams had arrived. The guy at my feet was still trying to catch his breath.

Now a couple people in bathrobes had ventured out to see the commotion. They wouldn't be able to see me because the van shielded us from view. Ryan hid behind the light and took a moment to shine it on the neighbors who covered their faces and retreated no doubt to call the cops. As blinding as that light was, they'd probably need to do so by touch.

Rollie stomped the dude to the ground and put a wicked looking K-Bar knife to the guy's neck. "Call off your partner."

I remembered I still had his .45 tucked in my belt.

"There he is!" Ryan said. I looked up and the light had swept across the big guy's face staring out of a second floor window of Fenster's house. He was clean-shaven, so I knew it wasn't Fenster with his stupid hipster beard. I aimed the suppressed weapon and fired two or three muffled pops at the glass, more to scare the guy than take him out.

It worked. I saw his bulky form a few seconds later flash past the front door and back into the house. Going for the back door, I guessed. What I didn't know was if he'd found Fenster first.

"We need to bail now!" I could hear sirens in the distance.

"What about him?" Rollie said.

I used my shirt to wipe my prints off the .22 and tossed it through the broken side window of the Mustang. I took the K-Bar from Rollie. The guy just stared at us. I wrapped a big handful of his greasy blonde locks in my fist and looked him in the eye.

QUICK FIX

I sliced through the hair with the seven-inch razor-sharp combat knife close to the scalp and threw the yellow clump onto his chest. "Next time it'll be something with veins."

The van was moving before we even got the door closed. I watched the Mustang start up and burn rubber in the opposite direction.

Chapter 21

Ryan's Van.

I checked my phone. Incredibly, it was still connected to Fenster. "Richard?"

I could hear muffled sirens in the background. Rollie kept watch for the Mustang or cops on our tail. Probably the neighborhood was still confused and trying to process what had happened.

"You there?" I thought I heard something else. "Are you okay?"

"Quiet." It was barely more than a whisper.

I realized he must be still in hiding. But he had to be alive to be frightened.

"They're gone. Are you hurt?"

"You sure?"

"We had to bolt. I saw the guy running after I threw some shots at him."

"The window? That was you?"

"Small caliber, suppressed."

"Suppressed?" He sounded like he might be in shock.

"A silencer. You know?"

"You shot my house? Why?"

"I had to get the guy out of your bedroom. It worked, didn't it? It was the blonde goon's gun. Do I need to tell you that's not standard issue with the Philly PD?" It occurred to me that while the cops would be excited enough about the hit and run, there probably wasn't a call for shots fired. That might have brought out a helicopter.

"It's safe to come out?"

"Should be. Where are you exactly?"

"Linen closet."

"You fit?" I tried to picture it. I'd need a walk-in closet to get my carcass hidden.

"Yoga three times a week. The police are on the street. Now what?"

I thought fast. "All right. You'll be safe until they leave."

"What do I tell them?"

"Don't lawyer up. They'll be suspicious." I thought about the state of his place and how it would appear from the street.

"And when they ask who shot up my place trying to kill me?" I didn't like the hysterical pitch in his voice.

"Calm down. Your front door is intact. Don't say anything about the back. If they see the windows just speculate it was a pellet gun or something. You heard a hit and run, like everyone else."

"What about the cars?"

"We're going to have to ditch the van soon. Describe them both. Maybe the others will get off the road."

"All right. Then what?"

I'd seen Ryan nodding when I spoke about getting rid of the van. I figured he had plans in place for another vehicle once this one had been identified. At least it was still running, but it had a hell of a gouge from Sally's car.

"As soon as the cops leave, you need to get in your car and meet us somewhere."

"Where?"

"Call me when you're clear and watch out for a tail. If you think someone is following then drive to the police precinct you suggested to me. You'll be safe there and we'll come get you."

There was a long pause and I checked the signal strength. It was fine. "You there?"

"I don't think so."

"What do you mean?"

"Sounds like the frying pan to the fire."

"Huh?"

"I can't trust the local cops. But I can trust the Feds." Fenster was regaining his confident tone of voice.

My heart sank, and for a split second I wished we had left the goons to finish the job.

"Richard. That's not safe."

He actually laughed at me. "You're going to tell me you and your merry band can protect me better that the FBI?"

Now my burner phone rang with an incoming call from Sheehan.

QUICK FIX

No thanks.

"No. You'll be just fine, you selfish ass, meanwhile Beth will be dead along with the rest of us and eventually you will be too, the first chance they get."

"How's that?" At least he seemed to have heard me.

"What you suggest is the last thing Sheehan wants. He's blowing up my phone as we speak and probably has Beth on the line so he can make her scream for me." As the words left my mouth I realized I wasn't exaggerating and then my stomach clenched so hard I thought I'd puke.

"But—"

"No. You'll take away our last leverage. Worse, you have no proof, just a bunch of death warrants for all the witnesses."

"I need to think about this. I can see the cops talking to my neighbors now."

"I gotta take this call. Whatever you do, get out of your house. He might come back tonight. He's nuts."

"I'll call you later," Fenster said.

"Oh, and Richard?"

"What?"

"You're welcome!" I screamed into the receiver. I needed to vent some of the emotion because this next call had to count.

* * *

Conshohocken, Pennsylvania

189

"I don't care what time it is. Make it happen," Ryan barked into his phone. "Call me right back."

I didn't know who he was talking to but it wasn't Hertz Rent a Car.

I was glad to see that Ryan was taking us out of the city. While we knew our neighborhood of Fishtown well, so did Sheehan, and he'd have eyes out for us everywhere. Also, we didn't want to run into the boys in the Mustang who were probably heading that way.

Ryan drove again. "Kyle, let's get it straight before you call Sheehan. His guy made me."

"I thought he might have," I said. "That puts the lie to me being too busy following you around to make that deal."

"Sure does." Ryan shook his head. "Damn, Kyle, I'm sorry. He's gonna be rip-shit angry, but remind him Beth is his only leverage against you."

The words only confirmed what I already knew and still felt like a kick in the balls. "We ought to let Bishop know and pray they haven't talked to him tonight."

"Try him."

I didn't feel any of us were on the same page. More like a clump of magnets forced together and ready to fly apart at the first opportunity.

* * *

"Bishop." I heard over the phone.

"It's Kyle. Please tell me you haven't talked to him yet."

"After the first five or six missed calls I didn't think I was going to like what I heard."

Good. *Very good.* I gave him a rundown of what happened with Fenster after Beth tipped him off.

"Wish she hadn't done that. Where is he?"

"Out of sight for tonight, we hope. I think we've got him under control."

"You think?" Bishop didn't sound like he'd done much relaxing in the intervening hours.

"Tell me all about all the lawyers you know who just do what they're told."

"Fine. Jump off that bridge when we come to it. You're going to talk to Sheehan?"

"Right now. We have to make our play."

'No way. We get the cash first. And I want to be there."

"No choice. At Fenster's place his guy saw Ryan with me. That cover is blown."

"Fuck. You sure?"

"Yeah. Couldn't be helped."

"I doubt that."

"Kiss my ass. You weren't there."

"So what are going to say to him?"

"I'll give him the terms and set a meet to exchange Beth for the money."

"You don't have the first clue what you're doing."

I felt my blood heat up. "Wrong. I faced more danger in the Sandbox than you ever did counting inventory in a warehouse, champ. And Ryan will be with me on the call."

"Call me right back when you're done and I swear if your plan sucks...."

It was late and he hadn't thought through his next threat.

"You'll sell two of the statues and cut us out of the deal?" I asked. Ryan stifled a laugh.

Checkmate.

"Just don't fuck it up." Bishop hung up.

Ryan grinned. "That went well."

"Rollie, we'll do this on speaker, hope you aren't offended by bad language," I said.

Rollie clapped his hands over his ears. I knew he understood he wasn't to chime in on the conversation. I also saw he had a pen and small notepad handy.

"Here we go. No pressure."

Chapter 22

Ryan's Van

We'd parked off the road where we wouldn't have any distractions. The inside of the vehicle was stifling despite the A/C being on full blast because the refrigerant was shot. Even so, we weren't about to open windows, given the upcoming conversation.

I dialed and expected the phone to explode with cursing as soon as I hit the *Send* button.

Instead it rang. And rang. Then we all heard the phone carrier's robotic voicemail. Ryan waved off leaving a message, not that Rollie or I were about to say anything.

I disconnected.

"Early to bed, early to rise?" Rollie quipped.

I wasn't smiling. My hands were sweating so much they stained my jeans where I kept wiping them.

"Psych job," Ryan said. "Call again."

Same thing.

We waited five agonizing minutes. I hit redial.

It picked up. "Danny?"

"Mr. Sheehan is indisposed. May I say whom it may concern?" Laughter in the background and the gruff voice spoke in a Philly-drenched attempt at a British accent.

"What are you talking about? Is he there? I thought he wanted to talk to me."

"He's otherwise occupied at the moment." More rough laughter.

"Can you go get him?"

No more crappy butler impressions. "He'll call you back. He said to tell you that if you want to fuck around and blow off his calls then he'd find another way to send a message. A big one by the sound of it." Loud guffaws and the guy hung up.

Heat and cold pulsed through me in alternating waves. Sweat rolled down my sides and my head began to pound.

Rollie gripped my shoulder. "More head games. We don't know anything. Don't let him rattle you."

I nodded, but I couldn't pretend. Sheehan had landed a direct hit. I was rattled, all right. My first thought was to get my hands on a few hundred pounds of fertilizer to turn into a truck bomb that I'd drive into his house.

Ten minutes felt long enough to turn my hair gray. Finally, the phone trilled.

"Can we get to business now?" I asked.

"We're on speaker? And who else is with us? Bet I can guess." Sheehan sounded like he was going to laugh.

"Yeah, Danny. I'm here, too. We're ready to put our cards on the table and end this thing." Ryan said.

"Cards, huh? I should have known you'd deal from the bottom of the deck, you piece of shit."

"I deserve that. I won't waste your time with apologies. But things weren't supposed to get out of control like they did. I didn't set out to screw you over," Ryan said.

I fought an urge to pop Ryan in the nose before I got back to contemplating my truck attack. Rollie looked like he'd hold Ryan down for me if I asked.

"Yeah, funny how shit happens, ain't it? Since we're talking cards your buddy needs to remember who holds the ace." I heard the flick of a lighter and an exaggerated drag and exhale of smoke. "That old cliché is true."

"What?" I asked, knowing it was just what he wanted.

"A smoke is good after sex."

"Congratulations," Ryan blurted out.

Ryan was slow on the uptake, but I saw Rollie's face go pale and then, as if the heat in my own face had warmed his skin, he flushed brick-red.

"You miserable cocksucker." I heard the words come out of my mouth, but it was like an out of body experience.

"Interesting choice of words there, Kyle. You might tell your ex that she ought to remember where she *doesn't* have teeth the next time she threatens to bite something off."

* * *

I'm not sure what happened next. Blackout? More like a red-out.

I came to, if that's the right term, squashed into the floor of the van. I felt hard pressure on my chest and legs and realized it was feet. My vision cleared like a curtain parting to Rollie crouched atop my chest with his full weight on my body. My arms were pinned at my sides and Ryan sat on my legs. I could barely breathe. An impromptu straitjacket.

"Wow, that sounded dramatic. You going to make it there, sport?" Sheehan mocked over the speakerphone.

Rollie looked down at me as if to ask the same question.

I nodded. Flipping out wasn't going to solve anything. Besides, truck bombs couldn't drive themselves.

Rollie and Kyle got off of me and the added air, stale though it was, cleared my head. "Yeah."

"Then you remember how you just felt when you thought it was only me. All she got was the back of my hand for her attitude. This time. Next time it won't be a slap, and will not just be me, she'll pull a train with the whole crew."

I felt some relief that she hadn't been violated, despite fresh rage that he'd hit her.

Ryan spoke. "Can we deal now?"

"I'm all ears," Sheehan said.

"All right. We, and by that I mean Bishop and Ratigan as well, are all together."

"Nothing worse than a cop who won't stay bought," Sheehan muttered.

"He saw reason and I hope you do too."

"Try me."

"Unless you want them instead, we have a second buyer for the statues."

"Your original customers aren't real happy," Sheehan noted.

I felt sane enough to contribute. "We know a lot of people aren't. The cartel got taken care of and your current *bankers* are counting on you to make it right."

"That isn't new information to me."

"We're offering a way out."

"Go on."

Ryan pointed to me to let me continue. "Day after tomorrow we give you the million you owe your people."

Ryan held up a finger and I understood.

"That ain't gonna cut it."

"I'm not done. We'll add another two hundred large on top of that."

"Why so generous?" But I could hear in his voice Sheehan was interested.

"Beth goes free or no deal," I said.

"That's it?" Sheehan said.

Then Ryan spoke. "That, and you leave everyone alone. Full truce. No retaliation and we're all done and live happily ever after."

"The girl, and you deliver one point two in cash then we smoke the peace pipe?" Sheehan asked.

"That's right," I said.

"And if that's not good enough?"

"That's the offer," I said.

"What if I said I talked to Bishop and he made me a better offer? And I don't even have to leave you alone."

I felt the red trying to rise up again and managed to cap it. "Then take your chances."

"My chances?"

"You turn us down and we go nuclear," I said.

Ryan jumped in. "Did the O'Briens okay kidnapping civilians? Since when? You got one guy in the wind ready to go to the Feds, how about us too?"

"You're up to your eyeballs, Ryan. My proof is stronger than yours. You too, Kyle," Sheehan said.

"I'm not afraid to get locked up." I probably deserved to anyway.

"Kyle, I'm glad I realized what a stupid punk you are before you jumped at the chance to work for me. You really want to push me? You realize there's no case without any evidence?"

We all knew what that meant.

"I'll put you in the ground," I said.

"Ooo, tough guy." Sheehan laughed.

Ryan spoke. "The O'Briens aren't a court. If they believe you're bringing Fed scrutiny back on their operation…."

"Yeah, yeah. I got it." Sheehan's tone was dismissive, but I also heard an edge in it that said the prospect worried him.

"How about we avoid all that and just let this thing go forward?" Ryan said.

"Why don't you tell me where this deal is going down and I'll take care of it myself? The cartel boss would still love those statues." Sheehan said.

"No point. We don't know where the sale will happen. Not yet. And Bishop doesn't have all the statues, either. See how this works?" Ryan asked. "You'll get more our way."

"Smart." I heard a touch of respect in Sheehan's voice. "But I still need something else."

My heart sank. I thought we'd been making progress. "What?"

"Give me that dipshit lawyer you rescued. He's a loose end I can't afford to have around. We could be done here if you hadn't fucked it up earlier tonight."

"We'll nail it down. Guaranteed."

"Well, as long as I have your word for it. How about his head on a stick?" Sheehan suggested.

"Tell me this, does Beth's life depend on his actions?" I asked.

"Of course. And not just hers," Sheehan said.

"Then know that I will do whatever it takes to make him understand." I meant that.

"Fine. Make it a million four and you own the lawyer's actions now."

Ryan spoke. "One point three million and we keep the prick in line."

"If I say yes, how do want to work it?" Sheehan asked.

"We'll give you a location and you bring Beth. We bring the cash. Straight swap."

"Just like that?"

"That's not enough?"

"How about I pick the location? We're still a little rough on the trust thing," Sheehan said.

"Not if we don't like your choice," I said.

Sheehan grunted acknowledgement. "Tell you what. We have what they call an agreement in principle. When you have the money in hand, you call me. If I get word that lawyer is going freelance or anything else, all bets are off. Got me?"

"Loud and clear." Ryan spoke before I had a chance.

* * *

"Bishop." He'd picked up quick enough to tell us we hadn't interrupted his beauty sleep.

"Looks like we're on with Sheehan."

"Was that why he kept calling?"

"You didn't speak to him?" I asked.

"If I had, do you think I'd tell you?"

I felt fresh rage surge in my chest.

"But no, I didn't. What did he say?" Bishop asked.

We gave him the basics.

"He wants the second sale location so he can hit it during the buy and get both the cash and the statues."

"He said that?"

"Pretty much," I said.

"What did you tell him?"

"He understands there won't be a deal until all the puzzle pieces come together."

"Thanks for not selling us out," Bishop said.

"You too, I hope," I said. "Just so you know, if he thinks we're setting him up, he'll punish Beth by…," my throat closed over the rest of the words.

"What was that?"

Rollie blurted out, "Scumbag rapist thug just like his old man."

"Shit. Sorry," Bishop said.

"I wanted you to understand," I said.

"I understand plenty. If we did let Sheehan raid the buy do you really think he'd let any of us live?" Bishop asked.

"Probably not. At least with our way we can arrange a proper head start."

"Agreed. All right I'll call him back and make sure he's clear that I can't tip him off even if I wanted to because I don't have the location from Ratigan," Bishop said.

"Sounds good. Going to be a long couple days." Ryan ended the call.

Chapter 23

Sitting on the side of the road I had another awful thought. Before we pulled over to make all our calls Ryan kept complaining about how the handling on the van was messed up from the wreck with the Mustang. It kept drifting to the left and he had to concentrate to keep the thing in a straight line.

It was bad enough that Rollie had joked that after everything we'd get pulled over for drunk driving. When we all thought about it, the cops probably were looking for a drunk driver for a hit and run.

What I thought of now was that we'd smacked that Mustang hard to cause other kinds of damage. "Rollie, can you check the guest of honor?" I pointed to the wrapped blanket that swaddled the statue.

He gave me a perfect "Oh shit!" expression and we all held our breath while he climbed over the back seat to take a look.

Rollie pulled the last layer off and I saw smooth black stone when he held it up. "Looks like the dog will still hunt."

We all breathed again.

"No problem. If it was busted, I have some Gorilla glue that'd fix her right up." Rollie smiled.

Ryan's friend called back, and I could see it was more good news.

"Yeah, I know where it is. Thanks, this is huge," Ryan said.

His friend said something.

"Yes, you only owe me two now."

I heard an angry buzz from his phone.

"Fine. Just one, okay? Later." He hung up.

"Boys, clean living pays off again. We scored another ride and even better, we have a place to ditch this pig."

"Speaking of clean, I could use a shower," Rollie said.

"I know. We'll go to my spot. I've been on the lam longer. Nobody goes home until this is over," Ryan said.

* * *

Conshohocken, Pennsylvania

"We're almost there." Ryan turned down a street and drove past a Public Works Building. Just beyond I saw a small used-car dealership. It was close to midnight and the place was closed, but Ryan hopped out of the van and I saw the rolling chain link fence gate was unlocked.

I got in the driver's seat and Ryan motioned where to go. The steering sucked at this point, and I imagined Ryan's arms must have been sore from the drive.

A garage door opened, and my instincts set my body on alert. It looked black inside until the headlights revealed a few old wrecks and an empty spot by a corrugated steel wall. I pulled in and parked it, now feeling exhaustion wash over me.

One guy walk out of a dumpy makeshift office. He wore a cap low on his head and didn't appear eager for introductions. He spoke to Ryan, who'd walked in behind us, in low tones I couldn't make out. He then placed a set of keys in Ryan's hands and slipped out a side door.

"No coffee?" Rollie whispered to me. "Mannerless prick."

"The maroon Blazer outside. Get all your stuff, and wipe it down, we're not coming back," Ryan said.

It didn't take long to move our things and the statue to our new ride. This thing had seen better days, but we all hoped it wasn't on any hot sheets. The cookie smell of the van was replaced by old Taco Bell.

But it started.

We drove to a run-down motel in Norristown where Ryan had a room. Judging by how lived in it looked I suspected he had a number of bolt holes around the area. The important thing was that we weren't in the heart of Fishtown. It was going on two in the morning and we were exhausted, yet none of us could sleep right away.

Ryan had called Bishop and given him the address. We'd decided that it made sense to stick together since Bishop couldn't go home either. Ratigan was keeping the sale location to himself and would call Bishop. Left unsaid was that we all wanted to keep an eye on each other. Ratigan had to fly solo in case the Colombians were watching him. Besides, he needed our statue and wasn't about to go near Sheehan on his own.

While waiting for Bishop I tried Fenster who wasn't picking up the phone. I hoped he'd at least gotten clear of his house with Sheehan on the rampage. I didn't say much on the voicemail other than to implore him to call and assure him we had a safe place for him.

* * *

Norristown

QUICK FIX

Rollie's snoring woke me up. My mouth tasted sour and my back ached from the stuffed chair I'd collapsed into last night.

I'd brought the statue over by the chair and when I couldn't keep my eyes open any longer had draped one leg over the thing. Ryan and Bishop seemed like they were trying to help now, but I'd be damned if I'd take any chances that the statue would sprout legs and walk off during the night.

I could hear someone in the bathroom and figured it had to be Bishop as Ryan was passed out on one of the beds.

I glanced at the clock and couldn't believe it was already seven thirty. Shit. Where the hell was my phone? Under the chair, it must have fallen out of my hand while I slept. I grabbed it and saw a text message had come in from Fenster.

Not home. Somewhere safe. Assembling the cavalry. Stay out of it.

My swearing woke up the rest of the group and I shared the message. "What do you think he means?"

Bishop came out of the bathroom scratching his pale belly. "It means he's bringing in the Feds."

"He said *assembling*. Maybe there's still time." I tried to call him back. No answer, so I replied to his text. *Richard. Wait one day. We have a deal to get her back.*

I tried calling again. Nothing.

The room felt stuffy.

Rollie was putting on clean clothes. My clothes were getting ripe after the last day. "Did you borrow those from Ryan?"

205

Rollie looked insulted. "Course not. I brought a bag. Marines taught me how to travel light." He had more than weapons in his duffel, it seemed.

"Here you go." Ryan tossed me a t-shirt and pair of shorts. I thought it would tear across the shoulders, but at least it was clean. The shorts made me look like I was about to go to a track meet.

"Looking good." Ryan laughed.

I checked the phone. Still no reply.

"We can't just sit here." Rollie gathered up all the clothes leaving Bishop in his boxers and t-shirt. "Let's wash these and Kyle and I will bring back some food."

I picked up the bundled statue.

"Where the hell do you think you're going with that?" Bishop asked.

"Don't you trust us?" Ryan smiled.

"No." I didn't smile back.

"That's no hood ornament. We've all got a lot riding on it," Bishop said. "Look at me. Do I look dressed to go hitchhiking with that lawn jockey under my arm?"

"Let him take it." Ryan sounded tired. "I want breakfast and I know he won't do anything dumb this late in the game."

* * *

I drove and checked the phone obsessively. Finally Rollie yanked it out of my hand. "Yer gonna kill us staring at that damn thing."

206

"Tell me if he responds."

Rollie spoke in a calm voice. "Don't put too much into the silence. Maybe the guy passed out like we did. He doesn't come across as the rugged type."

"He's not. But Beth said he's a pit bull in court. He might light up the Feds before we're ready."

"When is the last time you saw anything government-related move that fast? I figure they'll think he's crazy first."

"I don't know about that." But he had a point. It was hard to picture the FBI raiding Philly Irish mob establishments on the basis of one tip.

* * *

Just after noon we were back in our regular clothes and my fidgetiness had spread to everyone, including Rollie. The statue sat in the middle of the room where I could watch it.

We all jumped when Bishop's phone rang. He answered and began to scribble on a pad. "Okay, I know where that is. See you in twenty." Bishop tore the sheet off the pad. "Saddle up kiddies."

"About fucking time," I said. "Where?"

"A little place Ratigan rented. Near Valley Forge Park."

"You knew the place?" I asked.

"Not the house, but it is across the street from a local restaurant that's famous for its scrapple," Bishop said.

Ryan looked disgusted. "Never got a taste for it."

I could eat about anything if I was hungry. "And they have a parking lot with a good vantage point?"

"Bingo," Bishop said. "Grab the stone doggie and our gear."

Ryan drove and Bishop navigated. "So what's the play?" I asked from the back seat.

"Once we give Ratigan the last statue, he'll call in the Colombian buyers. They show up, verify the statues, and exchange the money. We watch the front and back of the place to make sure it goes down as advertised," Bishop said.

"What did he say about the buyers?" Rollie asked.

Bishop scowled and poked Ryan in the shoulder. "Ask him. I was in the dark when this little party got planned."

"It wasn't supposed to matter."

"Things changed," Bishop said.

"Ya think?" Ryan snapped. "Ratigan's fakes screwed me too. This part of the deal was really his thing. He's the expert who knows all the players in the underground art market."

"So what did he tell you?" Rollie asked.

"He said the buyer is a wealthy businessman who wasn't afraid to cut some corners to get what he wanted."

"Almost a little old lady from Bogota who just loves her some art?" Rollie quipped.

"He said the guy had been with the Colombian government at one time but was a developer now. Ratigan was kind of vague."

"That they had lots of cash to throw around was all you had to hear, right?" I kept seeing Beth's face.

Ryan took his lumps. "Something like that."

"So what happens after they get their artsy-fartsy puppies and scram?" Rollie asked.

"Ratigan is supposed to wait for us and we split up the cash," Bishop said. "He goes one way, I go another and you fine people rescue the fair maiden and secure peace in the land."

"And you trust him?"

"Fuck no." Bishop laughed. "We're adding a wrinkle."

I didn't like the sound of that, but I also thought the plan, as stated, was a recipe for disaster.

"I don't think Ratigan should be alone in that house. There's too much temptation for the buyers or Ratigan to get a cute idea about taking off with the dough," Bishop said.

"And you want to tag along?" I asked. I had visions of the two of them bolting with the cash.

Bishop shook his head. "Not me. If the Colombians even suspect a cop, the deal is toast." He pointed to me. "You'll go."

Chapter 24

Valley Forge

I recognized the red Explorer that Ratigan had been driving as we pulled into the driveway of a tiny gray shingled house that was little more than the size of a double-wide trailer. It sat just off the main two-lane road that cut through Valley Forge Park. The restaurant parking lot was directly across the street.

We'd dropped off Rollie who found a clump of trees to hide in while covering the back of the place. I could tell he must have missed sneaking through the woods as a former sniper. I'd seen a rifle case among his gear, but for now he just carried his pistol and compact set of binoculars.

At the front of the house I saw the venetian blinds in one window bend down and the dark outline of a face peered out. Ryan stayed with the car while Bishop took the lead. He knocked and the door opened right away.

Ratigan's skinny body stood in the doorway and I began to appreciate Bishop's thinking. The guy looked like a strong wind might break him in half. Any shady buyer would be tempted to rip him off.

"The interior decorator sent us." Bishop smiled.

"Where's the old guy?" Ratigan said.

I stepped forward with the statue in my arms, still wrapped in the blanket. "He's around."

It looked like Ratigan hadn't slept at all. He looked so tense he'd probably shatter if he tripped on the old threadbare carpet. It was an awful olive green and smelled so mildewed it might have been last vacuumed in the seventies.

I carried the statue inside. I cocked my head to give my good ear the best chance to hear any indication of others in the house.

The small place was dark and depressing. The drawn shades looked like they might crumble if I tried to raise them.

"Love what you've done with the place," I said. I spotted a battered couch in the living room. "Okay if I put this behind here with the others? Unless you want to show me where you keep the walk-in safe?" The top of the wood crate stuck out above the back of the couch

"Hilarious. Try sleeping here. My allergies are killing me."

"I have to ask…."

"Because it's cheap and you didn't guess the place, did you?" Ratigan said.

"Touché." I put the statue down carefully.

"Great. Now hurry up, they'll be here soon."

"Bishop?" It was his idea, so he could break the news.

"Kyle's going to stick around. We figured it couldn't hurt."

"No way." Ratigan shook his head so fast it looked like a blur.

"I'm not going to say anything other than *Good afternoon* or *Buenas tardes* if you prefer." I spoke enough Spanish to be dangerous at a restaurant, but that was about it. It couldn't hurt if Ratigan thought I knew more.

"This is my show." Ratigan looked right at Bishop, as if I wasn't even in the room.

"Not negotiable and we're wasting time. He's window dressing, that's all, but it's good if you show a little muscle," Bishop said.

"Just pretend I'm not here," I said. "You know, like you're doing right now."

"Keep your mouth shut and stay out of the way until I tell you to move," Ratigan said.

The little twerp's tone notwithstanding, I sensed some relief. I handed my cell phone to Bishop. "Hate to lose it if they get jumpy about devices that can record."

Bishop took the phone. "Have fun. We'll be close if you need anything." He slipped out the door. I noticed he never said how we'd signal them if something went wrong.

By the time we needed help it'd be too late anyway.

* * *

"You're sure about these buyers?" I asked. It was too quiet in here and the little whistling sound Ratigan's nose made while he breathed was bugging the crap out of me.

"Am I sure they're coming?"

"No. You think they're legit?"

"I'm here, aren't I?"

"Yeah, in a run-down dump more suitable for moving a suitcase of blow than holding a fine art auction."

"Discretion trumps decor, wouldn't you agree?" He asked.

"I guess. How likely are they to be unstable?"

"The buyer is a grateful for the opportunity. Truly, they were the better client to begin with."

I couldn't let that go. "Then what the fuck were you thinking? Do you have any idea how dangerous it is to piss off a cartel boss?"

He grinned. "I'm a quick study. Aren't we past apologies here?"

I agreed.

"Ryan can be very persuasive when he hatches an idea."

I wasn't going to let him toss that off so easily. "He twisted your arm?"

"As hard as he twisted yours, I'm guessing."

"Fuck you." Which was easier than admitting Ratigan was right. I coughed up some dust and spat in the dry kitchen sink.

"They were outstanding replicas." Ratigan seemed to look right past me, speaking as much to himself as me. "Some of my very finest work, more homage than ersatz."

"Fake is fake and your little error has innocent and not so innocent," I poked my own chest at the latter point, "up the creek."

We both heard an engine and squeak of brakes.

"Salvation arrives," Ratigan said.

* * *

We both looked out the grimy window and I was startled to see a silver Chevy Suburban dwarfing Ratigan's

SUV in the driveway. The windows were tinted almost black and I flashed back to some of the armored behemoths for VIPs we'd see in Iraq.

The doors opened and four men hopped out simultaneously. Like a well-drilled military unit. They were bronze-skinned, fit, and well-dressed in dark suits with generously tailored jackets, no doubt cut to accommodate a lethal assortment of hardware.

"I don't see a suitcase," I noted.

"I'll get the door, just follow my lead," Ratigan snapped.

I stepped back, sorry I hadn't brought a pistol, but then again a gun might invite an overwhelming response.

One of the men knocked on the door hard enough to rattle the hinges.

Ratigan fumbled with the lock and managed to open the door without hitting himself in the nose with it.

"Señor Ratigan?" The man stepped inside uninvited and three others crowded in behind him. They all looked like they could be soldiers with their close-cropped hair and starched posture. I noted bulges under the armpits of their suits. So far, no weapons in plain sight.

"Sí. Yes, that's me. You work for…?"

The lead man cut him off with a look. "Yes, we work for him." He fixed eyes as black as those basalt dogs on me and the men spread out at least as best they could in the narrow front hallway. "You were supposed to be alone."

Ratigan gestured to his back and mimicked a grimace of pain. "I hurt myself lifting the crate. He helped me carry them."

I didn't react to the story either way. They could think what they wanted.

One of the men behind the leader whispered into his ear. The guy continued to look at me now with a trace of a smile on his lips. "Señor Buckley?"

"No. I'm not Ryan Buckley."

The smile vanished and the man ignored me, but one of the other men watched me the entire time. They glanced at my hands and back to my face regularly. I decided to keep them out of my pockets.

One stepped forward and I allowed him to frisk me. A second man did the same to Ratigan. The guy must have felt my wallet but ignored it.

"Anyone else here?" the man asked.

Ratigan answered so fast I figured he must have worried I'd say something stupid like asking if I could frisk them back. "Just us. Have a look around, if you want."

They did. Two of them gave themselves the nickel tour of the dump. When they returned I noticed one brushing dust and cobwebs off his expensive-looking suit. "Nada," one said to his boss.

The leader nodded. "Señor Ratigan, we are in a hurry. Where are they, please?"

"Of course. Uh. Did you bring the payment?"

"We must verify the items. My employer was quite insistent."

"Certainly, but I thought while you did so we could count the funds," Ratigan said. "Or at least see them."

The man stared at Ratigan, who withered under the gaze.

I stepped forward and ignored the tensing bodies of the three henchmen. "The name's Kyle." I stuck out my hand. "And you are?"

He shook it and we did the hand-crusher thing. I could tell he was a tough guy, but he didn't drive and unload trucks for a living.

"Carlos." He settled for a draw and released my hand, and gestured to his three friends. "Smith, Jones, and Baker."

Of course.

"You're the art expert, are you?"

"Show me the statues."

Ratigan had recovered his wits and led the group into the living room. "In there. But don't touch them, you know what they're worth."

I stepped ahead of one of the men who had moved toward the crate behind the old sofa. "I handle them while they are still ours." I looked over at Carlos.

The goon reached inside his jacket and I thought for sure it was party time, but Carlos made a quick hissing sound and muttered in Spanish, "Déjalo!"

I picked up a small pry bar, opened the crate, and gently lifted out one of the black dogs. I placed it on the floor. I'm not sure what sort of reaction I expected. These folks didn't seem like connoisseurs, but the effect was electric.

QUICK FIX

Carlos spoke in rapid Spanish and one of the goons slipped outside.

"Go ahead, display the others." Ratigan tried and failed to sound commanding.

I was just thinking we should have kept one of the statues out of sight, but it was late for that idea, so there wasn't anything to lose by going along with Ratigan.

Ratigan stood by, looking like some sort of proud papa. "See?"

Carlos probably saw what I did in the things. To me, they looked like three jumbo doorstops, but that didn't mean he wasn't interested.

We all turned at the creak of the front door and in walked what I at first thought was a little kid wearing a saddle colored Halloween mask.

It was no costume. The man stood about four and a half feet tall with a wizened, cracked-leather face wearing a colorful South American style knit cap over long, tangled white hair. The guy barely glanced at Ratigan, me or the other Colombians. He stepped into the house, taking no notice of the dilapidated surroundings. His sparkling gaze lit on the three statues.

He removed the cap and approached them. Up close he towered over the two-foot sculptures.

"Señor Gomez will authenticate. If the first artifact is legitimate, we will bring the payment inside where you or your associate may count it. Under close supervision," Carlos said.

"Fine." Ratigan seemed transfixed by Gomez, who I'd already thought of as the Aztec Gnome.

His tanned skin held deep seams in his face and neck. The white hair looked like skeins of wool glued onto a catcher's mitt.

Gomez knelt before the closest statue, the one looking down at the ground that we called Underdog. First, he stretched his hands out like he was about to pray. Then he traced twiggy fingers up and down the outer surface of the stone. He continued like this, in silence, with his eyes closed until he'd gone over the entire figure.

Next, he placed his cap on the floor and put the statue carefully on its side.

The underside of the base of the statue appeared rougher. It was still the same solid black basalt but no high gloss polish.

Gomez pulled a small piece of coarse rock that reminded me of a pumice stone. It must have been a lot harder than that because he applied it to the interior of the base and rubbed gently. The rock was smudged dark from the rubbing and Gomez held it under his nose and inhaled deeply through his nostrils. He sneezed once and nodded, like he'd just sampled high-grade drugs. Then he crouched onto his knees and brought his face close to the base of the statue.

And licked it.

Gomez settled into a cross-legged seated position and smacked his lips as if he were savoring a new dessert. I wanted to laugh at the spectacle, but the way the Columbians had unbuttoned their jackets made me refocus on not getting shot.

Now Gomez stood the statue back upright and resumed his cross-legged position directly in front of the piece. He reached out, and I thought he was going to do his art expert Braille move again, but I was wrong. He closed his eyes and turned his head to press one ear against the stone. Then he drummed his fingers on the basalt up and down the figure.

It sounded like muffled rain on a sidewalk to me, but whatever song it made was music to Gomez' ears. His face split into a sparsely-toothed grin and he let out a whoop.

Gomez's message required no translation. Dog number one had made the grade. Carlos pointed to the other statues and Gomez prepared for an encore performance.

One of the guys, not sure if it was Smith or Jones (they probably didn't know either), stepped outside. He returned carrying a yellow bag that sagged at the bottom, while Gomez was still playing *I can name that statue in just five senses.*

"Kyle, go with Mr. Jones to the kitchen," Carlos said.

I glanced over at Ratigan and he stood transfixed by the Gomez show.

Speaking of counting, I hoped this cash wasn't in small bills or I'd never keep track all the way up to a million. The bag looked heavy enough.

Jones let me carry it into the kitchen. The table was coated with a thick layer of dust disturbed in a few places where Ratigan must have put things recently

I plopped the bag onto the table and waited for the okay from Señor Jones. He leaned against the kitchen sink behind me and part of his back was exposed to the grimy window. I tried to remember if Rollie was facing this side of the house.

Rollie had proven himself time and again on this bizarre adventure. He was no kid, but I liked to imagine

Rollie had a bead on the guy's back. More likely he just saw a bulky shadow.

Jones opened his jacket and dropped any pretense of subtlety. Resting inside a modified shoulder rig I saw a Mac-10 subgun. The weapon was chunky, inelegant, and highly lethal–especially within spitting distance of my vital organs.

Jones rested his hand on the butt so the gun could swivel into firing position right from the holster. I got the point. He could drill me before I could act on any cute ideas to jam him up in close quarters. I pantomimed dumping the contents of the bag out and looked for the go ahead.

He nodded, so that's what I did. The money poured out in bundles all over the table. A lot was just like the payment we got from the deal with Sheehan, banded stacks of hundreds with some fifties and twenties mixed in.

It was crap-load of cash, like last time and I began to set aside the big bills so I could get a ballpark. I separated out the ten-thousand dollar Ben Franklin stacks from the five grand Ulysses S. Grant bundles.

It added up fast, and I was hundreds of thousands of dollars into the count when I heard more whooping from the other room. Whatever was going to happen would be soon so I sped up, trying hard to ignore the bullet hose aimed at my spine.

At the halfway mark I could see the piles were roughly equal. Not exactly accounting board standard practice, but I'd decided we were close enough and now continued giving the wads of money a cursory effort while straining to hear clues from the other room.

Jones didn't waver and I really didn't know what cleverness I could muster that didn't end with me cut in half. Judging by the first two acts from the Gomez travelling appraisal show, we were holding up our end. The statues were the real deal.

But the Colombians were international bankers like I was a ballerina. Ratigan and Ryan sure could pick their customers.

I sped up the pace and if it wasn't a cool million it was damn close. I rushed the final wads of cash from the uncounted side of the table to the other. I looked over at Jones and nodded. "Estabien."

Jones didn't seem to care what I thought, and with one hand still on the weapon pointed to the pile with the other. "Put back."

"Sure, you bet." Like I was going to try to palm a couple twenties for my trouble. I held the bag wide open like a patient's mouth in the dental chair and began to shovel the bundles back into the canvas. Jones didn't take his eyes off me for an instant, not even when the caterwauling from Gomez told me that we'd gone three for three.

Apparently Carlos hadn't expected such a colorful outburst from his expert witness as I heard him hissing at the guy in Spanish to shut up. I walked back to the living room. Ratigan had a smug self-satisfied expression and looked over to me. "All there?"

"Yup." I set the bag on the floor and glanced up when the door opened and the two guys, Smith and Baker, I guess, came in with aluminum cases on rollers like carry-on luggage.

Gomez was off to the side beaming at the statues like he'd been reunited with old friends. He seemed almost oblivious to the rest of us.

The two men rolled the cases up to the statues and began unsnapping latches. They opened the cases and I saw they were foam lined and pre-cut to accommodate the statues.

They reached for the first statue and Gomez snapped out of his trancelike bliss. "Cuidadó!" He said in a croaking voice, admonishing the goons to be careful with his charges.

The men nestled the artwork into the foam liners and secured the cases. Two of them fit in a single case with the last dog going in the second case.

"Gentlemen, I'm glad you could meet with us today and that you are satisfied," Ratigan said.

Carlos held up a finger to put off Ratigan and whispered in Spanish to the men with the cases. They rolled the statues out the door and Gomez put his cap back on and followed without so much as a nod in our direction.

I was glad the bag of cash remained. I was less happy about Jones still standing behind me.

Carlos smiled at Ratigan. "Señor, won't you do us the courtesy of seeing us to the airport?"

Oh crap.

"Huh?" If Ratigan was acting, it was Oscar-quality stuff.

"Bring your payment with you of course." Carlos pointed at the yellow bag.

"I can't."

"I insist."

One of the other goons came back inside and stared at Ratigan. The guy had his hand inside his jacket.

"Can I give Kyle my keys? He can pick me up later. At the airport." Ratigan held up the key fob.

Carlos held out his hand and took the keys. "Go with Señor Baker. Now."

Ratigan walked forward like a zombie and picked up the cash. He met my gaze and I saw pure terror in his eyes as he left the house.

"How about we talk about a discount and you can get yourself something nice for the trip home, huh? You don't need him stinking up your nice ride." I said.

"We wish to have an uninterrupted journey. I'm sure you understand, Mr. Buckley."

All at once I sensed it was very important Carlos believe I wasn't Ryan. "I told you, I'm not Ryan Buckley."

"You have proof?" Carlos looked amused.

"How about a driver's license?" A dumb thing to have on a mission, but I figured if I was driving and we got pulled over I'd arouse less suspicion. Never thought I'd need it like this.

"Slowly." I heard from Jones behind me. I didn't bother to look to see if he had his weapon on me. I did as instructed and took out my wallet with two fingers.

When they saw it really was a billfold I slid out my real driver's license and handed it to Carlos. He studied it carefully.

"Adiós?" I heard from behind me.

I glanced to the side and wondered if I could make it to the old double hung window and dive through it. Not a chance. More likely I'd cut myself on the glass and break something right before getting shot to pieces.

Carlos looked up and flicked the card into my chest. "Sueño."

I ran the word through my limited list of Spanish vocabulary. I came up with *dream* right before a hard blow to the back of my head turned out the lights.

Chapter 25

Valley Forge

Dream. I clung to the thought and it became a nightmare where I was being buried alive. I could taste dirt and blood. Now I heard the sound of shovels biting into the dirt. It must have been hard dirt as the sound grew louder and changed. It sounded more like splintering wood. The dirt morphed into dust and mildew.

"Kyle!" I heard a voice that sounded like it came from the end of a tunnel. I spit some of the dust out of my mouth and managed to roll over. The back of my head throbbed and the pain seemed to soak through my scalp deep into my skull.

I opened my eyes and the light speared through my head. I could picture it passing straight to the other side.

I touched my head and felt a knot, but my fingers came back dry.

More splintering and footsteps.

Where?

Oh yeah. Valley Forge. That crappy house.

"Kyle?" Closer and louder. Now a figure stood in the opening to the living room.

The figure drew close and my vision began to clear. The headache had decided to stick around and I felt woozy but back on the planet. "Rollie?"

"You okay, kid?"

"Am I bleeding out anywhere?" I was half-joking. As the details began to filter back into my brain I wasn't sure why they left me alive.

Rollie checked me over. I noticed dirt on his clothes and his pistol jammed into his waistband.

"Aside from the bump on the back of your noggin, you're in one piece."

"Where did they go?" I asked. "They took Ratigan. And the money."

Rollie nodded. "I think they took everything except you but as to where, I don't know. Can you stand?"

"I know a way to find out." Jumping right up turned out to be a painful way, but I did begin to feel steadier on my feet. "Got a half-bottle of aspirin?"

"Yeah, but that goes to our next problem. It's in my bag in the SUV, which took off after those *businessmen*"

"What did you see?"

"Not that much. I was covering the back, remember? I heard all the car doors close and saw their Suburban roll out. A few seconds later I spotted our SUV leaving in the same direction."

"They left together?" My thinking still felt hazy.

Rollie shook his head. "Not like that. I think they saw Ratigan go with them and decided they better follow."

"The buyers forced Ratigan. So where are they now?"

"Good question. Nobody reached me and when it was quiet here I decided to check it out. I looked through a gap in the window shades and saw you plopped on the floor like the catch of the day."

"Now what? We just wait?"

QUICK FIX

"I don't suppose you have the keys to that thing outside?"

I remembered Carlos holding them. I checked my pockets just in case. "No, and I slept through hot-wiring in crook class. Damn."

"I didn't, but that doesn't work on newer models. Feel like hitchhiking?" Rollie looked around the house.

"Not sure I feel like explaining anything." I was still woozy. "The Colombians were a lot more hardcore than Ratigan and Ryan let on. Those guys were pros. Damn."

"You stay here and I'll get something for your head." Rollie handed me his gun and smoothed his hair.

"I was down to my last million, but I might still have a couple bucks." They'd left my wallet. I missed my phone, and then I remembered. "Damn, gave my cell to Bishop. I figured the goons would toss it in the reservoir. Do you have one?"

"Not good to have your phone go off when you're in hiding." Rollie pointed at the couch. "Tell the mice to make some room and rest for a minute. I'll be right back." Rollie walked out the front door.

I closed my eyes and the pain subsided a little. The next thing I knew I'd drifted off.

* * *

"Kid, wake up." Rollie sounded worried. I reached for the pistol and noticed he already had it. He was crouched by the window.

I had no memory of him coming back into the place and now I noticed the light outside was growing softer. How long had I been out?

"Car coming."

"Who?"

"It's Ryan's. Can't see who is in there yet," Rollie said. "It's Ryan and Bishop."

"No Ratigan?"

Rollie shook his head. "Bishop's hurt."

* * *

"Slow down. What happened?" I was feeling steadier on my legs but my brain wanted coffee or something stronger to pull the rest of the cobwebs off. Ryan had come in with Bishop leaning on his shoulder and now the cop had taken my place on the dusty old couch. He was sweating and grimacing but seemed lucid enough.

"You first," Ryan said.

I gave them my side of events right up to when Jones knocked me cold.

Ryan was pacing. Rollie elevated Bishop's leg which was bruised and swollen. He made him take a handful of the aspirins he'd brought back for me. Mine was just kicking in, the pounding in my skull down to tolerable levels.

"You sure they forced Ratigan?" Rayan asked again.

"You guys know him better, but why would he put on such a convincing performance for me? I still don't know why they didn't just kill me."

"They were supposed to be more civilized." Ryan almost spoke to himself.

"A classier bunch of crooks," Rollie said.

"Whatever." Ryan waved off the remark.

"So what did happen?" I asked.

"We saw Ratigan, carrying the bag of cash, get into the Suburban with the rest of them. When you didn't come out and they drove off we had to make a snap decision." Ryan sounded defensive.

"I wouldn't have been any good to you. Go on."

"So we headed east. I tried to hang back, but traffic was light and it would have looked strange if I crawled slowly enough for them to take a big lead."

Bishop spoke up. "The tint on the windows made it impossible to see inside."

Ryan continued. "They guessed something because about ten miles from here we were close to the I-76 on-ramp. Just before we crossed an intersection out of nowhere we got T-boned by an old station wagon. It was one of those tanks from the late seventies."

"Did you see the driver?" I asked.

"See him? We couldn't get him or that bitch to shut up," Bishop said.

"We got knocked across the road, damn near rolled over. Bishop was hurt."

Bishop interrupted, "My fucking leg."

I didn't see anything sticking out, but that only meant it wasn't a compound fracture. "Is it broken?"

"Probably just fractured. Speed work will be out for a while."

"We need to get you to a hospital," Rollie said.

"Bullshit. Can't take the chance, Sheehan's got eyes there. We're going to need to stick together to get through this. We've got problems."

That was already an understatement. "Tell me the rest," I said.

Ryan answered. "I got out first and the driver, a thirty-something Hispanic dude pops out of the car. I swear that thing would be a ringer in a demolition derby contest. The guy starts going off in machinegun Spanish, then a lady got out the other side and she was louder and faster than the man."

"She was right in my ear with that shit. Almost hurt worse than my leg. And all I could see was that goddamned Suburban vanishing down the road."

Ryan nodded. "Once I realized that they weren't hurt I turned to check on Bishop. He just started screaming for me to get back on the tail."

"Then the lady rolled through every Spanish curse I know and a bunch I don't," Bishop said.

Ryan jumped in. "While she's doing that, the guy stepped to the back tire and I heard a pop, whoosh sound. Then the guy and the lady jump into the wagon and lay rubber getting out of there. By now, a few cars have slowed with people offering to call the cops and an ambulance."

"I told everyone we called already and were fine," Bishop said.

"The last thing we needed was the police, especially with him on the job."

"That'd definitely get their attention. And Sheehan's," Bishop agreed.

"But the guy had spiked one of our tires. My own trick, do you love it? We drove on the rim of the flat just to get away from the approaching cops. By the time we were able to get the spare on the Colombians were long gone."

"We would have called you, but…," I said. Bishop returned my phone.

Ryan let out a long breath. "We're fucked. Those guys could be anywhere and that was our money for Sheehan."

"What about Ratigan?" Rollie asked.

Ryan looked at him like he was crazy. "He picked these guys. He told me they were businessmen."

"Looks like they decided to renegotiate," Rollie said.

"How do we know this wasn't Ratigan's idea all along? He's got the money all to himself and can afford to vanish, the Colombians have their prize and what does he care what happens to us?" Bishop asked.

"Pretty cold but possible," I said. "He looked scared for real but, either way, he and the money are with the Colombians. If they kidnapped him for a rip-off do you think they'll let him go? They could have killed me."

Ryan looked lost. "I don't know. Right now I'm just sure we lost our leverage."

"I don't think so," I said. I pointed at Ryan. "You got this mess started and you're going to do your part to fix it."

Chapter 26

Valley Forge

Everyone looked at me. "Take a look around here, Ryan. We're all beat to shit and you haven't got a mark on you."

"So?" Ryan said. "What's your point? I knew when to duck? We've all suffered."

"Sheehan wants his million back. Scrape your share together and let's finish it."

"Kyle, did the Colombians knock the math out of your head?"

"How much do you have left?" I asked.

"Half. At most and I'd have to dig into my savings." He waggled the keys to the battered SUV. "These beaters don't grow on trees."

That was right. Now I remembered Ryan telling me he'd split with Ratigan before the crap hit the fan. "You can have what's left of what you gave me… fuck, that's nothing." Dread rolled over me and my head throbbed. Forty grand wouldn't make a dent in what we needed.

"I don't have it, before you ask," Bishop said, "and nothing personal, but I'm not going to pawn the Rolex collection to hand over to a gangster. Be lucky to live through this myself."

I thought that was going to piss me off, but it merely fueled the waves of futility. We were what? Including the little sweetener we'd promised Sheehan, we were eight hundred grand short and needed it tomorrow.

We could rob banks from now until then and still come up shy. Forty-eight hours ago we tossed around numbers like that as if they were nothing. Hell, I'd had more than that in my hands a few hours ago.

"Kid, I only have enough to keep me in dog food and gas for the Blue Bomber until I kick the bucket, but you're welcome to it."

I smiled at him and felt a surge of gratitude and unchecked emotion that I decided to blame on the bump on the head. I shook it off. Not the time. "Don't deserve it. But thanks."

Ryan had stopped all his fidgeting. He was in full scheme mode. "Kyle, you need wealthier friends." He stared at me. "Or even temporary allies."

"Are you talking about Fenster?" But he was onto something. "Yeah. Well, he's sure no friend, but for Beth he might if he thought it would work." I mulled the idea over. "Only *money under the mattress* is just an expression. He lives in the real world, remember? It could take weeks to turn into physical cash."

"We don't know that. Maybe he's planning on paying a ransom himself," Kyle said. "Don't you think he loves her?"

"Not more than I do." Why the hell did that slip out? "That's not what I meant."

Rollie couldn't stand it. "You're talking about that little shit lawyer? Fenster? He's loaded, huh?"

"We don't even know where he is," Bishop said.

"We have to try. He's going to want to go with his plan to send in the Feds," I said. "We can't wait. If he's gone dark, this thing is over." Now the desperation squeezed my chest like a vise. "Unless."

"Yeah?" Ryan said.

I verbalized the thoughts as they entered my brain. "Sheehan doesn't know this phase was a disaster. We call him, tell him it's all good. And arrange the meet."

"And when it happens?"

I nodded. "Right. I carry the case. We stuff it with paper. And a bomb. Sprinkle some real cash on top and rig me with a detonator. When he turns over Beth you guys get her clear and I'll say something about staying to count it and I'll grab hold of Sheehan. I'll hold up the detonator and buy you time. Then when you guys are safe, I hit it and Sheehan isn't a problem anymore."

They all stared at me. "What?"

"Good," said Rollie.

"Good?" Ryan and Bishop said in unison.

"Yeah. Now that we've had the worst possible idea on the fucking planet we can hear all the better ones."

* * *

"If someone else besides Rollie wants to volunteer, I'm all ears," I said. "We created this mess. Beth has already paid a higher price than any of us and I don't think she or any of us will get out alive. I want to give her a chance and you guys, too."

Rollie actually looked offended that I didn't want to include him on suicide bomber duty. "I'm on Sheehan's shit list same as the rest. I know how his pea brain works."

"All right." I'd calmed down, but only a little. I didn't really have a death wish, and wanted mostly to force us all to come up with a plan.

Bishop sat up, and the aspirin must have started working because he was able to put his leg down without screaming. It was still swollen, but we weren't going to have to cut his pants off.

Ryan spoke. "Let's look again at our options. Sheehan's worst case scenario is a raid by the FBI because of their heat, but even more so because the O'Briens have a rule about kidnapping civilians. If he didn't desperately need the big payoff to get out from under the shitstorm with the O'Briens already, I think Beth would have vanished."

I hated to hear the words, but we were way past bullshit hour. He spoke the truth. "It'll be dark soon. Let me try to reach Fenster. Sheehan will be waiting to hear from us."

I called and got Fenster's voicemail again. "I'll try text."

RICHARD, ANSWER THE PHONE!!!!

And I got a reply right away.

How do I know who this is?

You'll know my voice if you answer.

Could be a trap.

"Well, you got him on board the paranoid train. Think he'll listen to reason?" Rollie asked.

I shrugged and tried not to type gibberish with my fat thumbs on the tiny keypad.

QUICK FIX

You know who isn't that high-tech. We need your help.
Answer and if you don't recognize my voice hang up and relocate.

OK

I didn't have to dial, the phone rang right away.
"Richard?"

"This better be you." Fenster sounded small and
terrified, like he was hiding under a bed somewhere. Maybe
he was.

"It's me. We don't like each other. You have a
restraining order against me. You throw like a girl and can't
take a punch. Shall I go on?"

"Thank God, it's you." I would have insulted him
more often if I'd realized how happy it made him.

"Where are you?"

"No way. He's after me. One of his men was waiting
for me at the office."

Made sense. "You know why, don't you?"

"It wasn't for a donation to the St. Patrick's day
parade!" He sounded borderline hysterical.

"Stay with me here. Are you safe for the moment?
You don't have to say where."

"I think so."

"Okay, good. Please listen. I messaged you earlier we
have a plan to get Beth back."

"How do you even know she's still alive?"

This wasn't the time for the harsh details. "I heard from her. I will again when I call Sheehan."

"Tell him I'm bringing the whole goddamned FBI down on his head!"

My heart jackhammered, but I forced myself to sound calm. "I think bringing the Feds in is a great idea."

Everyone looked shocked at that. I held up a finger. "But our timing here is critical."

"She's waited long enough!"

"Think about it. You're a lawyer. What kind of case have you got? Sheehan won't have her in his house. What do you think will happen if they call him in for an interview?"

"Interview?"

"Take a breath here, Richard. Have you ever heard of the FBI launching a raid with Hostage Rescue and all the bells and whistles based on a tip with, let's face it, thin or no hard evidence?"

He paused and for a moment and I thought he'd hung up.

"They might this time." But he didn't really believe it.

"Last thing. Where would they raid? Without some assurance where Beth is being held what's the point?"

"What's your plan, then?"

"He wants over a million dollars to set her free."

"What?"

"That's what he is saying. What he really wants is a way to get out of trouble with his own people."

"He wants it soon?"

"As soon as possible," I said. "Holding Beth is a big risk for him, but he'll jump at the chance to get out from under his problem."

"So you want me to get the money and the Feds will arrest him?" Fenster asked. "That could take a while. I can't get near my house or office."

In the house everyone huddled by the phone and I turned up the volume so they could hear Fenster without putting it on speaker, which might scare him off. "Don't worry about the money. We have it covered, and we'll free Beth and bring proof of Sheehan's involvement."

"Where is this supposed to happen?"

"Can't tell you." Which was true, as I didn't know yet. "But you have to promise not to try to get the Feds involved early. We don't have time to convince them and if they go in half-assed Beth is dead and we leave big targets on our backs."

"What if I say no?"

"I'll hang up, destroy this phone and move without you. Then you won't have to worry about Sheehan anymore. I'll kill you myself."

An even longer pause. "I still think you're full of shit and I blame you for everything that has happened. How do I know you won't fuck this up?"

"You don't. I'm her best chance and I also have help this time." I let that sink in a moment. "Richard, losing Beth this way would kill me, and when it is over she still goes home to you."

"You have one day. After that I'm going to handle this myself."

He hung up.

"Not enough cash, a hard deadline, and certain death for friends and family if I screw it up. Did I miss anything?" I asked.

"Yeah," Rollie said. "You meant to say if *we* screw it up."

The conversation with Fenster had done more than just crystallize the desperate situation. It had swept aside the remaining cobwebs from my knock on the head. "You guys are with me here?" I looked hard at Ryan and Bishop. It seemed I'd have to shoot Rollie to get him to back off.

Bishop forced himself to his feet. He grimaced in pain and took a few tentative steps. "Son of a bitch, that hurts, but I think better on my feet," he said.

"And what do you think?" Ryan said.

"Several things." Bishop continued to limp around the room. "Maybe this leg isn't broken after all, not that I'm going to turn into an action hero, but I'm in." He made a sweeping gesture. "Big picture is Beth or no Beth, Sheehan will hunt us down like dogs."

"I agree," Ryan said.

Rollie nodded and I saw no reason to feel otherwise.

Bishop continued. "Even if Ratigan were to show up, apologize and give us all his money that wouldn't satisfy Sheehan."

"No. It wouldn't," Rollie said. I saw by the look in his eyes that I wasn't the only one getting ideas. He took off his glasses and cleaned them with his shirt. "Old age is a bitch and that goes double for eyesight. Back in the day, I could drop a man at a thousand yards. Be lucky to hit a billboard at that range today. But get me inside a couple hundred and I could make it work."

"What are you saying?" I wanted to be sure.

"I wouldn't make this offer if it wasn't a Sheehan, but I got one or two more good ones in me. I keep my piece squared away. I'll take him out for you. You might want to duck after a couple rounds."

Ryan and Bishop smiled. I didn't.

"Even if we got the chance and Beth were safe, what do you think would happen next?"

Rollie paused, knowing the answer.

Bishop said it aloud. "A hydra. You cut off that head, deserving as it is, and two more replace it."

"And not just two," Rollie said.

Bishop nodded. "We'd be declaring war on the whole Philly Irish Mob. Right now we have the O'Briens on the sidelines, but they couldn't sit by and let an outsider knock off one of their own family."

"True. We'd add the remainders of Sheehan's crew to the rest of the O'Briens plus whatever bounty on our heads," Ryan said.

"What if he's already told the O'Briens what he did and asked for their help? Why not wipe us out and close the books on the whole mess?" I hated to think that way, but we'd only get one chance at this.

Bishop spoke. "The O'Briens don't have that rule out of the goodness of their hearts."

"It's bad business," Ryan said.

"Right. Targeting civilians isn't like hitting another wise guy where the beef stays in the family. It can get messy fast and I happen to know the Feds would love to have a legitimate excuse to turn them inside out," Bishop said. "They'd rather eat the loss and move on."

"I know Sheehan. That little punk is too proud to admit to the O'Briens that he's over his head. Plus, I think he's scared of them," Rollie said. "That's good, for Beth anyway, and he wants to show them that he can handle his business."

"But he's going to be doubly pissed when he tries to spend that cash," I said.

"If it were just me I might take that trade. Maybe go out in style hunting down the lot of them until they caught up with me," Rollie said.

"There's got to be another way."

Ryan spoke. "We're stuck no matter what. We don't have the money. Even if we fool Sheehan he's going to kill us on the spot the moment he looks at the cash. And like Bishop said, even if all the money was there I think he'd still come after us."

"Well if it's all the same to you guys, I'd just as soon deal with the consequences after Beth is freed," I said.

"You get her back and I'm okay going down swinging. I'll try to make them think I went rogue." Rollie said. "Been boring without Mary around anyhow. Might be nice to tell her some new stories when I get up there."

"Are you done?" I shook my head. "Don't be such a drama queen. But thanks."

The others laughed and it broke the tension. For a second.

"First things first. Let's get Sheehan on the line and set a meet. We can't plan squat until we know when and where," Ryan said.

Chapter 27

Valley Forge

We sat around the kitchen table in what we now called Ratigan's Nest. Ryan, Bishop, and Rollie huddled around the phone the same way as before. So they could hear the conversation without Sheehan knowing.

"I'm still not sure you should be doing this," Bishop said. "I've had some hostage negotiating training."

"When, back at the academy? Last century?" I snapped, then shook my head to tell him I didn't mean it. "I hear you, but I don't think he'll deal with anyone else and this won't be subtle. I'll hold my temper. I have to."

I made the call before I lost my nerve. They put me on hold and I made a conscious effort not to crush the phone if he came back on bragging about what he'd just done.

Finally. "You got any news for me, boyo?"

"I told you we'd call back. We have what we promised and are ready to deal."

"All of it?"

"One point three, all there in cash."

"Good man. I look forward to seeing for myself."

"How do you want to do this?"

"Let's see, Tuesday is bridge night and the boys are here for poker on Wednesday so how's next Thursday look for you?"

It was Monday night.

"No more fucking around. We have a brief window and it isn't our choice."

That got his attention. "What's that mean?"

"Our friend reached out to me, but I don't know where he is. He's going to the Feds and I convinced him to hold off for a day or two. We need to close the books and we all come out okay."

"You know if—"

"Yes, I got that. Loud and clear. Are you not still interested in the dough?" I fought to hold it together. "How about you skip bridge night and we end this chapter?"

All while I was speaking Bishop was staring at me and doing little nods of encouragement. I tried not to let him distract me.

"Okay. It's short notice, but we can make it work. You remember the warehouse when you and Ryan stuck me with those bobo chunks of rock?"

Ryan and Bishop made faces and shook their heads so hard I thought Sheehan would hear them over the phone.

"Warehouse? *Your* warehouse? Try again."

"Why?"

"Let's just say I'd prefer a place where you are less tempted to solve your problem by wiping us out. Something less private."

"What, 30th Street Station? How about right in front of the Liberty Bell?"

"No, I didn't mean that. I was thinking somewhere less claustrophobic."

"Than an empty warehouse?" He laughed.

"Less enclosed."

"Let me see what I can do. Don't go nowhere."

He hung up.

"Round one. I'll call it a draw," Ryan said.

"Now what?" I said to Bishop. Since he was an expert and all.

"We wait. But let's make use of the time. Ryan, we can't roll out in that heap." Bishop meant the battered SUV.

He was right. It ran, but besides being marginal transportation it also was part of another hit and run and might bring the last sort of attention we needed. I explained the lack of keys for Ratigan's Explorer.

Ryan nodded and pulled out his phone. "Never mind that thing. I know some people."

Bishop smiled and took out his own phone. "I know some people too, got some ideas."

Rollie shrugged. "Most of the people I know are dead."

* * *

We huddled up when the phone rang again, almost an hour later at about ten o'clock.

"Last offer and then I'm done playing," Sheehan greeted me.

"Go ahead."

QUICK FIX

"You know Aramingo, just before the Delaware expressway?"

I said I did. It was an intersection right in our neighborhood. Sticking close to home.

He gave me a house address about a block off of it.

"A house isn't exactly what I call wide open spaces," I said.

"Shut up and listen. We know everyone on the block."

When he said *know* he meant control. "And?"

"The house will be empty. Go in one at a time and see for yourself if you want. I'll leave the door open for you. You go upstairs to the roof; there'll be a ladder for you. We'll go to the one at the other end of the block."

I thought I understood. This was one of those row house blocks where the homes were connected without any space between buildings on the roofs.

"In the middle of the roof tops one house is only two stories instead of three so it will be like a moat or something. More ladders. We face each other. You see the lady, we see the green, and if everything's nice and friendly we go down to neutral territory and make the switch."

Clever. Out in the open but hidden from the street.

Bishop frowned, but Ryan nodded. Rollie started to grin. Bishop must not have known where Sheehan was talking about as he didn't grow up in Fishtown.

We knew the area intimately but, of course, so did Sheehan and it was obvious he'd been thinking about this spot a lot longer than an hour.

"All right," I said. "Tomorrow night?"

"No games and I see one cop and it's all over."

* * *

Back at Ryan's hiding spot, after he'd arranged for another vehicle, we planned until about midnight. We argued and tweaked and came up with something that might well get us all killed. But it was better than any other ideas.

The next morning we all huddled around Ryan's laptop screen while we studied the terrain. This was especially useful for Bishop who needed a crash course on the street and building layout. He took notes and made a shopping list of sorts.

I was glad to see that Bishop's leg appeared to be improved and despite the spectacular bruising from the hip to the knee, he was able to put weight on the leg and walk unassisted. We couldn't count on him to run and out of our group only Ryan was able to move quickly.

I mostly manned the phones in case Sheehan called in or someone else had to reach us. Ryan took Bishop and Rollie to Bishop's car, the generic looking one issued by the state. We'd all agreed it was a bad idea to try to go back to our respective homes in case Sheehan staked them out. We couldn't afford to let our guard down.

Bishop, it turned out, had lots of hiding places for gear he'd managed to cherry-pick during his tenure at the police storage facility. Rollie and Bishop worked closely on the equipment they'd be using. I'd insisted on being the point man for the exchange so they kept me in the dark on their plans.

I didn't see much of them all day.

QUICK FIX

Ryan spent the time working his network of shady contacts and scraping together the relatively meager funds we needed. Somehow we had to make it appear to be more than a million dollars in cash.

Speaking of which, we did allow some flexibility to our plan on the outside chance that Ratigan reappeared, with the cash. Nobody was holding their breath. Bishop had feelers out with friends of his with the State Police dispatchers in case there was any news. No luck so far.

* * *

By late afternoon Ryan showed up to his place in a bland silver Honda. "Ready?"

"I plan to do what I'm told. More importantly, are you guys ready?" I asked.

Ryan nodded. "We're in place. Just a couple kinks to work out."

That didn't sound good. "What kinks?"

"Relax. Okay, don't relax. How could you? It's going to be all right." I saw the yellow bags he plopped to the floor. They were heavy with something. "What do you think?"

"I already know they're bullshit," I said.

"Yeah, but take a look."

We were indoors, and daylight was still coming in through the widows. I unzipped the canvas bag and saw wads of bills, complete with bank bands. I flashed back to yesterday when I had the real thing in hand.

"The weight's good." I reached in and pulled out a couple bundles. The first was indistinguishable from the stacks I had handled while counting. "Okay...." The second stack felt different. The paper was too crisp and lacked that cloth quality of actual currency. I looked closer under the light and saw some of the fine writing. "Let's see, 'This note is not legal. It is to be used in motion pictures.'" I looked at Ryan. "That'll be the last thing I hear when Sheehan reads that out loud."

"Come on. Look again." He picked up the second bag and stepped into an unlit room and opened the door. He stood in semi-shadow and held the bag so it yawned open. He plucked out a pair of stacks. "Live." He held up a second one. "Memorex."

In the reduced light at a slight distance, they looked awfully similar.

Ryan tossed them back in the bag and shook it up. "Can you see the difference?"

I know I shouldn't have felt as comforted as I did. "Well not from here, no. But once I get my hands on them."

"Don't be giving away one point three million bucks so easily then. Treat it with the respect it deserves." Ryan turned serious. "Everything depends on this. You need to sell it. Beth has to be over to our side before they catch on."

The weight of it all that I'd somehow held off throughout the day dropped on me like an ACME anvil in an old Road Runner cartoon.

Ryan saw it and put on his best huckster smile. " heehan thinks you're just a lovesick truck driver."

I couldn't help smiling back at the description. "I'm not?"

"Not *just*. That's how we're going to win, partner."

Chapter 28

Fishtown

The sun seemed to hover in the air, mocking my impatience for nightfall so we could get started. Finally, what passed for darkness in the heart of a large city settled onto the area. Since it was a weeknight, most of the sensible and employed folks were wrapping up their days and getting ready for the next one. The streets weren't empty, but neither were they choked with traffic.

By quarter to ten there were just enough cars in the area for me to be suspicious of every one. Ryan drove and I sat in the back seat with the bags of cash. "You sure about the timing?"

"Don't rewrite the play on opening night, Hoss," Ryan said. He sounded cool, but I could see his tension by the way his gaze flicked to the mirrors. "Do your part and focus on Beth."

I could do that.

"This is us. See the cones they put out?" I saw in front of the house they'd blocked off a parking spot. Just like they'd guarded for that Mustang. I looked for that car before I remembered we'd wrecked it.

The houses were just as I'd remembered. Like a bunch of boxes shoulder to shoulder.

I spared a glance upward and thought I saw some movement on a rooftop, but it could have been my imagination on overdrive. The feeling of being watched was like electricity on my scalp. No way was I imagining that.

By reflex, I wanted to scan the street and sidewalk for improvised explosives, but stifled that unhelpful instinct.

"You'll know what to do. It'll be fine. I'll be in contact with Bishop. He's waiting inside, said so far, it's okay."

"Got it."

I sure hoped I did. I felt some better knowing Bishop had cleared the place.

"Keep the meter running," I said to Ryan, and carried the bags out of the car. He was to stay down here as a lookout and to drive Beth, Bishop, and me out of the danger zone following the transfer.

Even though my hands were full with the two bags, I wanted a weapon to protect the money. That idea had been nixed as another provocation that could lead to unpredictable outcomes.

I guess we'd see.

I made the twenty-five feet to the door of the house on the corner. I could see someone on the other end of the block standing, conspicuously casual, and figured he was just one of Sheehan's men dotting the landscape. One advantage we held is that we knew Sheehan would be stretched for manpower. He didn't dare reveal his activities to the larger Irish Mob, not outside his own trusted circle. However, that group still outnumbered us.

With a little luck that wouldn't matter, but I tried not to dwell on our recent supply of good fortune.

The door opened and Bishop nodded a greeting. I didn't say anything either until we were inside.

"We're good in here." The pistol holstered on his hip made me feel a little better.

"You bring one for me?" I smiled. Then I noticed the other dark object on his opposite hip was a radio and a thin clear wire snaked out of his collar into a low-profile earpiece.

"Sorry, you have to do this naked. We have to go by that dope's rules."

"Until we don't."

He nodded and grimaced when he started upstairs. I went to the front door and locked it along with the chain. "We're the only ones coming in until it's time to leave, right?"

"Good idea." Bishop looked mad. "We threw this together fast. I should have thought of that."

"Glad to help," I said. "You going to be able to move okay?" I pointed to his leg

"We'll see," Bishop said. "I had one Tylenol with codeine for lunch, just a bunch of Advil this evening. I can walk and talk. I haven't tried running or jumping so I don't know if those are options. We'll have to test it in combat."

I listened for any signs of a person in any of the upstairs rooms. I could see by the pictures and décor that it looked like a single older woman lived here. The comfy chair downstairs looked like the most frequently used piece of furniture. A glance in the kitchen showed a single teacup and spoon. A faint scent of garlic and clove hung in the air. I wondered where she was and how much warning she'd had before being booted out.

On the second floor I glanced into her bedroom and while the bed was neat and tidy, I saw one pair of slippers and in the bathroom one toothbrush.

Probably not much warning at all.

The third floor appeared to be used for storage. There were worn chairs and cardboard boxes stacked in one room, the boxes labeled with magic marker scrawling like, "Stanley's Uniforms."

I guessed the dark-haired gent in the old wedding photo on the lady's dresser must be him. I wondered what he would have said about all this if he'd been around.

Focus here, Kyle.

As promised, we saw a stepladder perched under a hatch style access to the roof. I went first and wriggled the hatch off like the top of a cardboard gift box. The cover moved easier than I'd expected, but I supposed Sheehan's people made sure it would not stick. What else had they done to prepare for us?

I climbed up and took the two bags, one at a time, from Bishop. I held out a hand and helped pull him up and over onto the flat roof. We kept low, the house before the drop on either side of Sheehan's so-called moat formed a low, wall-like barrier, a couple feet high. Otherwise we were out in the open on the silvery waterproofed tar roof. I felt the surface move slightly when I stepped on it. I imagined in the heat of the summer that material might soften underfoot.

Tonight the moon was out and the darkness was relative. The roof was dimly lit by ambient light. That was good. At least we'd spot them coming. We didn't see anyone at the moment, but my skin crawled so much I might as well have climbed through a roach nest on the way up.

My eyes adjusted to the dim light and now I was able to catch at least two heads silhouetted from rooftops across the street.

I made a more blatant pivot and one shape dipped down out of sight. No doubt they were Sheehan's people. On the one hand that was bad because it confirmed he had the numbers on us. On the other, their field craft was so piss-poor that I felt encouraged. I'd been watched by professional snipers, these guys were no more than street goons playing army.

"Nice spot for a kegger," I said.

"That's about how much I'm going to want later. You buying?"

"If I'm breathing." Neither of us laughed.

Bishop started to talk under his breath and just when I was going to turn my good ear toward him and ask him to repeat himself I realized he was whispering into a mic on his collar.

"We good?" I said.

"So far." We both heard a thump from the other end of the block. I couldn't see anything.

"Do we crouch?" I asked.

"They had some guys who could have started the party from across the street," he said.

"I saw them. So we wait?"

"Won't be long now."

The first thing I heard was Sheehan's unmistakable voice muffled by the distance. "Whatever you do, don't try to run. That first step is a doozy."

Now I heard a couple of his lackeys laugh. They seemed in good spirits and weren't making any attempt to disguise their approach.

"Here goes nothing," Bishop whispered.

The first figure I saw was familiar, the broad shoulders and blond locks stood out on Mustang Sally. Since we smashed up his car, maybe I'd just call him Sally.

The guy scowled at me and the two canvas bags in front of me. He turned back and nodded and now another person, one I didn't recognize, hopped over the low rise roofline.

He stood about twenty feet back from the edge of the *moat* which looked to be about a twenty foot drop on the roof of the only two-story home on the block. Sheehan had arranged an extension ladder at each end.

"You're Kyle, and you must be Bishop."

"Gold star," I said. "We're missing some people."

"You have it?" The second guy was sort of a runt, pale skin and dark short hair. He must have barely stood five-feet-six. His eyes darted around while he spoke.

"Right here." I nudged the bags with my foot.

"Show me," he said. His voice was surprisingly deep for someone so small.

I glanced at Sally and saw he'd unzipped his leather coat and brushed it back to reveal a pistol. No surprise there. I was sure Bishop saw it as well.

Bishop stood behind and to my side. He'd have a clear field of fire if it came to that.

I crouched down and unzipped one of the bags.

"Easy," Sally said, and I glanced up and saw his hand was wrapped around the pistol, but he hadn't cleared the holster yet.

I used two fingers to open the case wide and then tilted it toward the men to view.

A beam of light stabbed out from the runt who shone a mini-Maglite at the case.

I didn't worry about it at this distance.

"Same drill with the other one."

I repeated my actions making sure I moved with an exaggerated slowness for Sally's benefit.

"Very nice. Now drop 'em onto the roof below."

"Screw that. Where is she?"

"With you in two minutes if you deliver. Now drop the bags."

"Showed you too much already. I want to see her." I slid one of the bags toward Bishop. I noticed he'd quietly slipped his hand to his gun as well.

I felt like a lit match on a powder keg.

The runt tried to stare me down. When he realized he was wasting his time he shrugged, glanced at Sally and then gave a low chirping whistle. Now I saw them come from behind a brick chimney.

Adrenaline dumped into my body. I recognized Sheehan's pale hair and wiry build. He tugged a second person from the hiding spot and my heart thudded in my chest. Sheehan pushed the figure in front of himself and I saw what could be Beth, but her head was covered by a pillow case. Her arms were bound at the wrists in front of her.

I had an awful moment thinking all this was a sick joke and some other poor woman would be under that cloth. "Take it off, Danny."

The woman looked around at the sound of my voice.

"It's what we're all here for, isn't it?" Sheehan grinned, and his head looked like a skull in the moonlight. He reached up and snatched off the pillowcase with a sudden movement.

Beth.

She was terrified, and I saw a bruise on her cheek and a cut on her lip. But even in the dim light I could see the fire in her eyes.

"You okay?" I called over.

"I guess."

Fair enough. "Almost over." Then to Sheehan, "Your play. What's next?"

Sheehan pantomimed lifting my shirt.

I got the idea. I lifted it up nearly to my armpits as if I was a co-ed flashing some douche for beads at Mardi Gras, then I turned a full circle so he could see I wasn't armed or wearing a wire.

"Good. Now, like the man said, bags down on the low roof."

"I'll carry them myself, and only after she is down there first."

QUICK FIX

The low area was clever. Sally would have a fine angle on me, then again so would Bishop on Sheehan's men. We'd be below the others on the rooftops which at least improved the odds. Or maybe that was the idea and it was a trap.

I paused at the ladder. "Aren't you going to cut her arms free?"

"Nope. This one scratches." Sheehan turned his face and I could see the faint nail marks along his face.

"I can climb, Kyle." Her voice sounded strong.

"You sure? It's farther than it looks."

"Just get me the fuck out of here, okay?"

"Working on it." I remembered how that tone used to piss me off. Tonight it was like music.

I left the bags by the edge and started to climb down the aluminum extension ladder. I thought about Rollie working on his gutters. My head ached, but legs felt okay as I started down. Just before my face dipped below the roofline I said to Bishop, "Once I'm down kick them over one at a time."

Bishop never took his eyes off Sally. "You got it. Be careful."

I finished the descent, and the sides of the houses walled me in.

I heard the zipper for each bag being closed. Soon after, the bags thumped next to me on the low roof. I'd let them hit instead of trying to catch them.

"Here I am, all by my lonesome," I called up. From here, I could see Sally, then the runt popped into view and scurried down the ladder. Compared to my effort he'd made it look easy.

"You sure you want her climbing?" He asked me.

"Yup," I lied. I kept hearing that thump in my mind and imagining it was Beth.

"Let's get a closer look at that cheddar." The runt strode toward the bags.

"Not another step," I said, and he looked like he was going to ignore me until those darting eyes looked up, and I also saw Bishop had stepped to the edge and now stared at the guy.

He paused. "Not much point in going on here if the money isn't—"

"When she's down here safe. Don't fuck around," I said.

He gave me a shit-eating, "Who me?" grin and waved to Sally.

Beth, with her hands still tied, stepped to the ladder and began to back down the rungs. She was always a good athlete and I was relieved to see she was able to maintain her balance.

"Atta girl," Sheehan said from up top.

The runt stood at the base of the ladder. He held it steady, but I also understood that anytime he could kick the bottom out and send Beth crashing down. I breathed a little easier the closer she got to the bottom. After an eternity, she made it.

The runt took her by the arm. "Far enough."

QUICK FIX

I heard a metallic snick and saw the gleam of a steel blade in the runt's hand. Sheehan leaned over the roofline while supporting himself on the top of the ladder. I could see a pistol grip protruding from his beltline.

"Nice and easy here, 'boyo.' Everyone likes a happy ending, don't screw it up now."

"Can you untie her? She can't run off."

Sheehan nodded and spoke to the runt, "Go ahead."

Beth let out a little shriek when the blade cut through the twine in a blur. She rubbed her wrists, but I didn't see any blood. As for mine, it was boiling and I struggled to keep a lid on it.

Sally stood ready to act dividing his attention between me and Bishop up top. I found myself wishing I'd at least hidden a knife on me, not that I had any skill to speak of with a blade.

We were stuck on the roof and the only way off besides back up the ladders was to jump off the sides which would drop us over twenty feet onto the sidewalk. Not ideal and there'd be goons on the street to finish us off.

"Slide the cash and she can meet you in the middle. Nobody leaves yet," Sheehan said.

The moon dimmed as fat clouds passed in front of it. There was still enough light to see, but it took my eyes a moment to adjust.

I nudged one of the bags forward. "Half, and I see her before the other. Like you said, we can't leave."

"Okay. Send it." I kicked it across and tried to conceal my thumping heart. The ladder climb looked like a mile.

The runt released Beth's arm, but put his knife hand on her shoulder. "Stay." Like he was speaking to a dog. He reached down to open the bag while Beth still stood next to him.

Bishop called down, "Uh, uh. Earn it. Send her over." I saw him wipe his forehead with his sleeve. His other hand remained on his pistol. Sally looked like a metronome on crack with his head bobbing back and forth between the pit and Bishop.

"Go on, girl," Sheehan said. "Halfway only."

The runt lifted the knife arm and Beth walked slowly away from him and towards me. She was so completely composed that you might have thought she was crossing the street on the way to work. I left the other bag by the ladder and met her in the center. "I'm so sorry—"

She hauled off and slapped me hard across the face. The impact woke up all the contusions on that side, but before I could say another word she'd wrapped her arms around my neck and pulled me close for a bear hug. It cured all my aches for the moment and I took the opportunity to whisper into her ear. "When I tell you, get up that ladder and down the hatch fast as you can, no matter what."

Tears had begun to stream down her face, but I could see in her eyes she understood.

"Well?" Sheehan asked the runt who was poking at the contents and reaching for his flashlight.

Crap. What had we been thinking?

"The weight's good, but I won't know until I can count it." The beam snapped on, but the runt was still looking up at Sheehan.

"Take the rest and count it all, but it might rain soon. Let's get this show on the road." That was my signal to Bishop, in case he wasn't keeping up, that I was out of stall tactics.

I nudged Beth toward the ladder but whispered for her to walk slowly.

"I didn't. Hey! Don't move, bitch. We didn't say you could go over there." The runt trained the beam of light on her.

I picked up the second money bag and glanced up at Sally and Sheehan. Neither looked happy. "You trying to force my hand here, Kyle?" Sheehan asked. He gave a quick nod and Sally drew his gun but didn't aim it. Yet.

Fat drops of rain began to fall and they pounded a quickening drumbeat on the flat roof.

"Don't even think about it." I heard Bishop say.

"Wait! Here's the rest of the cash." I held up the bag I guess trying to obscure the view between Sally and Beth, though that was stupid. I did manage to draw their attention.

Beth made it to the bottom of the ladder and stopped.

"She's out of this when I say so," Sheehan started.

I didn't like the sound of that.

"Just take the money." I heaved the bag at the runt and it caught him off guard and hit him in the chest. It knocked the flashlight out his hand. I wasn't so sure about that knife.

"Beth, go!" I shouted loud enough for Bishop to hear.

Then everything seemed to happen at once.

Sheehan waved his arms and then nodded at Sally. "Do her."

A moment later I heard distant pops and Bishop cried out. Sally took aim with a two-handed grip on the pistol pointed right down into the pit.

I heard a series of pistol shots but not from Sally. His finger was on the trigger and I knew at once that we'd failed. He couldn't miss at this range and Beth wasn't halfway up the ladder yet.

Time slowed as Sally's finger seemed to squash against the metal of the trigger, pulling it backward.

Then Sally's chest exploded. His gun discharged with a flash but not before the impact had spoiled his aim. He didn't fire again as he dropped his pistol and glanced down at the hole that hadn't been there an instant before. He pitched forward and out of sight.

I heard the rolling boom, too sharp to be thunder, echo around the packed buildings. Then I heard more low explosions and the sound of sirens from the street.

At the first pistol shots, Sheehan had drawn his own gun, but when Sally went down and the sirens began to wail he seemed to think better of it.

"Double-crossing piece of shit," he said to me and clambered down the ladder facing the rungs. I heard more rifle shots and Bishop screaming in pain. One shot drilled a hole through the side of the ladder at the top. It wasn't all that close to Sheehan, but he slid down the rest of the way of the now-slippery ladder and his feet slammed onto the roof. I saw his gun fly out of his hand, and after a single bounce sail over the edge to the sidewalk below.

QUICK FIX

I glanced over to the other ladder and Beth was nearly at the top. Now red and blue lights washed over the area. I could hear cars screeching and garbled messages barking over loudspeakers.

"Gut him." I heard Sheehan say and the runt came at me like a wildcat. He still had his blade and if not for the little guy slipping on the slick roof, he'd have made good on Sheehan's order.

Even so, he swiped at me from his knees before regaining his feet. He left a huge slice in my windbreaker, and after a moment I felt warm blood down my side.

I backed up and noticed Sheehan, instead of flanking me, was busy tossing the money bags over the back side of the roof. He looked like he was going to jump, but skidded to the edge and reached over the roof lip. He pulled up a large, rolled-up rope ladder that had been attached to the roof just out of sight.

I continued to back up, but I was almost to the wall and the roof edge leading to the street. The runt grinned and slashed at every attempt I made to grab his arm.

Stupid. He knew what he was doing. The blade was razor sharp and it bit me the last time I tried to hit his arm.

I watched Sheehan begin his climb down the rope ladder.

"Your boss got away. You going to wait here with me for the cops?" I saw my comment did more than my attempts to grab him.

"Nah. Just been playing with you. You're out of room and time, bitch," he said.

He advanced for the kill, and no matter which way I moved the gleaming tip of that knife tracked me.

My side started to burn. Blood and rain soaked my left arm. I prayed this dance was giving Beth and Bishop time to get away, when I noticed Bishop had stopped screaming or shooting.

I felt my heels reach the edge of the roof. The runt saw it too. His teeth looked unnaturally white.

Then it hit me. I grinned back at him and spread my arms wide leaving my body open to attack. "Come and get me, you little shit. Stick it right in there."

I saw a flicker of doubt. He was just a step away. A couple feet and that steel was as good as through my heart. I wouldn't have a thing to say about it. He knew it.

"C'mon Speedy. You know you want to do it."

"You nuts?"

"Put me out of my misery," I waggled my fingers like I wanted to give him a hug, "and I'll teach you to fly."

I was in his head now.

"Cops are coming up here. You going to cut them, too?"

The runt had other ideas now and he backed away quick then moved to the rope ladder. He pointed the knife at me. "I can throw it, too."

I moved to the center of the roof and watched him descend. When he was out of sight I moved to the back edge and peered over from off to one side, in case he expected me right over the ladder. I didn't think he could really throw the knife. That was for circus people.

QUICK FIX

Wrong.

The runt was barely a third of the way down and when I peered over he hooked one arm through the ladder and let fly with that thing. The blade winked twice at me while it rotated in the air and I barely was able to flinch away. It stuck in the wood right where my face had been. The runt looked down and clearly decided it was too far to fall. He began a frantic descent, which slowed him down the way the ladder wriggled. He must have read my mind.

I reached for the knife, but the handle sagged downward as the blade worked out of the spongy wood. I made a desperate grab for the blade and was lucky to just nick my finger when the knife dropped to the ground.

"Tough luck, bro." The runt laughed and steadied the ladder.

"Little bastard, get back here." I scrambled over to the ladder. The son of a bitch was light. I finally had a place to vent my rage and used my arms to haul him back up.

He looked shocked when he felt the rungs move upward and realized what I was doing. He must have decided the drop was better than facing me without his knife, because he pushed away and released his arms.

I was still pulling hard when his weight came off and the ladder jumped upward in my hands. One of the rungs caught the guy's leg and I watched as his body inverted, then plunged about fifteen feet head first into the ground.

He didn't move, and from the angle of his neck I saw he wasn't going to again.

No sign of Sheehan or the money bags on the ground. I heard more tires spinning on the wet pavement and now the blue and red strobes were moving away. More sirens sounded in the distance.

I ran over to the ladder leading to our side of the roof and climbed as fast as I dared. The rungs were slick, but I was careful. If I fell I'd be useless.

At the top I didn't see anyone besides Sally's lifeless body face down on the roof across the way, but I did hear muffled voices.

I scampered across the roof to where it dropped a couple of feet, all the while looking over at the rooflines across the street. No sign of the other guys, and with all the commotion I hoped the Sheehan party had left for greener pastures.

Now I saw two figures at the hatch.

"Don't shoot, it's me." I could make out Beth and Bishop. They seemed to have trouble reaching the ladder below.

"We need help," Beth said. I must not have looked so hot. "Are you okay?"

"Yeah." Bishop wasn't. One of his arms was slicked in red and then I noticed he was bleeding near the waist. "Bishop?"

"I'm awake. Fuck, this hurts."

I started to reach for my belt to use as a tourniquet, but he stopped me. "I think the arm's just a graze. But I got hit in the ass. Believe that shit? The slug might still be in there."

QUICK FIX

I'd seen quite a few gunshot wounds over in Iraq when we'd make deliveries to hospitals. Any hit could kill him if it went through there into his abdomen. "You sure?"

"Feels like a hot poker, but the burn's not in my gut. Those rooftop jagoffs used pistols," He said. "Now we can't find the ladder."

I looked and could just make it out. It must have fallen over. Maybe Bishop kicked it by accident.

"I'll get it. Can you climb?" I lowered myself through the hatch.

"Wait," Beth said, but I already was trying to support my bulk with my arms alone. The key was not to land on the ladder or my touchy knee.

I dropped down and rolled like I'd been skydiving. I heard an odd pop sound and for an instant thought I'd torn something but not felt it yet. The stepladder was right next to me, flat on the wood floor.

A figure came out of the shadows holding a pistol fitted with a fat canister suppressor. He raised the weapon and then Bishop called down, "Freeze!"

The guy, some lanky white man, reacted instantly and snapped a shot at the hatch opening. It was a small caliber, probably a .22, and it made that same muffled pop, almost silent. Bishop pulled back, but his gun hand snagged and the weapon dropped to the floor.

I grabbed a rung on the ladder and yanked hard so it slid across the floor, ramming into the guy's legs and taking him off his feet. While he recovered, I reached Bishop's gun, grabbed it and aimed it at his face. "Drop it."

He did.

We didn't have time for prisoners, but I couldn't just execute him in cold blood. "Get the fuck out of here. I see you again and you're dead."

I didn't have to ask twice. I took the second weapon.

Between Beth and me we got Bishop down.

"I felt the wind when the bullet went by my face." He seemed surprised, "He ran?"

"I had your gun on him."

"Good thing you didn't try to shoot him. I was out of ammo. Keep that pea shooter handy."

"You need a doctor."

Bishop mumbled something, but it was clear he was woozy. I handed the .22 to Beth and picked him up in a fireman's carry.

He weighed a ton.

"Watch out for that guy. Our ride is downstairs."

Beth nodded and somehow we made it to the front door. The lock was broken and the security chain had been cut. How could Ryan have missed that happening?

I could still hear sirens, but they were a few streets over. Out here the street was strangely quiet. The houses on the other side were all dark and every one I saw had the shades pulled. Almost like the neighbors were conditioned to see and hear nothing.

Just outside the house I saw the gray car. Ryan was in the driver's seat, head down like he was looking at his phone.

QUICK FIX

We moved quickly to the car and I noticed two things. The first was that the streetlight was now out. The second was that Ryan was dead.

Chapter 29

Fishtown

Now the street felt like one big trap. Bishop had come around enough to warn us not to touch anything. We couldn't use the car anyway, as someone had removed the keys.

Up close, I could see the trickle of blood down the back of Ryan's neck. I suspected the wound came from the silenced gun Beth gave back to me. Now I knew why he hadn't warned us.

I didn't know how to feel about it, but I couldn't help him anymore and the rest of us were still alive.

"Hurry up." Bishop was leaning against me. "Ground game down and out, copy?"

Bishop's head was close enough to my good ear that I heard a tinny version of Rollie's voice from his earpiece. "Fuck! Bug out, Bomber on the way."

I noticed a helicopter in the sky on station with a spotlight shining a few blocks away. It was only a matter of time. But it wasn't the cops I was worried about.

Beth and I helped Bishop around the corner, and I racked my brain trying to think of a faster way to move. I saw headlights turn up our street. We heard a car approaching slowly. Hell with it, I picked Bishop up again and my muscles screamed in protest. I lumbered off the sidewalk and perched Bishop against a chain-link fence.

This streetlight worked fine and whoever this was would see us for sure.

QUICK FIX

"Beth, hide under that parked truck." I hated to leave Bishop, but needed to move if it came to a fight. I put my hand on the butt of the killer's gun and crouched by another car. The little gun wasn't much in a firefight but better than my fists.

Bishop mumbled into his microphone and the approaching car stopped. I glanced at the street and saw blue paint and then heard Rollie's voice. "Kid?"

"It's us."

* * *

Rollie turned the streets of Philly into his own personal racetrack. The car's wipers batted rain aside and I could feel the rumble of the Bomber's engine through the seat. The tires boomed off potholes and Bishop groaned each time, but the pain seemed to keep him awake.

The images flashed through my consciousness in a surreal montage. Rollie yelled at Bishop asking him where some friend of his was that could help patch him up.

At first Rollie was headed to the hospital, but I had to keep Bishop from bailing out of the car at seventy miles an hour.

Once Bishop gave him an address, Rollie stopped yelling at him long enough to tell Beth it was a pleasure to make her acquaintance along with a handshake while he drifted us around a corner. Then he started in on me.

"Where's Sheehan?"

"Don't know. He got away. He took the money."

I told him what happened.

"Well, he's in for a rude surprise," Rollie said.

"Why?" Beth was trying to piece things together on the fly and, considering all the insanity, I thought she was keeping it together well. She was in the back seat with Bishop and was pressing a clean towel against his wound.

"We bluffed the cash. No choice, our first plan to raise the money crapped out," I said.

"Maybe he got arrested. The police sharpshooter got that other man."

"There weren't any cops. Later, I'm sure, but that wasn't who got the goon on the roof," I said.

"Then who?"

"Guardian angel," Rollie said.

That didn't seem to sink in. "You're saying Sheehan is still out there and you guys screwed him?"

Rollie tensed behind the wheel. "In case you missed it while you were going up the ladder that tow-headed goon had you in his sights. Sheehan never was going to keep his word even if we had paid."

"We'll never know," she started but caught herself. "I mean, thank you, I'm new to this."

Then it hit me. "Rollie's right. The guy who shot Ryan did it before he broke into the house to wait for us. He took a shot at me when I dropped down."

Bishop spoke from the back seat, "They were going to do us all. And we're not out of it yet."

"If you're going to bleed to death can you wait until you aren't on my seats?"

QUICK FIX

"Bill me for the detailing, asshole," Bishop said. "Just tell me you got it."

"Sure hope so," Rollie said.

"Got what?" I asked.

"Not now. We're here." Rollie checked his rear view mirror compulsively while we roared east of the city into the suburb of Lansdowne.

We passed the huge Fernwood Cemetery and turned down a quiet street facing the property.

"Convenient if it doesn't work out," Rollie quipped.

"Fuck you, old man." Bishop sounded like he was getting weak again.

The front door opened and the guy sure seemed like he'd been expecting us. "Around the side." Hurry up."

* * *

Four hours later; Lansdowne

I rode the buzz of a couple Tylenol with codeine while I'd tried to focus on Rollie's debrief. We were in what amounted to a waiting room in the basement of this unlicensed, patch-up shop.

The owner, Rollie told me, was a disgraced MD who drank himself out of his license. He and his live-in girlfriend, a former nurse he met in AA named Cindy, now made ends meet catering to the underground needs of clients who valued discretion over board certification.

The guy's name was Crocker and he didn't care that he was known in shady circles as *Doc Crock*. He shared this unsettling fact before our treatment.

275

Nurse Cindy stitched me up, the cuts on my arm and side were more involved than I'd realized. She said I was lucky the guy missed the brachial artery. Adrenaline can be a great painkiller. So was codeine.

It looked like Bishop was going to be okay, but the guy took his time. Doc Crock even had Cindy bring out the slug to show us.

Now that she was back helping the doc close the wound and stabilize Bishop, Rollie felt free to talk. We explained to Beth how the arrival of the cops at the rooftop exchange was really staged by some friends of Ryan along with some police equipment provided by Bishop. Trying to get real cops to actually bust them would have only tipped off Sheehan and probably gotten her killed. As it was, the ruse was enough to scare off Sheehan's advantage in numbers to give us a chance.

It was all I could do to keep my eyes open, but before I drifted off I made sure that Beth understood that we were still in grave danger. It was crucial that Fenster didn't try to send in the cavalry either, or we'd end up putting targets on all our heads.

Chapter 30

The next morning; Lansdowne

"Wake up and get the fuck out of here!"

I pried my eyes open and nearly popped the stitches I'd forgotten about as I tried to raise my hands for a fight.

The yeller was Doc Crock, and some of the craziness of the night before seeped back into my brain. Beth was right next to me.

"Take it easy Doc," Rollie had snapped awake from his spot on in an overstuffed chair. "You charge extra for bedside manner?"

"Shut up. I took you in because you had the right friends."

"Yeah, and?" Rollie stood.

"You forgot to mention that you have the wrong enemies."

"You didn't ask," I said.

Nurse Cindy wheeled Bishop out. He was face down on a gurney with a sheet over his rump and bulky bandaging that made it look like he tried to wear an entire box of Depends at once.

"Hey, should he be moved?" Beth asked.

"He'll be fine. Make sure he takes all of these." He threw a bottle of pills to me with a handwritten label that looked like instructions to feed the cat on a post-it note. I saw something-
cillin and *3xday*.

"What about me?" I asked.

Cindy looked at me like I was stupid. "You've been cut before. Keep it clean and use antiseptic ointment." She peeked out the window. "Now go."

"And you were never here," Doc said.

"What set you off? What did you hear?" I asked.

"We have sources, 'kay? Scoot." Doc jabbed his finger toward the door.

Rollie stopped him from nudging Bishop off the gurney, which might have landed him on the floor. He was coming around but still pretty out of it.

"Tell me what you heard," Rollie said. "It could help us stay out of sight," he pointed to Bishop's bandages, "and avoid difficult questions."

The last seemed to penetrate. Doc stopped with the cattle-prod treatment long enough to give us the short version. "I heard that something went down in Fishtown, but once the cops showed up to what sounded like a war, they found nothing."

"That's it?" Rollie said.

"No. I also heard my person say that they saw Shamrock Sanitation and wondered if I had any work."

Jeez. The internet had nothing on these little neighborhoods. The name conjured a garbage truck with a big green clover logo on the side, but was really the nickname for the Irish Mob's cleanup crew. The unwritten rule was that if one of those guys was spotted going in or out of a place that they were invisible or else anyone who said anything soon disappeared themselves.

QUICK FIX

"What did you tell them?" Rollie's voice took on a steely edge.

"Why do you think I'm so excited now, dumbass? I said it was quiet. Now if you don't get lost, I'll call them back and say you threatened me."

* * *

Media, Pennsylvania

Less than an hour later, we pulled into a modest apartment complex belonging to a friend of Bishop's, not far from the State Troop office where he worked.

"My buddy is out of town and said if we leave beer in the fridge we can stay as long as we need."

On the way in Bishop did his best to walk under his own power. I wore a sweatshirt and tried my best to walk as though we were not survivors of a battle. Beth made us stop off at a drug store before we got there and in addition to some basic first aid and food, she found some makeup to cover her bruises. Tired as I was I felt my blood cook whenever I looked at them.

We ran into one old timer who couldn't miss Bishop's awkward stride and bandage-swollen rump.

"That looks painful." The guy wore a baseball cap that read *USS Forrestal.*

"Worst splinter I ever had." Bishop introduced himself with a fake last name and explained that his friend had okayed their use of his place.

Rollie spoke up. "We're here to get him settled and make sure he's on the mend."

The old guy nodded then Rollie leaned in close. "He didn't tell the whole truth,"

"Oh?" the guy was curious and I wondered what Rollie was thinking.

"It was a much more serious operation. They had to remove his whole head from back there."

Once inside, we did just like we'd promised and got Bishop stretched out on the bed with some coffee and his phone and pad of paper nearby. He had us close the bedroom door and began to make calls.

* * *

Rollie and Bishop were conferring in the other room while we finished getting dressed. I found the local news and saw no mention of what went on last night.

"Anything?" Beth asked.

"Nope. Nothing online either. Maybe Doc was right about the scene being cleaned up."

Images flashed through my head of the runt and Sally and especially Ryan. Did he really deserve to go out like that? Maybe. He wasn't innocent, but he was my friend.

"Past time to call Richard." Beth held out her hand for my phone.

She was right, but I still didn't feel ready for this. "What are you going to say?"

She stared at me. "That I'm alive? That I'm safe? I'm ready to go home?"

"You got one out of three." Rollie emerged from the other room and gave me a look that made me decide to hold on to the phone a little longer.

"What the hell are you talking about?" Beth looked at Rollie. "It's over. We're going to nail that maniac to the wall. And Richard is going to do it with my help and with or without yours."

Rollie's expression softened, but he stood his ground. "It's over when we can go home and sleep in our own beds without worrying about a knock on the door."

"Last time I checked, kidnapping and murder were illegal." Beth's jaw set in an all too familiar defiant pose.

"They have to make the case, and prove it," Rollie said.

"I'm more than happy to be the star witness." She turned to me. "Are you going to let me call Richard now? Or I am I still some sort of prisoner?"

That last comment cut deeper than the runt's blade. "Of course not. Just hear us out first." I handed Rollie the phone.

Rollie gestured for her to sit. "When I'm done explaining, we *need* you to speak with Richard. And you're free to go, but you won't want to. Not just yet."

She sat down.

I decided to let Rollie do the talking since he and Bishop had fine-tuned our plan. I trusted him to leave out the part where I was ready to give Sheehan his chance at me. We would finish him even if it meant I'd be the last casualty of this little war.

Rollie talked and Beth listened. When he was done, Beth was on board and I began to think I might just live through this thing after all.

Chapter 31

I felt like a peeping Tom sitting by Beth while she called Fenster for the first time since we'd freed her. I had to pity the guy; I knew how hard it was to sit by helplessly hour after hour. Based on her side of the conversation he was relieved, then angry. I felt like the whole situation sat on a knife edge while he tried to convince Beth that the right move was to sic the FBI on the whole Irish Mob.

Before Rollie and Bishop had explained their plan, I probably would have gone along with contacting the Feds, but as crazy as what they wanted to do was, we'd never rest with those mobsters gunning for us. Turning up the heat on the mob by bringing in the Feds would only increase the targets on our back.

Beth eventually put her foot down and told Fenster that she'd deny anything had happened if he went to the Feds on his own. Mad as he was, Fenster the lawyer recognized a moot case when he saw one.

She hung up and looked at us. "He's upset."

"That came through," I said. "Is he going to stay put?"

"He can be stubborn, but without me it's not like he has a choice, does he?" she asked.

"No, but that doesn't mean he couldn't try." I turned to Rollie and Bishop. "How long do you guys need?"

Rollie checked his watch. "We're burning daylight, but we could be done by this evening, couldn't we?"

Bishop stood up, let out a groan, but waved off support. Rollie handed him an old golf club— looked like a wedge— for a cane. "Can't take as many pain pills as I'd like because I need to keep the stupids to a minimum." He looked to Rollie "Yeah, I think we can get it all done and in place by then. Enough to make it work."

Rollie picked up the keys to the blue bomber. "C'mon, half-ass."

* * *

"So, now what?" Beth asked.

I didn't want to detail what we'd planned for fear of her changing her mind about helping us. Without her support we were dead. I owed her the whole truth, but for now she'd have to accept it on the installment plan.

"Now we have to approach the next stage very carefully."

"Which means?"

"I'm going to have to reach out to someone. Remember Meg?"

I saw by the way her mouth tightened that she remembered her just fine. "*That* Meg?"

I gave her a little nod.

"Meg Sheehan. As in psycho Danny's cousin? She was almost as crazy as he is."

She had a point. Danny's cousin Meg was cool if she liked you and if she didn't, well, she was a Sheehan. The first time we'd broken up she bounced right into Ryan's arms, so fast I'd wondered if there had already been something going on.

"Well, here's the thing now. We need someone on our side to make sure we don't get killed on the way to straighten things out. See?"

"Why would you trust her now?"

"Ryan." My ego could take it. Meg had liked me back in the day, but she'd been crazy about Ryan. He'd broken her heart, but being Ryan, she couldn't stay mad at him.

"Do you know where to find her?"

"Last I saw her she was an office manager for Sherwood roofing." They'd been a competitor way back when I was working for the union to please my dad.

"Really?"

"Drives an Escalade and lives in a hell of a nice house, so my guess is she hasn't completely cut all family ties. However, she seems to be trying to keep some distance from Danny's crew."

"Do you need me to be there?" Now she looked scared. I knew it wasn't of Meg herself, but because it might put her right back in the hands of the mob.

"No." Nobody would ever put her in that position again.

Chapter 32

The next day; Edgely Field in Fairmount Park; Philadelphia

Meg had agreed to meet me in a public area outside of Fishtown. I hoped that meant she was taking me seriously and this wasn't a trap. To be on the safe side, Rollie followed me in the Bomber and I drove the beater pickup Bishop's friend used to go fishing.

The cab of the old Ford reeked of ripe bait. Shiny, dry fish scales formed a sparkling galaxy on the battered black rubber floor mat.

Still, the truck ran and nobody was looking for it, so I couldn't complain.

I saw her black Escalade parked on the side, and I pulled in a few spots away. The driver's side window was open and a plume of smoke wafted out into the morning air.

I held a package under my good arm and left the truck so she'd be able to see me approach.

"Thanks for coming," I said when I reached it.

"Jesus, you look like shit." She flicked her cigarette out the window.

Meg wore a red sweater, and her thick, raven hair shone as much as the paint on her ride.

"You thought I was kidding, didn't you?" On the phone I'd used the term meat grinder to describe what we'd been through.

"Get in. I'm taking a big chance meeting you." I took that to mean that she'd asked around and heard a version of events.

"I need your help, and there are things you need to know."

"Just tell me, did you try to rip off Danny?"

"Which time?"

"Are you crazy?"

"Me? I'm just stupid. And more than a little desperate."

"But why? You *know* him," she said.

"Yeah. Wasn't my idea. Not the first time anyway. What did they say?"

"You and some other bums tried an amateur move on Danny and he had to take measures. This doesn't sound like you at all. Where's Ryan?"

No point sugarcoating it. "He's dead."

"Bullshit." But the way her face went bone white told me she knew I wasn't lying.

I handed the package to her. "Danny was going to kill us all and he just got to Ryan first. We fought back. In there is the gun I am sure was used to kill Ryan."

"Why are you giving me this?"

"Take it to the O'Briens. It's a show of our good faith. We don't want to go to the cops, but we need a guarantee they will end this war."

"I can't tell them what to do."

"You don't have to, just set up a meet and make sure they understand that we have insurance, the kind that would bring the Feds down on them." I explained how Danny kidnapped Beth.

"They'd never okay that."

"Exactly. Danny's off the reservation here. I'm not the only one who is desperate. We need off this ride before it gets worse."

"Why should I believe you?"

"We'll bring proof to them. As for you, you can do your own digging and find out what the Shamrock Sanitation boys were really doing. What we did that night and what we're doing now is self-preservation. But without an understanding from the O'Briens, Danny is going to bring heat down on them for what he did. We have a chance to stop it."

She peered inside the package and saw the pistol. The tangible weight seemed to harden her face and I saw the storm clouds gather in her eyes. "I'll call you. If you're telling the truth…"

I thanked her and left her in the Escalade with the package sitting in her lap.

She must have been pretty persuasive about getting answers on her own because she called me back before we finished lunch.

* * *

Fishtown

"Any chance I can convince you to let me go in alone?" I knew I was wasting my time and had to admit being glad my words would have no effect. Selfish, but there it was.

QUICK FIX

Rollie drove up the crowded street to the entrance of Heather Bakery, the worst kept secret in Fishtown. The place housed the toughest bakers in the world, and though they only made one or two kinds of cookies, the place did a thriving business. Several burly guys hung around the entrance and guarded the parking place in front.

"I love the valet service at this joint," Rollie said. "Kid, how many times do I have to tell you I'm in this to the end, whether I like it or not?"

"Have I thanked you enough yet? I don't think so."

"If we leave here under our own power you can buy me a bunch of beers." Rollie shut off the car and we got out. He took an aluminum briefcase from the back seat.

The goons looked us over and one glanced to the front door of the bakery. The door opened; it looked like the kind of place where the customer is always wrong.

"After you," Rollie said and I walked into a dark room.

The worn wood floor felt gritty underfoot, and the glass display cases showed a token tray of shortbread and lace cookies. The cash register looked like an antique.

The air smelled like stale ginger and cigar smoke.

A figure inside the place closed and locked the front door behind us.

"I hope you don't hurt the lunch crowd sales on our account," Rollie said.

A thin man, probably late twenties wearing a blue dress shirt and open collar, slipped into the room from somewhere behind the counter. "Put the case on the floor and open it. Slowly."

"Of course." Rollie did as he was told and it revealed a laptop embedded in the protective foam.

"Take it out," The guy said. He had thinning red hair and a diamond stud in his left ear. "And switch it on."

Rollie did. "You guys are tougher than TSA." The screen flickered on while the machine booted up to show a vanilla blue background and desktop icons.

Satisfied, the guy gestured to a pair of burly guys who proceeded to frisk us. I found myself hoping they wouldn't be as thorough as Bishop had been that time, but at any rate we weren't armed.

Outside of the computer, of course.

"This way."

We followed the guy and the other goons trailed us up a narrow staircase. Another guard stood in front of a thick interior door. I noticed a small closed circuit camera up in the corner of the ceiling.

Rollie saw it too. "Must be some cookie recipe."

I think this was the first time I'd seen him even a little nervous.

We stood in silence in front of the door. I kept my mouth shut even when I noticed one of the goons elbow the other and call attention to my bandages. They seemed alternately amused and angered by them.

I heard a tiny click and my mind jumped to the conclusion that my brains were about to decorate the door in front of me.

QUICK FIX

It was only the lock and the thin guy pushed the door open and held it for us. We stepped through and he closed it behind us, as I'd expected. The other goons waited outside.

"They'll be with you in a moment. Wait here."

Here looked like a lavish apartment's living room with red tooled leather couches and wing backed chairs facing a brick fireplace.

Off to the side of the fireplace sat a wet bar with crystal tumblers filled with amber liquid and glass shelves.

Rollie and I remained standing. I noticed the seats of the leather chairs bore the indentations of long use. I wasn't about to offend one of them by sitting in the wrong seat.

We heard footsteps approach.

"So tell me, why is it you aren't leaving our city in half a dozen small boxes?" William O'Brien, the older of the two brothers, stepped into the room.

At first glance he appeared unassuming, of average height with thinning hair but he had a compact build and a nose that had been broken more than once in the distant past. His eyes were a bright blue and his swollen hands bore the look of a retired boxer. Behind him his younger brother, Charlie, dwarfed William and had a full head of black curly hair, a paunch, broad shoulders, and thick arms. He had the exact same eyes as his brother with the same intelligent, yet predatory gleam.

"We got you curious?" Rollie said.

"Sit, please," William said. He and his brother turned the wingback chairs around to face the couch. Sure enough, Charlie's seat bore large deep indentations. "Kevin."

The skinny guy who brought us here worked to pour drinks of what had to be whiskey.

"It's a little early in the day for me," I said.

Kevin handed the tumblers to each of us as if I hadn't spoken.

The brothers raised the glasses so we did likewise.

"Slainte." It sounded like *Slawn-cha* the Gaelic word for health.

"You sure?" I asked.

Charlie drank half his glass and looked at me with a little smile. "It's just an expression."

"We want to hear what you have to say. And I salute your courage." William took another sip.

"We want peace."

"You have a strange way of showing it. Ripping us off and staging an attack on my men."

"Your men?" I asked.

"They're all mine, remember that," William said.

"I'm not here to argue about who started things. I think we all know. I was supposed to be a bit player and things got…. complicated."

"That they did. Or simple, depending on how you want to look at it," Charlie said. I couldn't tell if the whiskey or anger made his cheeks flush.

"I'm here to look out for this guy," Rollie said. "I didn't give a shit about his friend. He made his bed. My pal made a mistake."

"Your hands aren't clean. Try not to insult us too much. You're in our business now."

"True. And we want out."

"Not your call."

No," I said. "It is entirely your call, but we want to make sure you have the facts and the whole picture. When you do, you might see it differently."

William pointed to the laptop. "You have something to show us?"

"With your permission," Rollie spoke in a respectful tone.

"Go ahead," William said.

Rollie clicked on a few folders and a video player opened up to a still shot of rooftops from the church tower perspective.

"This footage is from the other night. I was the one behind the rifle and I added a nifty little camera so it could record everything I saw."

"We wondered if you were the shooter," William said. He turned to Kevin. "We'll be fine."

Kevin left the room.

"Thanks for the trust," I said and Charlie laughed at me.

"He's a hundred and you look half-mummy, half-piñata."

"We already know what happened," William said.

"You authorized Danny grabbing my wife?"

Now the two brothers exchanged a look.

"Your what?" Charlie asked. The color in his cheeks deepened and I felt hope that it wasn't all aimed at me.

"We're split up, and she had nothing to do with any of this shit until Danny grabbed her to force me to help him find Ryan. Things got more complicated for all of us when her lawyer threatened to go to the Feds, and we all know how much you would enjoy that."

"Bull. He knows better," Charlie finished his drink.

"Play the clip," William said.

The video was exactly as Rollie had described, a perfect view through the rifle scope, crosshairs and all. We watched the clip unfold with the scope panning to the guys on the roof across the street and us and then to Sheehan, Sally, and Beth. I noted that Rollie had placed the crosshairs right on the heads of the bad guys and carefully made sure they never settled on any part of Beth's body. Even so, he got very clear images of her face (once the pillowcase came off) and only a fool wouldn't realize that she was indeed a captive and this was some sort of exchange.

The O'Briens weren't fools.

Charlie threw his glass and cursed as it shattered on the fireplace bricks.

QUICK FIX

William sat in silence for the rest of the video. Rollie had made sure to let the crosshairs linger on Sheehan right up to when things got bloody.

"He was mine anytime I wanted, but we were trying to end the war not start a bigger one."

The camera image jumped when Rollie took down Sally with the first round just before the goon would have shot Beth. Rollie's point was underscored when he put rounds through the ladder rather than into Sheehan.

I was relieved that the Runt's near-fileting of me with his razor-sharp knife had taken place off camera.

Not long after, the camera tilted to the sky and then switched off. I assumed that was when Rollie had bugged out and headed for the bomber.

Rollie switched off the player and closed the laptop.

I saw a fierce gleam in Charlie's eye that sent fear crawling down my back. I glanced at William and was gratified that he looked concerned along with angry. His lips pressed together.

Rollie spoke. "This one is a gift."

"That means there are others." William's tone didn't make it a question.

"Many others, and know that as long as we remain safe and sound they stay secret. If anything happens to either of us, or our people, that changes."

"How?"

"Copies along with a full explanation will go to the media and more importantly to the FBI. Not just the local office, either. Several field offices, including ones I don't even know about, but the senders do."

"A dead man switch? What do you want?" William said.

"Peace. That's all. You leave us alone, this doesn't get out. You know it would give the Feds the perfect excuse to turn your operation upside down."

Charlie digested this. I could see he was boiling, but unlike his cousin Danny, his was a controlled rage. "Your wife could testify. That might be enough."

I tried to mirror his control. "That's part of the deal. She won't go forward unless we fail to come to an arrangement. She wants her life back too, get it?" The last hit me with a little pang.

"So you think you can waltz in with some presentation and just dictate terms?"

"No," I said. "We're just trying to offer a way out of this that doesn't compel you to solve the issue by making us all disappear. You know, in boxes."

"You also deserve to decide your next move with all the right facts. They change the math don't they?" Rollie asked.

William didn't respond, but the way he was listening I hoped he'd taken the full measure of what Rollie meant. Instead he shifted the discussion. "Speaking of math, what about the money? Danny told me most of the cash in those bags was bogus."

"That part was true. All that we had from the first sale was in there. We had a plan to raise the cash, but it turns out the second buyer was crooked. We got ripped off, so if you want to find the money, find Ratigan or the Columbians. Ryan might have known more, but Danny already slammed that door closed."

I thought they'd get angrier and assume I was lying. They just gave each other that look and then they stood up.

William spoke. "We'll give you an answer shortly. Until then you won't be touched. Go home and get some rest."

We left the laptop and got the hell out of there while we could.

Chapter 33

Two days later; Fishtown

Although I hated the waiting game, the time had passed faster than I'd expected. Mostly I'd drunk beer with Rollie and slept. The cuts were starting to itch, a maddening but good sign. My face was even healing up from the beat down Sheehan had delivered what felt like ages ago, but had only been a handful of days.

When Rollie and I stepped outside or went for a drive neither of us got that hair on the back of the neck feeling of being watched or followed.

Hard as it was, I tried to give Beth her space. I'd checked in just to make sure she was okay. She seemed all right and at least had reported no strange cars stalking her block.

Funny, Fenster had resisted from coming out of hiding until Beth texted him and told him she was standing inside his house.

We made sure Bishop was still all right. He was a tough guy and now moved around pretty well. No signs of infection, but he'd have a hell of a scar to show off if he mooned someone. He told us he was taking a leave of absence.

My phone rang and I saw it was Beth. She said something about meeting me at our old place. My first thought was that it was a trap, but she reassured me and I wondered if the place had sold. Mundane details of existence went on even in the throes of life and death escapades.

"We had a fight."

QUICK FIX

I didn't have to ask her with whom, and while I told her I was sorry she probably guessed I was lying.

* * *

Since our separation and impending divorce, I'd avoided the place as much as possible. On the advice of the realtor we left the little house furnished and staged for viewing, a re-creation of the home where we used to be happy together.

While it held the same furniture, it had been stripped of all the little touches that reflected our personalities. To me it looked like a well-embalmed corpse, perfectly preserved, yet devoid of spirit.

Beth came in not long after I arrived. She had a suitcase, and when I glanced out the door I saw the fading taillights of a taxicab.

She'd been brave for the stranger in the cab, but now the tears streamed down her face. I hugged her and listened. Standing in our old place together felt like I'd stepped into a time warp. The itching of my cuts served as a reminder of the present.

"Richard still wants to go to the police."

"Will he?"

She shook her head. "I made it clear I wasn't kidding about denying anything happened." She paused. "He got furious, it was almost like this was my fault," she said.

"Did he…."

"Oh, no. Nothing like that, but in a way it was worse. It was like he saw me as a different person. After all that happened."

"I'm so sorry." This time I wasn't lying.

"I have to do some thinking."

"Of course. I'll grab the couch. Nobody will get in without me knowing," I said.

* * *

Rollie called the next morning and I felt guilty for not telling him I wouldn't be home, like I was some kid breaking curfew. Then again, we didn't know if we had a goon squad gunning for us so I suppose that made a difference.

"Don't apologize, just get over here. Bring her."

"Why?"

"Got a special delivery this morning."

"What?"

"Just hurry up."

* * *

I brought Beth and was immediately relieved to see Rollie on his front stoop, alone and in one piece. He led us inside and a quick wink was the only acknowledgement he gave to what he must have assumed about last night. I'd straighten him out later.

On his kitchen table was a box and for a second I flashed back to the one that was there with a hank of Beth's hair. There was something in the box and a note.

It was a man's ring. It looked like a variation of the *Claddagh* Irish friendship ring, only with a skull in place of the heart. If I looked carefully on my face I might have had a matching contusion.

QUICK FIX

I read the note and all it said was, "Watch the news."

"Kid, I think we might be okay."

* * *

Cops had found Sheehan's body floating in the Schuylkill River. The news reports gave a surprising amount of detail. He'd been shot in both kneecaps and then in the back of the head, execution-style.

All the speculation surrounded a gangland assassination, yet the police had no leads and no suspects. Reputed Irish mob figures, the O'Brien brothers, had no comment other than a request for respecting their privacy in this time of loss of their dear cousin.

* * *

One week later

Beth remained in our old house, but once we'd gotten our answer from the O'Briens I went back to Rollie's at her request.

She stopped by his place and carried an envelope with the logo from Fenster's law firm on it. I was surprised at how disappointed I was to see the final divorce papers.

"Thanks for bringing me these yourself, I guess."

She smiled. "Open it."

I did and saw a bunch of legal jargon, but it wasn't a decree of divorce or whatever they called it. "Is this...?"

"Yup. Richard agreed to drop all charges."

"You mean my assault?"

301

"The assault, the restraining order, everything. He said to tell you this is for what you did at his house when things got crazy. I don't think he wants to be your buddy, though."

I saw that there was a cc to Delivergistics. "Huh. So this means I'll be able to get my old job back?"

"Yup."

I glanced at her hand and noticed she wasn't wearing her engagement ring. Nor was she wearing her wedding ring from me. "You're still at our place?"

"For now. We had a long talk. A bunch of them, actually."

"Yeah?"

"The upshot is that he's not going to try to go to the Feds or anything like that."

"Thank God."

"Yeah," she took a breath. "The other upshot is that we called it off."

"The wedding?"

"The all of it. He said he couldn't trust me if I didn't back him up."

"But—"

"I know, but I decided it was just as well it could be his idea. It doesn't matter. Truth is, I felt the same way about him the way he kept pushing."

"What do you want to do?"

"Now that not getting killed isn't a full time job?"

"Right," I said.

"I need to get my bearings again. My head's going in too many directions at once."

"I think I realized I wasn't as ready to split up as I thought," I said, which wasn't what Id expected to say when I opened my mouth.

"Maybe I wasn't either." She bit her lip. "So much has happened, and it doesn't fix everything that was wrong before. I was in such a hurry for what I thought would be a better life that I left behind more good stuff than I realized," Beth said.

I smiled. "I'm not sure what that means."

She laughed, which was a sound I'd missed.

"Keep the house, Kyle."

"I don't understand."

"I won't need it. We can figure out us later, right now I need a change of scenery. Getting away from Philly is a good place to start."

"Where will you go?"

"The firm has offices around the country. I was thinking Denver might be a good place for a fresh start."

"So you'll want me to sign the other papers then?"

"Would you come to Denver with me if I asked?"

Part of me wanted to leave that minute. I sure liked the idea of getting away from the area for a while. "I was ready to die for you. I still would. I'll always love you, but I'm not sure if we're right for each other anymore."

She nodded, and I could tell she was thinking the same thing.

I continued. "Tell you what. You have the address. If you send me the papers to make things final, I'll sign them without complaint. If you don't, that's okay too. Let's give it a few months and see where we are."

"I can do that."

"I was thinking after I mend up I might pull some shifts back in the Sandbox. It pays well and is probably safer than Fishtown."

She laughed again.

"Maybe I'll stop by and see you before I leave the country," I said.

"I'm going to miss you." She didn't look mad like she used to when I told her I was going overseas.

"You'll be fine. Colorado? You'll be shacked up with a nice pot farmer in no time."

"I'm sure. And you'll wind up staying in Iraq with a harem and twenty kids."

"I think I need a nap already." We hugged goodbye and I knew we were okay.

But I wondered if we'd ever be good again.

Chapter 34

Three weeks later; Fishtown

I didn't keep the house. Not a week after I'd told the realtor to take it off the market she got an offer that wasn't the same old lowball crap I'd rejected for months. This was a fair deal and Beth, now in the middle of her move to Denver, agreed. At the end of it all we'd be out from under the mortgage and I'd split what was left with her. I gave my share to Rollie, and called it advance rent.

"Jaysus, I'll be dead and buried before you use it all up," he joked. "I'm a single man, you know. It might cramp my style having you underfoot."

"I'll make a great wingman, you'll see. You give me the ugly friends."

Rollie cracked up then he turned serious. "I saw Bishop this morning."

"Yeah?"

"It'll hit the papers tomorrow, but he said the cops found Ratigan's body."

"Where?"

"A pond near Valley Forge. Needed dental records to ID the corpse. The state police will say foul play of course, but Bishop tells me they don't have a clue. He had to give them a statement because they talked to everyone who'd worked with the guy."

"Now we know. Ratigan didn't double cross us the second time."

"Nope, just bit off more than he could chew."

"Bishop didn't say anything about Ryan, did he?"

"No. I don't think we'll ever get an official declaration for him, or any of the others," Rollie said. "When I was a kid we called those Shamrock Sanitation guys the opposite of the Canadian Mounties. 'They always *lose* their man.'"

Rollie avoided talking about Sally or the runt. I saw the guy in dreams all the time.

One time, after many drinks, I asked Rollie if he ever got nightmares. All he said was, "They get bored and haunt somewhere else eventually."

I was glad my old boss, Cliff, at Delivergistics didn't have me on the polygraph when I had my reinstatement hearing with him. It was the only area I had to lie about when I said I didn't know where Ryan was and hadn't heard from him in a while. Technically true, but also, a crock of shit.

I'd been right about opportunities back in the Sandbox. These days if there wasn't a buildup and a boom for contractor logistics folks there was a pullout and drawdown and we were the hired help to scale down the forces. Then things would more than likely heat up again and back to another buildup. Rinse, lather, repeat.

Even after all that happened I'd miss Ryan. Especially overseas. It was still hard to stay mad at the guy.

All this time I'd blamed him for getting me into this mess, but it was my temper that led me into trouble and Ryan was just peddling easy answers to a willing sucker.

Ryan's luck finally ran out and I sure didn't get the answers I expected, easy or otherwise.

I didn't know where things would wind up with Beth, but maybe I'd learned to start asking the right questions.

QUICK FIX

Whatever happened, I was sure glad we'd both get the chance to find out.

ACKNOWLEDGEMENTS

I would like to thank my wife, whose tireless support has made it possible to continue my writing. Many thanks also to early readers whose comments and insight helped shape this book in its early days including Connie Garcia-Barrio, and Bill Rolleri.

I want to recognize the outstanding cast of editors, Jacque Ben-Zekry of Modify Editorial and proofreader Michael Dunne. Finally, thank you to Malcolm McClinton for the great cover art!

Note from the Author:

Thanks so much for reading. If you enjoyed this book I'd greatly appreciate a review on Amazon or Goodreads. They can go a long way to help reach new readers.

If you have a question or comment you can reach me directly at gregsmithbooks@yahoo.com.

You can follow upcoming releases and author doings at my Facebook page here:

https://www.facebook.com/J-Gregory-Smith-Author-297074464674/

You can also find my author page from Thomas & Mercer here:

https://www.amazon.com/J.-Gregory-Smith/e/B002VW9IIU/ref=dp_byline_cont_ebooks_1

ABOUT THE AUTHOR

J. Gregory Smith is the bestselling author of the thrillers *A Noble Cause* and *The Flamekeepers*. He also writes the Paul Chang Mystery series including his breakthrough novel Final Price and the sequels, Legacy of the Dragon and Send in the Clowns.

Prior to writing fiction full time he worked in public relations in Washington, D.C., Philadelphia and Wilmington, Delaware. He has an M.B.A. from The College of William & Mary and A B.A. in English from Skidmore College.

He lives in Wilmington, Delaware with his wife and son.

99424643R00193

Made in the USA
Columbia, SC
09 July 2018